THE STRING
OF PEARLS

Also by Joseph Roth

The Radetzky March
Confession of a Murderer
Job: The Story of a Simple Man
Flight without End
The Silent Prophet
Weights and Measures

Also by Michael Hofmann

Translations

The Legend of the Holy Drinker by Joseph Roth
Right and Left by Joseph Roth
The Man Who Disappeared by Franz Kafka
The Story of Mr Sommer by Patrick Süskind
The Double Bass by Patrick Süskind
The Film Explainer by Gert Hofmann
The Lord Chandos Letter by Hugo von Hofmannsthal
Death in Rome by Wolfgang Koeppen
The Good Person of Sichuan by Bertolt Brecht
Blösch by Beat Sterchi

Poetry

Acrimony
Corona, Corona
Penguin Modern Poets 13
After Ovid: New Metamorphoses
(editor, with James Lasdun)

THE STRING
OF PEARLS

Joseph Roth

Translated from the German by
Michael Hofmann

Granta Books
London

Granta Publications, 2/3 Hanover Yard, London N1 8BE

First published in Great Britain by Granta Books 1998

Original title *Die Geschichte von der 1002. Nacht* by Joseph Roth

A CIP catalogue record for this book is
available from the British Library.

1 3 5 7 9 10 8 6 4 2

ISBN 1 86207 087 3

Typeset in Bembo by M Rules
Printed and bound in Great Britain by
Mackays of Chatham PLC

634898

INTRODUCTION

It is rare for an author to make such multiple, almost contra-dictory claims on us as the Austrian novelist Joseph Roth (1894–1939). As a chronicler of the Jazz Age you can set him alongside Scott Fitzgerald; with Malcolm Lowry, he is one of the great poets of alcoholic decline; and his work brings back the 'Vanished World' of Jewish culture in Central Europe as much as that of the photographer Roman Vishniac. His memorial to the Dual Monarchy (the Empire of Austria and the Kingdom of Hungary; '*kaiserlich und königlich*'; '*k. und k.*'; '*Kakanien*' in Musil's playful toilet term of which Roth disapproved), spread over many sad and adoring novels, is a wonderful complement to Musil's monumental comedy, *The Man Without Qualities*. He is a novelist of exile, and of personal destiny and responsibility; a French-influenced fabulist (Stendhal, in some versions; Proust in others) and the prose heir to Heine; a poet of *Stimmungen*, of public pomps and private melancholy, but a writer of plots as much as anyone this century.

Each one of Roth's thirteen novels doubles and triples,

presents aspects of two or more of the above, like a domino or a piece of a jigsaw puzzle. The reach and the fullness of these books, which are rarely long and never dense or heavy, is quite extraordinary: they seem to defy literary physics. This is something to do with Roth's combining of static and dynamic elements, of rapid, often catastrophic twists of plot, and luminously beautiful pageants; between one set of covers, sometimes on a single page, you get the caricatures of Grosz, the semi-abstract gorgeousness of Klimt, and the free-wheeling, home-made, modern inventions of Paul Klee. Reviewing a book of Roth's once – it was *Zipper and His Father*, but it could just have easily been any of the others – I wrote:

> There is an almost bewildering profusion of Rothian tropes and archetypes in this book, so that one wonders if the same novel can contain the elderly married couple, the surly son, the rich uncle from Brazil, rejection by one's beautiful bride and one's ultimate flight to another continent.
>
> (*Times Literary Supplement*, 3rd February 1989)

The barriers between the books come to seem just about the least satisfactory thing about them. (*The String of Pearls*, for instance, is set mainly in Vienna, like *The Emperor's Tomb*; as in *The Leviathan*, someone remarks that pearls are unlucky; and like *The Legend of the Holy Drinker*, it deals with the effects of sudden wealth and a poor protagonist, though separately, not together.) This is why, thirty, forty, fifty, sixty years after Roth's death, books of his are being brought out for the first time; why, since the 1950s, the Kiepenheuer edition of his works has gone from three to four to six volumes; why his unfinished novels, *Perlefter* and *Erdbeeren* (*Strawberries*), are being published and collections of his journalism are coming out, and why translations of his books continue to appear in many languages (Gallimard, for instance, published their *Conte de la 1002ième Nuit* in 1973). Joseph Roth is a writer of whom one cannot have enough. That's why Nadine Gordimer wrote:

> No other writer, not excepting Thomas Mann, has come so close to achieving the wholeness that Lukács cites as our impossible aim.
>
> (Introduction to *The Radetzky March*, Penguin, Harmondsworth, 1995)

He is worth reading *in extenso*. No one more so.

The String of Pearls (*Die Geschichte der 1002en Nacht* in the original, *The Story of the 1002nd Night*) was the last novel of Joseph Roth's to appear. It was published some time in 1939 – sadly, it is not even clear whether it was in his lifetime or not, I have seen it claimed both ways (he died on 27th May in Paris) – by the Dutch firm of De Gemeenschap. Not that it mattered very much, as the entire stock was destroyed in May 1940 when the Germans occupied The Netherlands.

In order of composition, though, it preceded *The Emperor's Tomb* (1938), having been written in 1936–7. Some copies of an early version of the book were even printed and circulated in 1937, and from this version translations were made into Polish and Yiddish and distributed in Roth's native Galicia. However, Roth – distracted, to put it mildly, by personal and political anxieties, by a difficult tour of Central Europe, and also by *The Emperor's Tomb* – was slow to deliver a revised and edited version of the book to De Gemeenschap. Once the Germans had annexed Austria (the *Anschluß*, in March 1938), Roth and his publishers agreed that *The Emperor's Tomb* - which reflects these events in its shattering last pages – was the more topical and commercial book (a type of thinking, even in these circumstances, never entirely suspended!), and so *The String of Pearls*, revised and shortened, was put back a year.

The delay left the publisher free to complain to Roth, rather ungallantly (on 10th September 1938):

> If we had been able to supply copies of *The 1002nd Night* early in 1937, Austria would still have existed, now we can't distribute there or, most, probably in Czechoslovakia either. (Note that the reps have been paid commission for orders in those places than cannot now be filled.)

I don't know of another instance of an author being reproached for the disappearance of his market! Still, to give De Gemeenschap their due, I don't suppose having Roth as an author was an unalloyed joy either, and German *émigré* literature in the 1930s owes a great debt to generous and plucky Dutch publishers for bringing out books in tiny editions (about one-twentieth of their previous levels in Germany) and a foreign language to serve a small, often penurious, politically divided and geographically scattered readership, and without much hope of an ultimate reward.

As with other late books by Roth, one's first reaction should be amazement and gratitude that it exists at all, given the news of *Kristallnacht* and the creation of concentration camps, and the annexation of the Sudetenland and Austria. Roth's personal circumstances during these years – the frequent changes of abode, alcoholism, the dispersal and deaths of friends, the wreckage of his emotional life, and worries about money and health – would not have enhanced his production either. To think of these things is to invest the conception and the beginning of the book, 'In the spring of the year 18––, the Shah-in-Shah . . .' with an alarming, Nelson-like heroism: the raising of a telescope-cum-kaleidoscope to a sighted eye. It was 1939 or, as you can say in German, 'one wrote, *man schrieb*, 1939', and here was a man who was no fool and no escapist and knew exactly what was going on, writing wise and witty dialogue for a Shah and his Chief Eunuch – and then a paean to Vienna when, as he must have felt, the city had been taken away from him for the rest of his time, and when he must have known no one living in it would have been allowed to receive a copy of it.

That's perhaps the first thing to note about *The String of Pearls*: it's a celebration of and a valediction to a city. It memorializes Vienna. Its world, as Roth's friend, the novelist Hermann Kesten beautifully put it, is that of 'an exotic old-Austria, a kind of vanished, fairy tale Wild East'. It is full of the names of its streets and cafés and hotels, its food and drink, its modes of transport and its amusements, its shops and businesses – the trinity of haberdashery, *Trafik* (small, I think, government-licensed shops that sell stamps, stationery, cigarettes and newspapers) and panopticum, the topical waxworks and proto-cinema-equivalent. It has its speech and its forms, the myriad ranks of civil servant, the grovelling and cynical politeness that makes a 'Herr Redakteur' of the gutter-journalist Lazik, 'Herr Doktor' of the money-grubbing dandy Pollitzer, and even a 'Captain of Horse' of 'poor Taittinger' (and what a strange epithet that is!). The injection into all this of the extra-ordinary Orient, the 'Shah-in-Shah' and his 'Serene suitcases' makes it all the more consciously odd, so that even the regular Austrian greetings, 'Grüß Gott!' and (for intimates) 'Servus!', retained in my translation, are somehow precisely jarring. And of course there is the Danube too and the great park and fun-fair (familiar from The Third Man) of the Prater. The String of Pearls seems to begin with Schnitzler and finish up as Hórvath; to start off as the city of La Ronde (Der Reigen), where a corrupt and appetite-driven society preys on itself beautifully and effi-ciently, where, to use another Austriacism, the situation is 'critical but not serious', and end as the tawdry and terrifying tragedy of little people (like Tales from the Vienna Woods or Faith, Hope and Charity).

It is a sort of Ronde, The String of Pearls: the way characters are named, move into focus, act and are taken off; the way it begins in Teheran and ends in a waxwork imitation Teheran-an-der-Donau; the way it is structured as a fairy story that has swallowed a novel. In one sense of the word, it is a 'panop-ticum' (literally: 'see-everything'), not the waxworks that Taittinger ends up buying that finishes him off financially, morally, perhaps even, in a curious way, artistically – but a Dickensian cross-section of an entire society, and at a third of the length of Dickens. Think, for example, of the unobtrusive parade of professions that are represented in the book: the army, the Church, the law, government, banking, journalism, diplo-macy, medicine. It ranges from the top of Austrian society almost to the very bottom, encompassing steep, mostly down-ward movements. It brings a terrifying wise clarity to a tangled imbroglio. The mechanism of the book is the characters' failure to understand themselves and each other: it is full of moments of dim revelation, not acted upon; of involuntary bursts of speech; of incomprehensible narrations (Taittinger to Dr Stiasny, Frau Kreutzer and Trummer to Taittinger, the Eunuch to Schinagl); of the writing and signing of documents. 'Evidently he had been trying to write something', is the writer's sardonic farewell to his 'poor' hero. Understanding arrives by the same post as calamity. Wherever there is a wound, there is money. The only thing that is really unaffected by the whole chain of transactions is what catalysed it: the string of pearls. And even that, it should be remembered, is the price the Shah pays for his error and disillusion, and its value is quietly quadrupled in the course of the book.

It strikes me too that the whole novel is instinct with the conservative's horror at social change. I suspect this is because Roth is writing about – half-celebrating, half-criticizing – something that no longer exists, and he wants to show that grim and glittering social hierarchy as an intact pyramid, functioning at full power. Hence, to aspire is as hopeless as to decline. As long as they remain stuck in the forms of the rigid '18– –'s and the ritualized encounters between high and low, whether in the brothel, the army, the corridors of power or the Court, the characters seem to live in amber. But then contacts are made that are hard to legislate for: the Shah espies Countess W.; Taittinger his Mizzi; Mizzi her madame. Money comes into play, putting a false value on everything, collapsing the society and destabilizing the characters. It is an index of folly and alienation: in Lazik, in the Shah, in Frau Matzner, in Mizzi, in Taittinger. There is a whole series of chance encounters that ought never to have happened, between characters who should have been unaware of one another's existence, in places they should never have set foot. The separation of social spheres is lifted, the Chief Eunuch goes to the brothel, Frau Matzner sets up as a retired spinster in a good part of town, first Lazik and later Frau Kreutzer and Trummer present themselves in Taittinger's hotel, until finally all distinctions are removed, money incessantly changes hands, each may talk to each, and a cat may look at a king. There is a kind of squeamishness in the idea – for Roth – of the multiple functioning of the Prater: the place where Taittinger, in his pomp, used to ride out on Pylades (such an inspired mistake: the friend of Orestes, the *locus classicus* of friendship, Horatio to his Hamlet, the person Taittinger so badly misses, and whom Zenower – almost another philosopher – just fails to become for him), doubling and tripling as an aristocratic game park and the place where the Viennese plebs go for their revels (in the aptly named 'Second Café'!) and where at night the bushes teem with ill-assorted couples. It is the 'unlucky' pearls that set all this rolling.

A little note on the Shah: there was a historical visit – a celebrated one – not just to Vienna, as Roth has it for the purposes of his novel, but to all of Europe. It took place in 1873 – two centuries after the Siege of Vienna in 1683, when the Ottoman invasion was turned back, an event referred to by the Shah in the beginning of the book. The historical Shah in question was Naser-od-Din. The diary he kept on his visit – admired for the simplicity of its language – was widely translated and published at the time. A recent German republication of it, under the racy title *A Harem in Bismarck's Reich*, makes it sound closer to Roth than it actually was. (I owe my knowledge of it, and the sight of an English copy, to James Buchan.) In it, as in *The String of Pearls*, the Shah experiences heat and rain, a storm at sea, but also such things as a trip round the Krupps armament factory, the sight of a garden hose ('tubes of india-rubber in use for watering the lawns and plants') and various conjuring displays. Curiously, he finds 'Austria is the country of all others that bears the bell for [the] beauty and comeliness [of its women].' This first visit was followed by others; and there might have been more had the Shah not been assassinated in 1896 – partly, no doubt, on account of his pro-European policies that seemed to be selling off his country to Western interests. (It's an old story.) Roth would certainly have known about him and his visits; in what detail I can't say.

We are told that history often repeats itself as farce, and it is a striking feature of *The String of Pearls* that things in it are often enacted more than once: there is Frau Matzner's miserliness and then Mizzi's; Taittinger's resignation from the army and the 'Super Arbitration Commission'; the haberdashery and the panopticum; Silberer and Gollitzer, and then Pollitzer (!); Stiasny and Kalergi; two sets of train journeys; two nights with Zenower in the bar; and most obviously, the two visits by the Shah to Vienna which frame the book, and indeed, two versions of the Shah, in flesh and in wax. The low form, the extra form – as in the *1002nd night* – is what gives things their final pathos and their final meaning. Taittinger, a notably unliterary type, who doesn't read and who dies in the attempt to write, can survive the first 'low mimesis' of his story – in Lazik's deathless prose – but the second, in wax, a 'true image', does for him. It is the vehicle for his final insight – anagnorisis in tragedy theory – into his own waxiness, as it were: his stiffness, his shallowness, his lack of life. 'There was something attractive about wax figures,' Taittinger muses: it's because he is one himself. The artist, Tino Percoli, a stand-in for Roth, creates, as he self-deprecatingly puts it, 'monsters'. He could do more, but it's what the public wants. Anyone reading the German word 'Ungeheuer' would think of the Nazis. The gulf between '18––' and 1939 is closed.

Even within Roth's *oeuvre*, *The String of Pearls* is a strange book: frothy, highly decorated, full of money and costumes and ambience and light, a pitiless morality with the cruelty of fable. The novelist keeps skipping ahead of the reader, into ever more distressing and constricting settings and situations – but he never stops skipping. Its scenes and images live in the memory: in this short book there is enough for many books. One might remember the storm at sea (a masterpiece of psychology), the Lippizaners at the Spanish Riding School (more articulate than any of the human characters), the yellow leaf on Frau Matzner's purple hat (like an image from Klimt), or the scene – one of the best in all Roth, for my money – in which Xandl confronts his father in the Carpathian pub. Whatever it is, it's more than you get in most books.

Michael Hofmann
London, January 1998

I

In the spring of the year 18--, the Shah-in-Shah, the great, exalted and holy monarch, the absolute ruler and overlord of all the lands of Persia, began to feel a sense of malaise of a kind he had never experienced before.

The most renowned doctors in his Empire were unable to explain his condition. The Shah-in-Shah was most alarmed.

On one of his sleepless nights, he summoned to him his Chief Eunuch Patominos, who was a wise man and knew the world, for all that he had never left the court. He spoke to him as follows:

'Friend Patominos, I am sick. I'm afraid I may be very sick. My doctor tells me I'm healthy, but I don't believe him. Do *you* believe him, Patominos?'

'No, I don't believe him either!' said Patominos.

'Do you think I might be gravely sick, then?' asked the Shah.

'Gravely sick – no – I don't think so!' replied Patominos. 'But sick! Definitely sick, Sire! There are many sicknesses.

Doctors don't see them all, because they are trained to look only for physical ailments. But what good to a man are healthy organs and a healthy body, if he pines in his soul?'

'How do you know I'm pining?'

'I ventured to guess that you were.'

'Then what is it I'm pining for?'

'That,' replied Patominos, 'is something I need to think about for a while.'

The Eunuch Patominos pretended to think, and then he said:

'Sire, you are pining for exotic foreign climes; for example, for Europe.'

'A long journey?'

'A short journey, Sire! Short journeys are more fun. Long journeys may endanger one's health.'

'And where to?'

'Sire,' said the Eunuch, 'there are many countries in Europe. It all depends on what one is looking for.'

'And what do you think I should be looking for, Patominos?'

'Sire,' said the Eunuch, 'how can a miserable fellow like myself have any idea what a great ruler should be looking for?'

'Patominos,' said the Shah, 'you know I haven't touched a woman for weeks.'

'Yes, Sire, I know,' replied Patominos.

'And do you think that's as it should be, Patominos?'

'Sire,' said the Eunuch, drawing himself up a little out of his hunched posture, 'that, surely, is something that a person of my particular type can know but little about.'

'I envy you.'

'Indeed,' replied the Eunuch, now fully and plumply upright. 'And I feel sorry for other men with all my heart.'

'Why do you feel sorry for us, Patominos?' asked the monarch.

'For many reasons,' replied the Eunuch, 'but especially because men are driven to the pursuit of variety. And that is a treacherous objective, because there is no such thing as variety.'

'Are you telling me that I should go somewhere in pursuit of variety?'

'Yes, Sire,' said Patominos, 'to convince yourself that it doesn't exist.'

'And that of itself would cure me?'

'Not the convincing yourself, Sire,' said the Eunuch, 'but the experiences gathered on the way to such a conviction.'

'What gives you your insight into these matters, Patominos?'

'The fact that I am a castrate, Sire!' replied the Eunuch, with a low bow. He proposed a remote destination to the Shah. He suggested Vienna.

The ruler reflected: 'Muslims have been there once before, many years ago.'

'Sire, they were unfortunately unable to enter the city. Had they done so, St Stephen's Cathedral would have had not a cross, but a crescent moon on top of it!'

'It was all a long time ago. We are now at peace with the Emperor of Austria!'

'Indeed, Sire!'

'Let's go then!' decreed the Shah. 'Inform my ministers!'

And it all came to pass.

The Chief Eunuch Kalo Patominos sat and presided over the women, first in a first-class railway carriage, and later in the bow of a ship. He watched the red setting sun go down. He spread out a carpet, prostrated himself on the ground, and began to murmur his evening prayers. The party reached Constantinople without incident.

The sea was as placid as a baby. The ship, itself a babe in arms, floated gently and sweetly out into the blue night.

II

For two days the Shah's bridal-white ship cruised on the blue sea. No one dared tell their great master that they were waiting for word from the Persian Ambassador in Vienna. After a day and a half, the Shah became restless. Although he took no interest in the ship's course, he couldn't help noticing that the same stretch of coastline kept reappearing. It also struck him as peculiar that such a powerful ship needed so much time to cross such a small sea. He summoned his Grand Vizier and indicated his dissatisfaction with the slowness of the crossing. He merely indicated it, he didn't expressly state it. Not trusting any of his servants on terra firma, he trusted them still less when they were all bobbing around on the water. He was still in Allah's hands of course, but a little bit in the Captain's too. And whenever he thought of the Captain, the Shah got a little restless. He didn't like him at all, mainly because he had no memory of ever having seen him before. You see, he was by nature extremely suspicious. He was quick to suspect even men he knew well and saw often; how much more so then such men as he did not know or could not remember? Indeed, he was so suspicious that he was even at pains to hide his suspicion – in the childish belief, common to many great men, that they can outsmart their servants. And therefore he merely hinted to his Grand Vizier that this protracted sailing around struck him as a trifle odd. The Grand Vizier, recognizing that his master was at pains not to voice any mistrust, gave no signs of detecting any.

'Sire,' said the Grand Vizier, 'I too find it puzzling that the crossing of this sea is taking us so long.'

'Indeed,' said the Shah, as though it was only the Grand Vizier's remark that had alerted him to this slow progress, 'indeed, you have a point: why *are* we making such slow progress?'

'That's something one might ask the Captain!' said the Grand Vizier.

The Captain came, and the Shah asked: 'When are we finally going to reach land?'

'Great master,' replied the Captain, 'the life of Your Majesty is sacred to us all! More sacred than our children, more sacred than our mothers, more sacred than the pupils of our own eyes. Our instruments tell us a storm is imminent, however tranquil the sea may appear now. With Your Majesty on board, we must take infinite care. What is there more important to our lives, to our country, to the world, than the sacred life of Your Majesty? – And I'm afraid our instruments are warning us of a storm, Sire!'

The Shah looked up. The sky was blue, taut and radiant. The Shah thought the Captain was lying to him. He did not say so, however. He said: 'It seems to me, Captain, your instruments are no good!'

'Certainly, Sire,' replied the Captain, 'instruments are not always reliable!'

'Just like you, Captain,' said the Shah.

Suddenly, he spotted a tiny little white cloud almost on the horizon. In truth, it was barely even a cloudlet, it was a puff of mist, the mere ghost of a cloudlet. The Captain noticed it too, at exactly the same moment – and he hoped a miracle had come to his aid, and that he and his lie and his lied-about instruments would suddenly all be vindicated in the eyes of the Master of the True Faith.

But exactly the opposite happened. For, tiny and faint though the little wisp of cloud was, it still managed to exacerbate the fury of the Shah. He was so pleased to have caught his Grand Vizier and Captain both lying to him – and then Nature herself had come along and given birth to a cloudlet (which might go on to become proper clouds!) and so had given credence to what the lying instruments were saying! An angry and intent Shah observed the busy mutations of the cloudlet. It spread a little. The wind frayed it. Then it knitted together more tightly than before. It looked like a veil that had been tied in a knot. It lengthened. After a time it grew firmer and darker. The Captain was still standing behind the Shah. He too was observing the changing shapes of the little cloud, but with gratitude rather than anger. He was making a mistake! The Shah spun round furiously, and his face reminded the Captain of a dangerous, purple, hail cloud. 'You're making a big mistake,' the great ruler began in a soft, almost toneless voice that came up from the uncharted depths of his soul. 'You're all making a big mistake, if you think I can't see through your treachery. You're not telling me the truth! What's this talk about your instruments? You want me to believe they're predicting a storm? My eye is more reliable than any of your instruments. There's clear blue sky all around us. Rarely have I seen such a clear blue sky. Open your eyes, Captain! Tell me, can you see the faintest sign of a cloud anywhere on the horizon?'

The Captain was greatly afraid, but still greater than his fear was his astonishment. And greater than either of those was his uncertainty. Was the King's rage feigned or real? Was His Highness testing him? Who could tell? He had never served the Shah before and didn't know his particular habits. The Captain had heard occasional reports that the Shah liked to feign anger to test the honesty of his servants. Unfortunately the poor Captain now seized on that one particular – not overly characteristic – trait of his master, and decided to be honest. 'But Sire,' he said, 'Your Majesty's eyes have just lit on that cloud on the horizon.' And the unhappy Captain went so far as to point his finger at the little cloud, which had by now become a proper blue-black cloud that was making for the ship with alarming speed.

'Captain!' roared the Shah, 'are you telling me what's in the sky? Do you call that bit of heat-haze a cloud? Can't you feel the burning sun?'

Just then, something unexpected occurred. The cloud, which in a matter of seconds had become a louring, rain-swollen, black and blue thundercloud, blotted out the sun, and the world was plunged into darkness.

The Captain spread his arms wide, and his trembling lips made no sound. It looked as though he were saying: Sire, I deeply regret this, but I have had to let the sky speak on my behalf. It is just about to reply to Your Majesty's question.

Of course the Shah couldn't fail to notice the way the sun

had gone dark. He wasn't quite sure whether to be pleased by
the honesty of his servants, who had accurately and truthfully
reported the approaching storm, or to be annoyed with himself
for being so mistrustful. He felt there was a chance he might
betray his own confusion, which was something he wanted to
avoid at all costs. He therefore ordered: 'Show me your instruments, Captain!'

As they walked along the deck, the Shah leading the way,
the Captain following, the sky darkened still further, leaving
only a narrow blue strip to the north-east. To the west the
clouds were an angry purple, directly overhead they were a
little lighter and milder, and to the east they thinned to a positively encouraging pallor. Three steps behind the Shah, the
Captain was in the throes of real terror. This time it wasn't, as
before, the fear of his master and the lie he had told, but the
fear of Allah, the master of the world, and of the storm he had
so foolishly said was coming. It was the first time that the
Captain had had the honour of welcoming the Shah-in-Shah
on board his vessel. What did he know about the niceties of
diplomacy, the good Captain? For twenty years he'd been sailing the seas on the same cruiser of the Imperial Navy, the
Ahmed Akbar. He'd been through plenty of storms, and in his
younger days he had served on sailing ships, it was on sailing
ships that he had learned his craft. Not once since he had
come to the throne had the Shah found it necessary to cross the
sea. And now the poor Captain had the dangerous distinction
of ferrying the mighty king over the water for the first time in
his life. 'We mustn't reach the coast of Europe in the pre-
scribed time,' the Grand Vizier had told him. – 'His Majesty is
very impatient by nature, and wants his wishes to be fulfilled
the moment he opens his mouth. But you understand,

Captain, there are diplomatic obstacles to be overcome. We need to wait for a reply from His Excellency our Ambassador. Until we have it, it would be best to steam up and down the coast. If His Majesty should happen to ask you, tell him you're afraid there may be a storm on the way.'

Thus the Grand Vizier. And lo: there really was a storm on the way. His instruments hadn't predicted it at all. It was only his lie that had predicted it, his lie and nothing else! The Captain was a believer, and he was afraid of Allah.

They went into the Captain's cabin. It contained few instruments, and none of them had anything to say about the approaching storm. There was only a large compass of British manufacture that was screwed into a round table. The Shah leaned over it. 'What's this, Captain?' he asked.

'A compass, Your Majesty!' said the Captain.

'I see,' said the Shah. 'Have you no other instruments?'

'Not here, Your Majesty, they are next door, in the engineer's cabin!'

'A storm, then?' asked the Shah. He didn't feel like looking at any more instruments and besides, he was now in the mood for a storm.

'When is this storm going to come?' he asked pleasantly.

'After sunset, I should say!' said the Captain.

The Shah went off, followed by the Captain. When they stepped up on to the quarterdeck, it was almost black. The watch officer raced up to them. He reported to the Captain, using strange expressions the Shah had never heard before. The Shah walked on, leaving them to it. He stepped up to the railing, and with real delight watched the furious onslaught of the waves. The ship started rolling. The world started rolling. The waves were green, black, blue and grey tongues, all edged with white. A powerful queasiness suddenly gripped the Shah. A strange monster was rummaging and squirming in his insides. He remembered how he'd felt like this once before, when he'd been a boy and very, very sick.

The Captain was prey to a double agitation: first his Lord was indisposed; and second the storm he had so frivolously and mendaciously predicted, was drawing ever nearer. The Captain wasn't sure which he should attend to first: the storm or his master's condition.

He decided to give his attention to the Shah. This was the more prudent option in any case, as he had already given the order to steer as close to the shore as possible. The Shah was lying on the quarterdeck, wrapped in several blankets. His personal physician – whom he cordially hated and who, in his opinion, was also the only man in his life he could not escape – was crouching over his sick master. He did the obvious: he administered valerian to the Shah. The first heavy raindrops fell on the soft velvet tent that had been put up over the Shah. The wind jingled the rings that connected the tent to three metal supports. The Shah felt a little better. Lightning was flashing outside, and he listened blissfully to the thunder. His infirmity was leaving him, and no wonder! The ship was almost motionless, barely two sea miles from the shore. Only the sea slapped against its sides in rhythmic fury.

This storm had been sent to the Grand Vizier by special grace of Heaven. Delegates in nippy little motorboats reached Constantinople in the middle of the night. At about nine o'clock the following morning they returned, in the same boats. The Shah was still asleep. They brought with them the telegram from the Ambassador in Vienna: His Majesty was expected. Everything was ready to greet him . . .

The storm abated. A fresh, sparkling sun shone as brightly and cheerfully as it must have done on the very day of its creation.

The Captain shone and sparkled too, and the Grand Vizier. The ship made for Europe, full steam ahead.

III

His Royal and Imperial Apostolic Majesty received the news of the Shah's visit at eight in the morning. Two hundred years had passed since the most terrifying of all Muslims had laid siege to Vienna. Only a miracle had saved Austria then. But now, more frightful by far than the Turks, was the threat to old Austria from the Prussians, and, even though they were almost more infidel than the Muslims – being Protestants – God performed no miracles. There was no longer any reason to fear the sons of Mohammed more than the Protestants.

A new and still more terrible era was beginning – the Age of Prussia, the age of the Janissaries of Luther and Bismarck. Their black and white banners – colours, both, emblematic of mourning – displayed not a crescent but a cross; only it was an Iron Cross. In their hands, even Christian symbols were deadly weapons.

All this went through the mind of the Austrian Emperor as he was told of the impending visit of the Shah. Similar thoughts occurred to the Emperor's ministers. All Vienna was abuzz. There were whisperings in ministries, in ante-chambers and behind closed doors, in meeting rooms and corridors, in editorial suites and cafés, and even in *chambres séparées*. Everywhere, people were looking forward to the Shah's visit.

On the day the Shah–in–Shah's train was expected at the Franz-Joseph Station in Vienna, four companies of a guard of honour and two hundred policemen on horseback and on foot, blocked off all the approach roads. The punctilious hospitality of His Royal and Imperial Apostolic Majesty had seen to it that every carriage of the train that was taking the Persian ruler to Vienna had been painted white, a bridal white just like the ship the Shah had boarded in Constantinople. A company from the regiment of the Hoch-and Deutschmeisters was drawn up on the station platform. Bandmaster Josef Nechwal ordered the Persian national anthem. Cymbals and tambourines made more of themselves than was strictly required for the Persian national anthem. The kettledrum, loaded on to the back of an otherwise docile and music-loving mule, didn't want to be left out either; and the mule trembled from time to time, as though in rebellion; but neither the drummer nor the bandleader Josef Nechwal noticed it. All his thoughts were on the military decorations that were hanging in the window at Tiller's.

The Emperor felt ill at ease in the unfamiliar uniform. It was hot, too: one of those precocious days in May that seemed to anticipate summer. The glass roof over the platform shimmered in the heat. The Emperor rather took against the anthem. Still, he listened to it with respect – with evident respect . . .

When the Shah alighted, the Emperor embraced him perfunctorily. The Shah inspected the guard of honour. The bandleader called for the Habsburg anthem, 'God Save the King'. The Persians stood rigid.

Carriages were boarded and driven away. Behind a blue wall of soldiery, the populace cried out their huzzahs. The horses of the mounted policemen became jumpy and, much against the wishes of their riders, kicked out. There were twenty-two injuries. The police report in the *Fremdenblatt* merely noted three instances of people 'fainting' from 'emotion'.

I V

These three instances did nothing to dampen the enthusiasm of the people of Vienna for the visit of the great Shah of Persia. All the people who had witnessed his arrival and survived it intact – including those who had fainted – went happily back to their homes; as happily as if they had been given some personal reason for rejoicing. Even the railwaymen and the porters were happy as they sweated. For the great Shah of Persia had arrived with a great many heavy cases. They filled no fewer than four ordinary freight wagons, which, however, had failed to be attached to the bridal-white court train of His Majesty in Trieste. The Aide-de-Camp of the Imperial Master of Ceremonies, one Kirilida Pajidzani, paced up and down the platform in agitation, with the stationmaster Gustl Burger in close attendance. The telegraph chattered away incessantly in the stationmaster's office. Poor stationmaster Burger understood not one syllable of the French that the Imperial Aide-de-Camp jabbered away in. The only man who might have been able to help in this desperate situation was standing at the buffet of the first-class restaurant, feeling enviably bored. This was Baron Taittinger, Captain of the Ninth Dragoons, currently on indefinite leave of absence from his regiment and attached 'on special secondment' to the Court and Cabinet Office. The Baron had his elbow on the bar and his back to the window, and turned from time to time to take grim pleasure in the spectacle offered by the ridiculous stationmaster and his Persian colleague, Kirilida Pajidzani, whom Taittinger had already privately dubbed the 'Jannissary'. The clock over the bar showed it was past two o'clock. At half past four, Taittinger had a rendezvous with Frau Kronbach, at Hornbichl's. She was married to a soap manufacturer, a Commercial Councillor, and lived in Döbling. Frau Kronbach was his passion, or so he liked to imagine. He had once told himself she was his passion, he had called her his passion, and he proved it to himself by being faithful to her. She was, in actual fact – not to beat about the bush – his second grand passion.

So there he was, leaning on the bar, Captain Taittinger. Every now and again he looked out of the window, then up at the clock above the blonde barmaid who served him, and who was, in his estimation, merely one of the pieces of equipment you needed to run a properly functioning railway service. It made him happy to watch the two men running around in their agitated state outside, the 'Janissary' and the stationmaster. Unfortunately, he was obliged to wait until the Shah's luggage had arrived, and Frau Kronbach was obliged to wait too; it was a shame. Still, there was nothing to be done about it.

At last, it was already half past three, and the Captain had taken a sip of his fourth Hennessy, the special train came in, hissing with the self-importance of an express although it consisted of just four wagons. They contained the luggage of the Shah of Persia.

Taittinger chose this moment to rush out on to the platform. He grabbed the stationmaster and said: 'Get a move on, man! This delay is a scandal! His Majesty was here an hour and a half ago! You can't keep His Majesty waiting like this! Disgraceful! It's disgraceful, stationmaster!'

And not waiting for a reply, the Baron turned to his Persian colleague Kirilida Pajidzani and said in the fluent French of the Dual Monarchy, which seemed to consist only of vowels, 'Ah, punctual! How punctual! You know we have the most punctual railways in the world!' Railwaymen and porters ran up. The stationmaster took personal charge of them; the Captain, meanwhile, was briefing his Persian colleague about the amazing, positively Oriental wonders of Viennese nightlife.

The Persian listened with a smile on his face, the sort of indulgent smile that easygoing men of the world always put on when they're being gracious. This indulgent smile finally showed the Baron whom he was up against. This 'Janissary' was actually anything but. He gave off the dear old familiar aroma of worldly duplicity; the Baron took to him immediately.

Quickly, the Baron reclassified the Persian as 'charming' – which was his highest term of approbation. For him, human beings could be one of three types: first were the 'charmers'; then the 'so-so's'; and third and lowest were the 'bores'. Kirilida Pajidzani – no doubt about it – was the 'charming' sort. And, all at once, the Baron was able to pronounce his tricky name so expertly it was as though he had moved among Persians ever since he'd been in short trousers. 'Monsieur Kirilida Pajidzani,' said the Captain fluently, 'I'm so sorry you were kept waiting for so long. These trains! These bloody trains! But we'll find the fellow responsible! Don't you worry!'

To show the Persian he meant business, he went up to the

stationmaster and said loudly: 'This is a right balls-up, Station-master, if you don't mind my saying so!'

'Captain,' replied the stationmaster, 'it is a balls-up, but it's not one of mine, it was a balls-up in Trieste.'

'I don't mind if it's Trieste or Timbuctoo,' said the Captain, raising his voice a little more. 'The point is His Majesty got in a good two hours ago, and he's still not in possession of his luggage!'

Stationmaster Burger, now beginning to worry about a possible demotion, struggled to remain calm and friendly. He had a sudden inspiration and said: 'The Serene suitcases have just arrived, Baron!'

'That's as may be,' jeered the Captain, 'but they're still not where they ought to be!'

It took another half an hour before the twenty-two mighty trunks of His Persian Majesty had been loaded up. Not until that had been accomplished could the Baron leave the station. Luckily, the carriage that had been assigned to the Grand Vizier's Aide-de-Camp was still waiting. With an exquisite display of awkwardness, Taittinger addressed Kirilida Pajidzani: 'Would it put you out greatly, I have orders –'

The Persian didn't let him finish his lie, but said right away: 'I was going to ask you to do me the honour of allowing me to escort you to wherever your duty requires you to be.'

They got into the carriage. The luggage went on ahead, in three wagons drawn by heavy Pingau bay horses. They had driven for some time when the Captain stood up, tapped the liveried driver on the shoulder and said: 'Will you stop at Hornbichl's.'

The driver raised his whip to show he'd understood. It traced a Yes! in the air and gave a soft crack. Relieved and cheerful, Taittinger fell back in the cushions, next to his 'charming' Persian comrade.

The carriage stopped outside Hornbichl's. The Baron went behind the hedge at the right of the garden – to the 'lover's nook', as he'd called it for ten years now. The wife of the Commercial Councillor had been waiting for a quarter of an hour. She had never seen her lover in full dress uniform before – they had only been carrying on for some four months. She was so dazzled by the helmet with the gold crest that all the reproaches she'd been collecting for the past fifteen minutes flew out of her head. 'Oh,' she whispered, 'at last, at last!'

V

For the next few days, Captain Taittinger hardly left the side of the charming Kirilida. In the course of the hours they spent together, it emerged that the charming Kirilida was completely informed about everything, even more than the Grand Vizier. And it was possible to discuss everything with him, too. For example, one learned that the Grand Vizier was actually not as averse to drink as one would surely have expected. In fact, quite the contrary: the Grand Vizier was continually in breach of the laws of Islam.

Over two afternoons, Captain Taittinger acquired more and harder information than Professor Friedländer the renowned Orientalist, who had been taken on as an expert consultant by the Reception Committee, had been able to glean in the course of a lifetime of study. Professor Friedländer was a teetotaller. And that's what happens when a man doesn't drink, thought Baron Taittinger.

Poor Professor Friedländer hardly knew what to do with his accumulated expertise. He was even on the point of questioning his own memorandum, despite the fact that it was based on impeccable research. But the Professor, after twenty years of Oriental studies, now had to have it broken to him by Baron Taittinger that some Muslims – including the Grand Vizier himself – occasionally took a drink. His Aide-de-Camp, Monsieur Kirilida, whom Friedländer met once in the company of Taittinger, had read none of the classics of Persian literature. Even the Chief Eunuch, according to Baron Taittinger, liked to send the palace footmen out for ordinary mugs of beer from Wiesenthaler's over the road, and drank them no differently than, say, your average Christian tailor. Still more perturbing than Taittinger's revelations were articles by wholly unqualified journalists, which were full of the most egregious falsehoods about life in Persia and Persian history. Professor Friedländer tried in vain to acquaint the various editors with the facts by detailed rebuttals of these stories. The only result of his efforts was that the journalists started dropping in on him at the department and at home for interviews about Persia. A few even started going to his lectures.

Unfortunately, the parade in Kagran was spoiled by a sudden downpour. The Shah lasted no more than fifteen minutes in a draughty tent whose three crimson sides flapped maddeningly, bellying out and allowing the rain to trickle through. He was no great devotee of military spectacles. While he looked on distractedly as the magnificent uhlans galloped across the slick green meadows like an orderly storm, he could feel the remorseless drip of rain falling, at irritatingly regular intervals, on his tall fur hat and on the scarlet collar of his pitch-black cloak. He worried for his health, too. He trusted European physicians still less than he did Ibrahim, his own Jew. He was surrounded, and felt hemmed in by alien generals who were used to all weathers, and weren't bothered by the rain. The horsemen waved their sabres. Martial tones blared from wet trumpets and were beaten out of drenched calfskins. The infantry was still to come, and then the artillery. No! He'd had enough. He stood up, and with him the Grand Vizier, his Aide-de-Camp, and the entire retinue. The Shah walked out of the tent and into the pouring rain. He ducked his head to get away from its clammy blows, while all the others – he cursed them inwardly – held their heads up, as if they were walking in bright sunshine. He made for where he hoped to find the safety of his carriage. With instincts honed by peril, he quickly found it. He got in without looking round. His suite followed. Two generals remained on the platform, engrossed in the military spectacle, preferring their troops to the Shah. The parade was ruined by the weather. In spite of this, that day each of the soldiers from the Vienna barracks was given a dinner of roast pork, boiled potatoes and peas, with Pilsener beer and a packet of Hungarian ovals to follow.

It rained the next day too, but that didn't matter. Today's venue was indoors, in the Spanish Riding School. As the exotic visitor had shown himself not to like fresh air the day before, the box in the Riding School was lined with thick, genuine Persian carpets, weavings from Shiraz, ancient stuffs taken down from the Palace walls and soft red velvet cushions; and the door jambs had leather strips nailed to them to keep out any draughts. The whole large arena felt almost unbearably close. The Shah threw off his cloak. His heavy fur hat weighed oppressively down on his head. He regularly mopped the sweat off his brow with his pink silk handkerchief. His retinue all did likewise, partly to show that they too felt the heat, and partly because they really did feel the heat. On this occasion, though, the Shah of Persia did not walk out prematurely. He kept two thousand eight hundred horses in his stables in Teheran. They were finer and considerably more valuable than the women in his harem. In his stables he had Arab stallions whose backs shone like tawny gold; greys from the famous stud of Jephtahan, with hair as soft and light as down; Egyptian mares, a gift from the breeding stables of the mighty Imam Arasbi Sur; horses from the steppes of the Caucasus, a gift from the Tsar of all the Russias; hefty Pomeranian chestnuts, bought for a lot of money from the tight-fisted King of Prussia; half-wild horses just lately imported from the Hungarian Puszta, still unused to the hand or voice of man, and throwing off his best Persian horsemen.

But what were all these beasts compared to the Lippizaners of the Spanish Riding School? The military band, standing on a platform facing the Imperial box, played the Persian anthem, followed by 'God Save the King'. A rider in Persian dress – of a kind that the Shah had only ever seen in portraits of his ancestors and never once in Persia – with a lofty lambskin cap braided with thickly worked gold threads on his head, a short blue cloak with gold embroidery thrown over one shoulder, in red kneelength rawhide boots with golden spurs, and with a scimitar at his side, was the first to enter the arena. His grey was caparisoned in scarlet. A herald in a white silk uniform and white pumps strode out in front of him.

Straightaway, to the strains of a Persian melody that seemed largely unfamiliar to the Shah – it was actually a little effort of Nechwal's own – the grey began to perform a sequence of positively witty steps. Thighs, hooves, hindquarters and head: it was thoroughly graceful. Not a word, not a sound! No instructions whatsoever! Was it the rider controlling the horse, or the horse the rider? There was silence all round. Everyone held their breath. Even though they were sitting so close they could practically reach out and touch horse and rider, they followed the spectacle through opera glasses and lorgnettes. It couldn't be brought near enough. The grey pricked up its ears: it was as though it took pleasure in the silence. Intimately and proudly and curiously its large, dark, moist, intelligent eyes surveyed the ladies and gentlemen seated all round it − not at all in the expectation of applause, like a circus grey. Just once it looked up at the box of His Majesty the Shah of Persia, as though to ascertain for whom it was doing all this. With aristocratic hauteur it raised its right foreleg, only a little, as though greeting an equal. Then it described a circle, as the music seemed to require. Thereupon, it gently set its hooves down on the red carpet; but suddenly, at the sound of the cymbals, it produced an astonishing − but elegant and, even in its show of exuberance, perfectly measured − leap, stopped dead, waited a second for the sweet sound of the flute and then, when it finally came, followed it by a gentle and velvety trot, with a hint of a zigzag to suggest the mazy inscrutability of the Orient. The music stopped briefly. In that time, one could hear only the soft, delicate impacts of the hooves on the carpet. In the great harem of the Shah of Persia − so far as he could remember − not one of the women had displayed as much loveliness, dignity, grace and beauty as that grey Lippizaner from the stud of His Royal and Imperial Apostolic Majesty.

The Shah sat through the rest of the programme impatiently: the silent elegance of the other animals; their grace and cleverness; their slender, wonderful bodies, conducive to feelings of devotion, brotherhood and desire; their powerful gentleness and their sweet power; and the Shah thought only of the grey.

He told his Grand Vizier: 'Buy the grey!'

The Grand Vizier hurried down to the stables. Stablemaster Türling, mustering as much dignity as any Royal and Imperial Minister, said: 'Excellency, we don't sell. We give – if His Majesty our Emperor will allow.'

And no one dared to ask permission of His Majesty.

VI

They rose. The ball was due to begin in fifteen minutes.

The assembled ladies and gentlemen, drawn up in two rows in the ballroom, awaited the arrival of His Majesty. From time to time a stifled cough emerged from the breast of one of the older gentlemen. It was a cough that was more sheepish even than the cougher himself, who held a silk handkerchief in front of his mouth. One of the ladies whispered something to another. It was hardly a whisper, it was the merest breath, and yet in the silence it sounded like a hiss.

In the silence the soft thump of the heavy black rod on the crimson carpet sounded like hammering. Everybody looked up. Unseen hands drew back the white, gold-framed double doors, and Their Majesties came through. At the other end of the room, the court orchestra played the Persian national anthem. The Shah gave out greetings in Oriental fashion, touching his hand to his brow and breast. The ladies curtseyed, the gentlemen bowed low. The two monarchs, host and guest, strode on as through a field of bending corn. Both smiled, in

29

accordance with protocol. They smiled to right and left even though no one saw it. They smiled at fair and dark tresses alike, at smooth pates, and sharp partings.

Three hundred and forty-two wax candles lit and heated the room. The great crystal chandelier in the middle bore no fewer than forty-eight alone. Each little candle flame was reflected a thousandfold in the burnished oval of the dancing parquet, making it appear as if the floor were lit from below. The Emperor and the Shah sat together on a scarlet-covered dais, on two broad thrones of polished ebony, that looked as though they'd been carved from the deepest night. Beside the Emperor of Austria stood the Court Chamberlain. His heavy, gold-embroidered collar sucked and drank and insatiably swallowed the golden candlelight, reflected it back, gleaming and glittering, grabbed the light and generously redistributed it, competing with the candelabras and even surpassing them. The Shah was flanked by his Grand Vizier, in a black uniform. His black moustaches hung down in dreadful majesty – heavily and massively over his mouth. He smiled from time to time, at regular intervals, as though some external agency were controlling his facial muscles. The assembled ladies and gentlemen were presented to His Persian Majesty in order of rank and station. He looked closely at the women, with his childish, glowing eyes that contained everything his simple soul had to offer: hunger and curiosity, vanity and lechery, pleasantness and cruelty, pettiness and also, in spite of everything, majesty. The ladies felt the hungry, curious, vain, lecherous, cruel and majestic stare of the Shah of Persia upon them. They trembled slightly. Without realizing it, they were in love with the Shah of Persia. They were in love with his black cloak, his red, silver-embroidered cap, his curved sabre, his Grand Vizier, his harem, all his three hundred and sixty-five wives, even his Chief Eunuch and the whole country of Persia: they were in love with the Orient.

And just then, the Shah of Persia was in love with all of Vienna, all of Austria, all of Europe, all of Christendom. Never in the course of a life not exactly lacking in love and women had he felt such a degree of arousal – not even when, many years ago and still a boy, he had known a woman for the first time. How was it that the women in his harem at home were a thing of indifference, even irritation to him, while these women here, in Vienna, seemed to belong to a different race, an unknown people that were as yet undiscovered? His tanned face reddened imperceptibly, his pulse quickened, tiny beads of sweat appeared on his smooth, unwrinkled, youthful, inno-cent, bronzed brow. He quickly dabbed his eyes with his green silk handkerchief. He put it back into the deep pocket inside his sleeve, and his deft, slender fingers began to play faster and faster with the string of large blue Gurdi pearls on his left wrist. Even those cool jewels, that had always calmed and soothed his fingers, now felt irksome and hot to the touch.

Thus far, the women he had known had been of two kinds: either naked bodies or arrangements of drapery. But here were both together, at one and the same time! A gown that seemed to want to fall of its own weight, and yet clung to a body: it was like a door that wasn't locked and wouldn't open. When the women curtseyed to him, the Shah caught a glimpse of cleav-age and then the downy hair on an exposed neck. And that split second in which the ladies raised their skirts with both hands before bending at the knee, had something indescribably modest and at the same time fabulously indecent about it: it was like a promise they had no intention of keeping. So many doors that weren't locked and that may not be opened! thought the Shah of Persia, the mighty proprietor of his harem. Each one of these half-open and yet inaccessible women was more enticing to him than his entire harem, containing three hundred and sixty-five unenigmatic, unmysterious, indifferent bodies. How inexhaustible the amorous arts of the Occident must be! What sophistication and subtlety in the refusal to veil a woman's face! What was there in the world that was more mysterious and more naked than a female countenance! Their lowered eyelids betrayed and concealed, promised and deferred, laid bare and refused. What was the glitter of the diadems they wore in their hair, compared to the black, brown or blond shimmer of that hair itself, and then the array of different tones among those colours! Here was a black that was the colour of a midsummer night, while there was one as hard and matt as ebony; this brown was touched with gold, like the last dying rays of the sun, while that was reddish like the kingly maple leaf in late autumn; this blond was as bright and breezy as the laburnum in a spring garden, while that was as silvery and crisp as the first frost on an autumnal dawn. And to think that every one of these women belonged, or would belong, to one single man! Each one of them a closely guarded jewel!

No! The Shah could not think of that now. Embarrassing, troubling imaginings! He had come to Europe to enjoy the singular, to forget the plural, to trespass on individual property, to break the local law, just once, to experience the pleasure of unlawful possession and taste the particular, sophisticated pleasures of the European, the Christian, the Westerner. When the dancing began – the first number was a polka – his senses rioted. For seconds at a time, he closed his large, beautiful, shining brown, innocent doe's eyes, ashamed of the hunger and curiosity that radiated from them. He loved them all. But it wasn't their sex he was after. He felt a longing for love – the eternal male longing for the adored, the divine, the goddess, the one and only. All the delights that a woman's sex could afford he had already experienced. There was only one thing lacking: the pain that the one and only can provide.

So he went about choosing her. Gradually the women in the room were eliminated. In this and that and the other one he found more or less obvious flaws. Finally, one was left – his one and only. It was Countess W. Everyone knew her.

Young, blonde, attractive, and blessed with eyes one might best describe as resembling violets with a forget-me-not look, she had been, ever since her first coming-out ball three years ago, the cynosure of all eyes, a creature universally worshipped and desired by men. She was one of those women who in those bygone days, were revered and adored for no other reason than their sheer beauty. One looked for a moment and felt so richly rewarded one felt like saying thank you.

She was a late child. Her father was one of the oldest servants of the monarchy. He lived alone with his mineral collection on his estate in Parditz in Moravia. At times it escaped him that he had a wife and a daughter. In one such period, when he had just received a sample of a rare malachite from a friend in Bolzano and his family was the last thing on his mind, he was called upon by a department head in the Treasury, some fellow he didn't know. This was Count W. He was not, as the old man had hoped, an inamorato of minerals but merely of his daughter. Now, to any common or garden lump of quartz, the Old Master of Parditz would at least have taken his pocket magnifying glass. But in the case of the young man who had come for his daughter, he merely flashed his lorgnon. 'By all means!' he said then and there. 'I hope you'll be happy with Helene.'

The young wife loved her husband, even though she retained an occasionally fond, occasionally irksome, memory of the charming Baron Taittinger, on secondment for special services. She'd been just a girl at the time and while she appreciated all his good points – even when he was speaking, he seemed to be dancing – she had felt so threatened by him that one day she began to meet him with distinct frostiness. Poor Taittinger had sufficient imagination to believe himself deeply and passionately in love; but not sufficient stamina to await the standard outcome of passionate courtship in those days. He was a cavalryman, on secondment for special services, and proud with it, so – especially once he had spent an hour in the girl's company in the course of which she had told him to leave and she wasn't in the mood to speak to him further – he convinced, himself, that there was no shortage of such girls, and that his own honour was worth something too, and perhaps more than this.

That, then, was the final 'break' between them, a fact which made him sufficiently 'melancholy' as to go walking through Sievering one day. What did he care about Sievering? It was worse than boring: it was 'deadly'. However, a day later, it had become 'charming'. And that was on account of Mizzi Schinagl.

VII

Regrettably, the times in which our story is set are already so far distant that we are unable to establish with any certainty whether Baron Taittinger was right in his opinion that Mizzi Schinagl could have been Countess W.'s twin sister or not.

As he strolled mournfully, even abjectly, through the streets of Sievering, he made the ridiculous decision to purchase a clay pipe. And so he went into the shop of Alois Schinagl. He expected to find an elderly, dignified gentleman. The door set off a jangling bell. That too came as no surprise to Baron Taittinger. But what did surprise, nay, even alarmed him, was that, instead of the old pipe man he had expected to find, there appeared behind the counter a being who looked utterly familiar to him: if it wasn't Countess W. in person, it had to be her sister. He decided to take his time inspecting the pipes, although this wasn't something he knew much about.

The pipes were absurd and their prices were absurd. But while ostensibly examining them, bringing each one to his mouth, blowing through the mouthpiece – as he remembered once having seen his dear old Papa doing, the late Court Councillor Taittinger, when he'd accompanied him on a pipe-buying expedition to Olmütz – out of the corner of his eye he was fervently observing the delicate face of the *doppelgänger*. There was no doubting the similarity with Countess W.: the same violet eyes with the forget-me-not expression; the same hairline over a low brow; the same ash-blonde chignon on the neck, in evidence each time the girl turned round to fetch another pipe off the shelf; the same fluttering eyelids and the same sweetly mocking smile; the same sharp canine teeth that showed each time she smiled; the same movement of the hands, and the same lovely dimples on either side of her elbows.

The golden buttons on his Captain's uniform gleamed more brightly in the shop as darkness fell outside. The pipes were still perfectly visible, but the girl, Countess W.'s double, became uneasy, all alone in the shop with the strange officer, and she lit the gas jet over the cash desk to the right of the display. The light guttered slightly at first. Taittinger bought fifteen pathetic clay pipes. In addition he asked, 'What does your father do, miss?'

'He's the stove maker, Alois Schinagl!' said the girl. 'The pipes are just a sideline. Most of our customers come about stoves. We don't get many callers in our shop; most people already own pipes.'

'I'll be back tomorrow,' said Baron Taittinger. 'I get through a lot of pipes.'

He returned the following day with his valet, and bought no fewer than sixty pipes.

Three days later, he was in Sievering again: he found it 'charming'. It was three o'clock on a Saturday afternoon, and this time Mizzi treated him like an old friend, even though he was wearing civilian clothes for the first time. It was a warm and golden day. Mizzi locked up the shop, got in the hansom cab, and they drove to Kronbauer's.

Three hours later she was explaining to the stranger that she was sort of engaged, really. Engaged to Xandl Parrainer, hairdresser and wig maker by trade. They stepped out together every Sunday.

These details bothered Taittinger not at all, in fact he barely comprehended them. He got the impression the girl was recommending a local barber to him. 'By all means!' he said. 'Send him along! Herrengasse 2, first floor.'

VIII

Before long, Taittinger was bored with Mizzi. One day she told him she was pregnant, and that condition was even worse than boring: it was tedious.

The consequence of this realization was that Taittinger sought out a solicitor. Taittinger loved neither Countess W. nor Fräulein Schinagl who looked like her. He loved only, as usual, himself.

As was customary in those days, the solicitor recommended a haberdashery. All the gentlemen he advised had set up haberdashery businesses. And all the ladies concerned were doing very nicely, thank you.

And so the Baron took a couple of months off, and went to stay with an uncle of his mother's in the Bacska, where no post could reach him.

Nor did any of the fervent love letters that Mizzi Schinagl incessantly wrote, reach him. She sent these love letters to the only address she had for Taittinger: to the Herrengasse, number 2. There Taittinger's secretary, Dr Maurer, a fair judge of handwriting, duly tore them all up, unread.

By the time Baron Taittinger returned from the Bacska, Mizzi Schinagl's haberdashery shop had been set up in the Porzellangasse and was open for business and Mizzi herself was in her ninth month.

She gave birth to a son, and called him Alois Franz Alexander. Alois Franz for his natural father; Xandl for her fiancé, the hairdresser.

The haberdashery was doing well, and the hairdresser was still prepared to marry Mizzi. She too craved a quiet and decent existence. Only, while she contemplated such an eminently sensible outcome, her heart and head were full of love, and it was love for Taittinger. She was thrilled with her child. Not for one moment did she give up hope that Baron Taittinger would come to view the fruit of his loins. But Taittinger did not come.

When Xandl was three years old, Mizzi Schinagl made the acquaintance – by chance as it were, on a park bench in Schönborn – of a friendly gossipy woman, who told her about a house on the Wieden where she would be well looked after, and fine gentlemen went there, and what was a haberdashery anyway, and what kind of life was that, unmarried, with a child and a haberdashery. What kind of life was it? The same thought had often occurred to Mizzi Schinagl, word for word

'What sort of gentlemen go there?' asked Mizzi Schinagl.

'Some very distinguished gentlemen,' replied the woman. 'I can give you their names, I just need to get the list.'

She hurried off and got the list.

Mizzi herself didn't know what made her go round to Frau Matzner's house the next day. What did she care about Frau Matzner? What had she ever heard about Frau Matzner? It was summer, the end of summer. It was very hot. Late, frivolous blackbirds still whistled on the green lawns in among the cobbled streets. Six o'clock struck as she stood in front of Frau Matzner's house, 'Josephine Matzner, Masseuse, 2nd floor, ring three times' it said. She rang three times.

A positively overpowering scent of lilies of the valley, lilacs, violets, verbena and mignonette met Mizzi. Before she could tell what was happening, she was standing in the so-called pink room: the curtains in the windows were pink silk; the curtains in front of the door were pink silk; the walls were covered in pink roses; even the doorknob was a pink porcelain rosebud.

One day, or rather one evening, in walks her beloved Taittinger. He's been a regular in Josephine Matzner's house for some years.

When he spotted Mizzi Schinagl there, he wasn't surprised – as many another man would have been in his place – he tried instead to find a suitable way of opening the conversation. He couldn't remember what his solicitor had finally settled on Mizzi Schinagl, whether it had been a laundry, a millinery or a haberdashery. What he was fairly certain of, though, was that Fräulein Schinagl had had a girl child by him, and a polite inquiry after her welfare seemed in order. '*Grüß Gott!*' he said, 'How's your little girly doing?'

'We have a boy!' said Mizzi, and she blushed for the first time in several years, as if she'd been lying rather than telling the truth.

'Oh, right you are, it's a boy!' said the Baron. 'Terribly sorry!'

A little later he ordered champagne to drink a toast with Mizzi to this boy child of his. He didn't hear most of what Mizzi was telling him about the boy. He didn't hear that he was being well looked after by Frau Schyschka, who came from

Bielitz-Biala, but was pretty reliable all the same. She was also running the haberdashery, which was doing fairly well. Thus far, Mizzi Schinagl was quite pleased with how things were going. She wore a low-cut white silk dress, and checked her right garter from time to time, obviously to make sure that the money she'd made earlier, a ten-gulden note, was still there. Even though she knew that the Baron had only come to Josephine Matzner's out of old habit, she began telling herself after her second glass of champagne that it was entirely on her account. Before long, the Captain too would have sworn he had only come today to see Mizzi. The Baron had a small and sloppy heart: it was both negligent and easily moved. He still felt very fond of Mizzi, and wondered why he had left her. He even desired her, which posed rather a problem for him: it seemed bad form to buy a woman he had once enjoyed for nothing, give or take a haberdashery. But, then again, it was as bad, if not worse, to go with one of the other girls right under Mizzi's nose, so to speak. In the hope of negotiating all these imponderables, he gave Mizzi some money immediately – a golden five-gulden piece. She took it, spat on it and said: 'Let's go upstairs, I've got a nice cosy little room!'

The Baron went into the cosy little room, and stayed there till midnight, full of memories. He promised he would come again often, and he kept his word. He didn't know if he was blessed or cursed; if he loved Mizzi or the Countess; if he even loved anyone at all; if he was still the old Taittinger or not. He was practically on the point of putting himself in the third and lowest class of person: the category of 'bore'.

I X

The Mighty Sovereign of Persia, Lord of three hundred and sixty-five women and of the five thousand three hundred and thirteen roses of Shiraz, was not in the habit of suppressing a whim, let alone a desire. No sooner had his eyes chosen Countess W. than he beckoned to his Grand Vizier. His Grand Vizier leaned forward over the back of his chair. 'I have something to tell you,' whispered the Shah. 'I want,' the Shah went on, 'that young woman, tonight, the silvery blonde, you know the one I mean.'

'Sire,' the Grand Vizier made bold to reply, 'I know the one Your Majesty means. But it's, it's –' The word was 'impossible', but he knew that such a word might well cost him his life. Instead he said: ' – it's rather difficult to organize these things here so quickly!'

'Tonight!' said the Shah, to whom nothing he had ordered seemed at all unreasonable.

'Tonight!' his minister confirmed.

There was a break in the dancing. The King and his servant

returned, slow and dignified, to their places. The Emperor gave them a friendly smile. The music started up again. The dancing recommenced.

A little before midnight, Their Majesties rose, and vanished, the double doors behind their twin thrones swallowing them up.

The Shah waited in a side room. Directly opposite him, so that he can examine her in detail, is a silver figurine of Diana on a round black base. She strikes him as a faithful copy of the woman he desires. In fact, everything in the room reminds him of her: the dark blue sofa, the wall covering of pale blue silk, the lilac in the tapering majolica vase, even the crystal candle holder, the wonderful curve of the four-footed candelabra with its four slender little arms, and the silver pattern on the deep blue velvet carpet at the feet of the King of Persia. He's waiting, he's waiting! And the Shah is not used to waiting.

Unfortunately, he is made to wait. Barely twenty yards away, a conference is in progress. Its participants are the Grand Vizier, the Imperial Chamberlain and His Majesty's Aide-de-Camp. They decide to include the Chief of Police in their councils. Still, no solution can be found: the Grand Vizier wants his friend, the Aide-de-Camp Kirilida Pajidzani, to be present too – he sends for him, people start looking for him. He can't be found, the young, handsome, high-living Pajidzani.

What is at issue? The question is: which takes precedence, the laws of decency or the laws of hospitality?

The Lord Chamberlain declined firmly and with dignity; the Emperor's Aide-de-Camp likewise. Naturally enough. Both gentlemen thought it was out of the question to pass on to His Majesty the rather remarkable request of his noble visitor. But it was equally out of the question to refuse the noble visitor anything he asked.

Finally the Chief of Police said a suitable man must be found, someone on the Privy Committee. And no sooner had the phrase 'Privy Committee' been uttered than the Imperial Chamberlain called out Taittinger's name.

It was decided to take a break. Two gentlemen went into the Blue Room to the waiting Shah. He was sitting quietly in his chair, toying with his pearl bracelet, and merely asked: 'When?'

'It's only a matter,' lied the Grand Vizier, 'of finding the lady. She's disappeared amidst the confusion of the ball. We are looking for her with every man at our disposal.'

Meanwhile, 'every man at our disposal' was actually not hunting for the lady of the Shah's desires at all, but for Taittinger.

The Shah gesticulated. 'I'm waiting,' he said.

There was patience and understanding, but also an edge of menace in His Majesty's voice.

One of the worldly spies whose task it was to watch over the comings and goings, the morals and habits – the loose morals and bad habits – the friendships and *amours* of those at the top, reported to the Chief of Police that for the past hour Baron Taittinger had been in the vestibule of the theatre, engaged with the daughter of the wardrobe master, Wessely. The Chief of Police went straight there. The Captain of Horse, on secondment for special services, got up to answer the door. He was not in the least bit worried about being caught in the act – such mis-behaviour seemed to him not only unavoidable but positively imperative – but he did not want the world to know that he had been dallying with the Wessely girl, whose father was a mere wardrobe master. Poor Taittinger had no idea that the spy Vondrak had had him under observation for a long time.

Taittinger straightened his tunic and went to the door. He recognized the Chief of Police, concluded therefore that he must know about the Wessely girl already, and made no effort to shut the door after him as he stood in the corridor.

'Baron, will you come with us right away!' said the Chief of Police.

'Bye, darling!' he called over his shoulder through the open door.

As he climbed the shallow flight of stairs with the Chief of Police, he did not ask what all this was about. He already sensed it must be exceptionally tricky and hush-hush, something to do with his special secondment.

Oh no, his secondment had not been by chance. Under normal conditions, he might prove a disappointment, but under exceptional ones, his imagination got to work. The three gentlemen sat in the little room looking perplexed and vacant, exhausted from thinking, pale with worry, almost sick with anxiety, when in breezed Captain Taittinger. And after they had told him of their worries in whispered French, he cried out – no differently than if he'd been playing cards – in his usual army German that seemed to evoke all seventeen nations of the Dual Monarchy simultaneously: 'But gentlemen! The solution is staring us in the face!'

The three of them pricked up their ears.

'It's staring us in the face!' repeated Taittinger. In a flash, in the selfsame instant he'd heard that Countess W. was involved, an odd hatred that he'd never felt before had woken in him, a kind of ingenious vengefulness, an extremely inventive, highly imaginative, practically poetical vengefulness. And this now burst from him: 'Gentlemen!' he said. 'There are many, many women in Vienna, innumerable women! His Majesty the Shah – not to say that he displays bad taste, quite the contrary! But His Majesty has evidently not had the opportunity to appreciate that there are certain, shall we say, approximations.'

He was thinking of himself and of course of Mizzi Schinagl. It suddenly struck him – and struck him for the first time in his smooth and insouciant life – that he had lost all heart and all bliss for ever. An inexplicable hatred of Countess W. gripped him, as did the wish – which he found still less explicable – that the Shah might actually have his way with her. An unprecedented bewilderment raged in his soul: even as he wanted the woman he had loved and thought he was just beginning to love again to be disgracefully offered up to the Persian, he simultaneously wanted to avoid such a shameful episode at all costs. He suddenly understood that he was still unhappily in love; that unhappy love had made him vengeful; but that he also had to preserve the object of his love and his vengefulness as if she were his alone; that he wasn't even allowed to offer up the beloved woman's *doppelgänger*, i.e. Mizzi; and that, despite everything, and however circuitously, he had to betray, sell, humiliate and curse her.

'It's an easy thing, gentlemen,' he said, and as he spoke he felt shame and pleasure at the same time, 'it's an easy thing to find doubles in life. Probably every one of us – isn't that right? – has one. And ladies have their lady doubles, and why wouldn't they? Ladies have lady doubles, some of whom may be, how shall I put it, ladies of the night. The Chief of Police will understand me! – Thereby we can save ourselves a great deal of trouble. Or should I say, we should save ourselves any *embarras* to His Majesty, as well as all our perplexity and the possible appearance of inhospitableness.' '*Embarras*,' he thought, was stronger than 'embarrassment'.

The assembled company took his meaning right away. They merely looked, with a little concern, in the direction of the Grand Vizier, but his steady, polite smile never faltered. He would not – this was clear to them all – let it appear that he had understood. He too admired the Captain's resourcefulness and imagination. 'The gentlemen are agreed then?' he asked in French, as further demonstration that he could not have understood the proposal that Taittinger had delivered in German. 'May I go and inform my master?'

'We will find the lady as quickly as possible, Excellency!' said Taittinger with a bow.

Five minutes later, the few tenacious onlookers who were still standing around outside, in spite of the late hour, in the vague and sorry hope of seeing a count, an earl, or even an archduke getting into their coach or hansom cab, saw no fewer than eighteen gentlemen in tails and top hats all come out at once. Alas, though, these were no princes. They were agents from the special section, so-called 'Specials': spies, observers and students of the *beau monde*, the *demi-monde* and the underworld. The two constables who were on duty outside the entrance, however, knew very well who they were. They whistled for cabs, and the gentlemen piled into them.

All these men, as already mentioned, knew the ladies and gentlemen who moved in the three worlds: the *beau monde*, the *demi-monde* and the plain old underworld. Their Commander was one Sedlacek. Before leaving, he had assured the Chief of Police: 'Do not worry, Excellency! In half an hour, an hour at the most, I'll have the Countess here in front of you, or at any rate her spitting image.' Sedlacek was a dependable fellow. He needed no photographs. The faces were all in his memory. He knew Countess W. He knew Baron Taittinger. He knew of the Captain's hopeless love for the Countess. He knew the manner in which the Captain had consoled himself, too. He knew Mizzi Schinagl, her present whereabouts, and not just that: her background, her father, and the shop in Sievering. But despite all this – and in contrast to the Baron – he was of the opinion that Mizzi Schinagl bore no particular resemblance to the Countess so desired by His Persian Majesty, not least because she had probably changed greatly, and not for the better, from her time in Frau Matzner's house. But she remained a possibility, a stand-by, in case his men were unable to come up with a better likeness elsewhere.

Everything seemed – for the moment anyway – to have been sorted out, and for the next hour, or half an hour, the gentlemen involved, or perhaps entrusted with the affair, hoped for a little respite. Instead, something occurred that was without precedent in the annals of the court history of the Dual Monarchy: the guest of the Austrian Emperor reappeared in the ballroom. News of this was straightaway relayed to the band leader, and the orchestra straightaway struck up the Persian national anthem again. The effect on the celebrants was deadening.

The Shah, though, saw nothing, heard nothing, greeted no one. After a few minutes, he simply began mingling with the guests. He wandered around the room. He didn't notice how the people in front of him melted away, clearing a wide avenue wherever he went, splitting the world in two, as it were. The orchestra played a succession of Strauss waltzes, but the mood in the room remained glacial.

Baron Taittinger spotted him right away. He knew immediately who the Shah was looking for. Time was ticking on, the 'Specials' would be due back soon. What had to be avoided at all costs was the Shah actually speaking to the Countess within, say, the next half hour. The Shah of course couldn't be removed from the ballroom. Therefore the Countess would have to be sent home.

In order to bring this about, the Baron decided to have a word with Count W.

He went up to the little table where the Count was seated, alone. He didn't like dancing. He didn't like gambling. He didn't even like drinking. His only pleasure was jealousy. He loved it, he lived by it. It gave him a savage satisfaction to watch as his wife danced. He hated men. He thought all men were after his wife. Of all the men he knew, Captain Taittinger was his absolute favourite. He was the only one he had managed to finish off, to dispose of, to see off: he was no longer in contention.

Taittinger came straight to the point.

'Count,' he said, 'I need to have a word with you. Our Persian visitor has fallen in love with your wife!'

'So?' said the cold-blooded Count. 'That's hardly a surprise. Plenty of men are in love with her, my dear Baron!'

'True enough, my dear Count, but the Shah, well, you know the Orient!' He said nothing for a while. He gazed fervently, violently and imploringly at the cold, brutish, fair-haired face of the Count, a kind of albino carp . . .

'But you know the Orient!' he began again, feeling quite desperate already.

'The Orient doesn't interest me,' said the brute, and his watery blue eyes scanned the room for his beautiful wife.

For God's sake! thought Taittinger. Has he really no idea

what the Shah is about? How can he be so indifferent? He's so
jealous the rest of the time.

'You know, I don't mind about the Shah!' said the Count.
'My jealousy doesn't extend to Orientals.'

'No, no! Quite, quite!' cried the Captain. Never in his life
had be been in such a pickle. Moreover, a little voice inside him
had begun to say it was all his own fault! All of a sudden he felt
the stifling heat from the candles, a luminous simoom, and his
own folly on top of it, which was making him boil. He started
to sweat, from fear mainly. It had to come out, he couldn't
bottle it up any longer. And in a fit of desperation, he came out
with the sentence: 'I'm telling you, we have to get the Countess
out of the ballroom for a while!'

The Count, who had been sitting there so dully and
brutishly, suddenly reddened. Rage darkened his pale little eyes.
'I beg your pardon!' he cried.

Taittinger remained seated. 'Please listen to what I'm telling
you,' he said. He summoned the last of his strength, and continued: 'What is at stake here is the honour of your wife, of
yourself, of all the ladies assembled here in this ballroom. The
gentleman from Teheran must not be allowed to meet the
Countess tonight. Look at the way he's stalking about the
room. He is His Majesty's guest. He is a crowned head. He is
on a diplomatic visit. He will stop at nothing – unless we
manage to trick him. Within half an hour, perhaps even fifteen
minutes,' the Captain looked at his watch, 'the danger will have
been averted. Count, I beseech you, be calm, and allow me to
have a five minute tête-à-tête with the Countess.'

The Count sat down, cold and pale once more. 'I'll go and
get her!' said the Captain. He stood up, feeling relieved, but still
a little apprehensive.

X

The danger was not over yet. It was not a straightforward matter – finding a suitable way of explaining to a woman the fact that the Shah wanted her, so to speak, on a plate. Clearly the woman couldn't be told the whole story. The Chief of Police, in discussions with the Minister of the Interior, smiled warmly at the Captain, as if he hadn't seen him for some days. The Minister made his excuses and left immediately. The Captain asked: 'Has Sedlacek come back yet?' The expression on the face of the Chief of Police was one of complete astonishment.

The next instant, the penny dropped for Taittinger. The Chief of Police had no knowledge of anything, and would deny all knowledge to the end of his life. So the Captain merely said: 'Well, I'm on my way, then!' and left as fast as circumstances would allow. He understood that the Chief of Police would deny everything, but as yet had no idea of the full repercussions of his plan. He made straight for the Countess. 'Your husband sends me,' he said.

Everything seemed to go well. The coach drove up. Countess W. and her husband got in. Before the Count could give any instructions to the coachman, Taittinger, with presence of mind born of desperation, called up: 'To the Prater, man! Their Lordships want some fresh air!'

Whereupon, as the wheels rolled soundlessly off, and only the gentle, stylish clatter of the two chestnut horses was heard, the Captain was ashamed of his pathetic cry. I must have had too much to drink, he thought, or else I've lost my mind.

But he hadn't lost his mind: his prognosis had been accurate. There was no need to give Franz Sedlacek detailed instructions and descriptions. He had sufficient resourcefulness.

Neither he nor his men had been able, in just under half an hour, to find a woman – or as Sedlacek was pleased to say: 'a party' – to offer His Majesty in place of the lady he had chosen. There was only one thing for Sedlacek: to fetch Mizzi Schinagl from the renowned establishment of Josephine Matzner.

He had hurriedly pulled her from the embrace of an old forester, and taken her, as she was, which was in a little garter-length red number, in the hansom cab with him. There was enough time on the way to give her her instructions. 'Keep your mouth shut,' he said. 'If he asks you your name, say: Helene. Act dumb. You don't understand about anything, you're a Lady, got that? Can you remember what it was like with your first boyfriend? Make an effort and concentrate! Try it for me now if you like! Only act it out, of course. I'm on duty. Well?'

Sedlacek left her in the cab with the roof up. A policeman stood guard over the lonely vehicle, which was parked some ten steps away from all the others. Mizzi Schinagl shivered.

They had to find her a ballgown, silk, sky blue, *décolleté*, plus corset, pearls and diadem. Sedlacek thought of everything. His men, four gifted operatives, had spent the last quarter of an hour digging around in the costume department of the Burgtheater. The nightwatchman stood over them with his lantern. Four formally dressed ghosts in tails, with canes in their hands and top hats on their heads, crashed about in the midst of the dreamy array of theatrical props. They grabbed at anything that was pale blue and seemed silky. Their pockets bulged with artificial pearls, glittery, fiery diadems, fake flowers, forget-me-not-blue garters, sparkling brooches. It all came off very efficiently, in a way that very few things in that state ever did. In another short while – and to untrained Oriental eyes the accommodating Schinagl would look almost like a Lady. She waited in the dressing room of the Court Official Second Class, Anton Wessely, whose daughter Taittinger had only recently had to leave with such abruptness.

All else was effected under the veritably refined direction of Sedlacek, and with the assistance of the flexible Aide-de-Camp Kirilida Pajadzani. His Persian Majesty was conveyed in a sealed coach, followed by Sedlacek in a cab, to the house of Frau Matzner. If one of the regulars had happened by at that time, he would have had no option but to suppose the house – and indeed the whole of the street – had been transformed by magic. The house slept, the street slept, the lights were out, the whole world seemed blotted out. Only the narrow and impartial section of sky over the rooftops was still awake, with its twinkling silver stars.

The interior of Frau Matzner's house was similarly transformed. All its denizens were locked away in their rooms. Frau Matzner herself had the keys. Dressed in her dove-grey, high-necked and high-toned gown, and standing in gloomy lighting she had gone to considerable trouble to create by means of various fabrics and drapes, all to conceal the rather common décor, she resembled the ghost of a taciturn chambermaid, come back to life after hundreds of years. With a deep bow, she welcomed the pair on their arrival: Mizzi and His Majesty. There was no sound and nothing could be seen clearly. His Majesty the Shah must have had the impression of having arrived in one of those fairy-tale Occidental castles his thirsting imagination had evoked over the course of many years in Teheran. He really believed it. Altogether more innocent than, say, some European Christian arriving in Persia at round about that time, and supposing he had discovered the secrets of the Orient merely by peeking into a perfectly ordinary public brothel, His Majesty that night was enchanted by the secrets of the Occident he thought he had finally managed to uncover. So it's not the case then – he said to himself in his charmed simple-mindedness – that these magnificent women here are the exclusive property of their husbands! Of course – he went on – they have no harems as such; but how much more delightful, charming and appetizing love is without a harem! . . . You don't buy the woman – you're actually made a present of her! So all the while these Occidentals preach virtue and monogamy, they not only unveil their wives – they lend them out to others!

That night, His Majesty, the Shah of Persia, became finally convinced that the erotic arts of the West were considerably more sophisticated than those of his native land. That night, he tasted all the delights that cannot come to a man from a familiar, native love, but only from one that is unfamiliar, exotic, strange. The methods that the spy Sedlacek had advised Mizzi Schinagl to adopt were indeed exotic to the ruler of Persia. He was no European, he had a harem of three hundred and sixty-five women. There are that many nights in a year. Whereas here, in the house of Josephine Matzner, he had but one.

Sedlacek spent the whole night waiting outside in a cab. Don't imagine he was one of those feeble, undependable characters capable of going to sleep before their job is done. On the contrary, never was sleep further from his thoughts, never had his eyes felt so watchful! It was in his character. What was at stake was not recompense; commendations; promotion. Dark deeds needed to be done, and they were to remain forever shrouded in secrecy! He wasn't someone hanging around hoping for a tip!

When the Shah awoke the following morning, he found no one in the bed next to him. He looked around in surprise, almost in panic. From the dark green canopy over the bed hung a tasselled rope. It had seen considerable wear. He gave it a tug, in the vague hope that it might make some noise somewhere. He was not mistaken. It was in fact a bell.

Many other men had used it before him.

XI

A clement blue morning sky arched over the city. The dew in the gardens had a freshness and vivaciousness that mingled with the warm, dry aroma of the crisp new-born loaves and rolls being carried in the baskets of bakers' boys.

It was a spring morning of radiant beauty. The poor Shah saw nothing of it. Guarded rather than escorted, by two alert members of his retinue, he trundled through the smiling streets in a closed carriage. He was in a bad mood. The previous night's adventure was a pleasant memory, but in his healthy simplicity he had hoped for a great and hallowed experience; something that would have worked a transformation in his soul, of his ways of seeing and hearing and feeling. It was, to put it bluntly, the biggest disappointment of his life. He had had in mind a splendid celebration, and it had turned out to be a humdrum little party. What had he really learned about European love? He no longer loved the city as he had the previous evening. Indeed, the whole of that evening now struck him as a glittering deception. The longer the drive went on, the riper the beaming day became, the more the monarch's soul clouded over, and the more bitter grew its taste. He remembered the wise words of his Chief Eunuch, who had warned him that desire and curiosity were an illusion. There was considerable rancour in his heart, and a longing to do penance. He felt like a boy who, after just an hour, has broken his new toy.

To his attendants he said not one word. If he had spoken, it would have been to say that the world that only a few hours ago had been so rich, was now suddenly empty. But was that really the kind of thing he could say, the Shah, their master?

The moment he returned, he summoned his Chief Eunuch to him. Was he happy here? the Shah asked him while he calmly scooped out half an orange. There was a warm and homely, one might almost say, Persian aroma in the room, from the strong coffee His Majesty had drunk a little earlier. It was prepared over a pretty little open flame, in a special earthenware pot. The flame was still burning: it looked like a sacrificial fire.

The Chief Eunuch replied that he was happy here, he was happy wherever he could be near his Shah. Old liar, thought the Shah. Still, the flattery pleased him. He said: 'I've half a mind to punish you for your lying, and make your life less agreeable.'

'His Majesty is merciful always,' said the Eunuch, 'his punishment would only make my life still sweeter.'

'How are my wives?' asked the Shah.

'Sire,' replied the Eunuch, 'they are eating properly, they are healthy, they sleep comfortably in large, comfortable beds. Only one thing makes them unhappy: that their Lord doesn't visit them!'

'I don't want to see another woman, not this year, not next

year. That European didn't make me happy either. You were the only one who predicted that. Does a man have to be castrated to gain wisdom?'

'Sire,' replied the castrate, 'I know foolish eunuchs; and whole men who are wise.'

This was an insult, and the Shah sensed it. 'What would you do if you were disappointed?' asked His Majesty.

'I would feel hurt, and I would pay, Sire. Disappointments are costly.'

'Indeed they are!' said the King. He called for his hookah and was quiet for a long time.

During this period of silence, he made up his mind to go home. He didn't like it here. The West offended him. It didn't live up to what he thought it had promised. Gloom spread across his soft, yellowish face, making it, in spite of his youthful glossy black beard, that of an old man.

'If it wasn't that you were castrated, I wouldn't mind changing places with you,' said the Shah. The Eunuch bowed deeply. 'You may go!' said the ruler; but then straightaway he called: 'No, stay!'

'Stay!' he called once more, as though afraid that even his castrate might slip through his fingers. He alone, in the whole of the Shah's retinue, was capable of selecting the most subtly appropriate and the most magnificent of gifts. Eunuchs have something courtly about them.

'I have a job for you,' said the Shah. 'I want you to take a present to the Lady from last night. I want it to be worthy of Our Majesty, but also of your own discrimination. Make sure no one from my retinue sees you. You must find the house and the woman by yourself. I wash my hands of the matter. I'm relying on you.'

'My Master may have every confidence in me!' said the Chief Eunuch.

He had already accomplished tasks in his life that were more demanding and more sensitive. Since his arrival, he'd been on good terms with the lackeys and footmen, and he was well able to distinguish between the avaricious and the bribe-able, and between the clever, the useful and the foolish. He didn't speak their language, but everyone understood his: the language of money and signs. The Chief Eunuch made his meaning perfectly clear.

It was a simple matter to find the way to Mizzi Schinagl. Everyone on the staff knew where the Shah had spent the night. What was less easy was finding a present of the right sort, one that would express his master's power and his own good taste. He thought about it for a long time. He didn't know the lady. He imagined she must occupy a lofty station. He decided on a heavy triple-string of pearls. Their value seemed a suitable price to pay. Accompanied by the court lackey Stephan Lackner, he drove up to Frau Matzner's house the following afternoon.

The visitor was not expected. Frau Matzner was still in her nightgown, and Pollak the piano player was in flannel long johns and slippers. The Chief Eunuch, in Western dress so discreet and conservative and navy blue that it looked almost like an attempt to make its wearer invisible, was not so ignorant that he didn't immediately realize where he was. It took neither familiarity with Europe nor any distinct sexuality to grasp Frau Matzner's line of business. He regretted the exquisite pearls in their silver case.

Mizzi was sent for. She arrived with a couple of pins holding up her tousled-looking hair, her face thickly powdered, and having just pulled on her red dress. A couple of hooks at the back were not done up. This made her stand with her back to the door she'd just come through: she stood there like a condemned man waiting for the firing squad to put him out of his misery.

Standing thus, she accepted from a fat gentleman in a navy-blue suit, a bunch of orchids, a silver case and a long and incomprehensible oration. Once or twice she nodded or gulped. Not even Frau Matzner, who might have bucked her up with a look, was present. Frau Josephine had run out to get dressed. When she returned, ready for anything, the ceremony was unfortunately already over, and the dark blue gentleman was in the process of leaving. He recognized Josephine Matzner immediately, in spite of her transformation, took out his purse and presented it, with a slight bow, to the lady of the house. The purse was light. No wonder: it contained only gold pieces.

The following day, when the Chief Eunuch reported back to his master, the Shah asked whether the Lady had said anything.

'Your Highness,' replied the servant, 'she will never forget you. I could see that quite clearly, even though I couldn't understand her words.'

XII

Many people, contented or dissatisfied, were to remember the Shah for a long time to come. For he had distributed largesse and honours as he had seen fit, without taking advice from his Ambassador, and without any regard to the rank and station of those he had honoured or rewarded.

The only truly unhappy man among them was Cavalry Captain Taittinger. For the very day after the distinguished visitor's departure, his 'special service' was abruptly terminated, and he was ordered back to his regiment.

The whole sorry tale disappeared into oblivion: or rather, into the secret files of the police. No one will ever know why poor Taittinger had to return to garrison with such haste.

In his small garrison town in Silesia, however, there was nothing to distract the Baron from reflecting on the wretched episode. He had sufficient insight to draw some superifical conclusions and formed, as he saw it, an exceptionally harsh opinion of himself: in his own estimation, he was now no longer 'charming'.

From that time, he also began to drink. It crossed his mind to write to Countess W. and ask her forgiveness for betraying her to the Persian. But he tore up first one draft of a letter, then another, then a third. Whereupon he drank even more.

His dreams kept returning to the moment when he was walking down the stairs and met the spy coming the other way, doffing his hat to him. He saw himself sliding down a smooth ramp of stone. He took no more pleasure in women, his duties bored him, he didn't get on with his comrades, the Colonel was dull. The town was dull, and life was even worse. There wasn't a word for it in Taittinger's vocabulary.

He slipped and sank even lower. He felt himself doing it. He would have liked to talk to someone about it, perhaps to Mizzi Schinagl who also appeared in his dreams. But he felt too torpid and too dumbstruck to be able to say anything honest and truthful. So he didn't talk. And he drank.

As for Mizzi Schinagl's great euphoria, it lasted barely three weeks. The whole of Frau Josephine Matzner's establishment shared in it. All Sievering was enraptured when they heard from the old pipe-seller Schinagl that his daughter had joined the suite of the Shah of Persia, and was thinking of moving to Teheran. It was in such distorted form that the news of Mizzi's Oriental adventure reached Sievering. There was no shortage of intermediaries and rumour mongers. First wind of it came from the hairdresser Xandl. No one believed him. He was so offended by this that he beseeched Mizzi to go to her father and tell him herself. Finally she agreed to do so. She drove up in a two-horse carriage. When she got in, Xandl sat beside her, and stayed there most of the way. As they approached

Sievering, though, he moved to the back seat, facing Mizzi.

It was an emotional, even a heart-rending reunion. Old Schinagl was weeping. Barely six months had passed since he had assured the whole of Sievering that he had disowned his daughter, and didn't want to see her again as long as he lived. But what can a man do in the face of money? Old Schinagl embraced his disowned daughter in full sight of everyone.

As Mizzi Schinagl walked out of her father's shop, the throng opened up before her. She was a touchingly pretty thing, in her dark green dress, with a wide-brimmed blue hat and a pale grey parasol in her hand. The people of Sievering could wish for no fairer queen for their Persian friends. She smiled and waved as she got in the carriage, and once more Xandl the hairdresser climbed in opposite her. The driver cracked his whip smartly and discreetly. Away rolled the cab, away into the city, and Mizzi waved with a white handkerchief. Old Schinagl stood in his doorway, weeping.

This was far from being the only exalted hour in the new life of Mizzi Schinagl. She had many such – indeed, her days were entirely made up of lofty and elevating hours.

The pearls were lodged with Efrussi's Bank, there was no need to worry about them. But when good fortune breaks in upon the life of a poor, helpless girl with the force of a natural disaster, it gives her a lot to think about! She needs to make a new life for herself. Xandl junior needs to go to a boarding school so something can be made of him – she wants him to be a fine gentleman when he grows up! How should she repay Frau Matzner? Or Xandl, her fiancé? Should she remain in Vienna? Wouldn't it be better to move somewhere new? Perhaps abroad. Monte Carlo was a possibility, and in the *Kronen-Zeitung* they wrote about Ostende, Nice, Ischl, Zoppot,

Baden-Baden, Franzensbad, Capri, Merano. It was such a big world! Mizzi Schinagl didn't know where any of these places were, but she knew she could get to them. Her sudden wealth excited people; but it stunned her. Confused visions of spa towns, furniture, houses, châteaux, servants, horses, theatres, gentlemen, dogs, garden fences, races, lottery numbers, dresses and tailors filled her nights, when she couldn't sleep, and her dreams when she could. She had long since stopped meeting clients. Josephine Matzner gave her advice, though she too was stunned by the magnitude of the good fortune that had befallen her girl. Still, she had sufficient commonsense left to give Mizzi some sound advice.

'You should marry Xandl,' recommended Frau Matzner, 'he can open a big hairdressing salon downtown. Put some of your money in the haberdashery. Put some in my establishment. Do everything by the book. Put your boy in the Church orphanage in Graz. If you get bored with Xandl, take a lover! You're swimming in money, but you must organize it properly. If you don't you'll spend it in short order, and in two years you'll have nothing left. Take my advice, I want the best for you!'

But Mizzi Schinagl was in no position to take sensible advice. She sometimes thought of a husband, but it was the unattainable Captain Taittinger. One of her pet fantasies was that he could resign from the army and marry her, now that she was so rich.

Gwendl the Jeweller estimated the value of the pearls at around fifty thousand gulden. Efrussi's Bank had advanced her ten thousand gulden using them as collateral. Even her bank account alarmed and stunned poor Mizzi Schinagl. She went around with a thousand gulden in notes stuffed into her stocking. She kept another hundred in the form of ten gold pieces in her purse. A further hundred, in silver money, were in the care of Frau Matzner.

One day, Mizzi felt she had to see Taittinger. This feeling came to her with such violence that she got a cab, drove to Grünberg on the Graben, and bought four dresses on the spot. She had three of them sent home, and put on the one that was her favourite. Then she drove to the Herrengasse, to that dear, familiar address. There she learned that the Captain had been ordered to return to his regiment. She felt an even greater confusion. It seemed to her now that, but for the stunning and enrapturing storm of good fortune, she would have been able to hold on to the love of her heart, the only man she really loved.

Her next obsession was the idea that she had to visit Taittinger in his barracks. She told Frau Matzner she had to go and find him. 'You'll write to him first,' said Frau Matzner, 'you don't just turn up on a man's doorstep. Nor do you throw yourself at him willy-nilly, least of all when your net worth is more than his.'

Mizzi Schinagl wrote to tell Taittinger that she had become rich, that she missed him, and when could she visit him.

Baron Taittinger received her letter in the regimental office. The handwriting looked familiar; but for several weeks now he had felt an antipathy towards it. He put the letter in his pocket, unread, and decided to look at it later. But he only got to bed at three, having been in the Café Bielinger. He came across it two days later – and then only because his valet had emptied his pockets.

To the Baron, the idea of seeing Mizzi Schinagl again seemed too awful. She reminded him of his foolish error. Ideally, he would have liked the whole episode to disappear from his life altogether. But is it possible to rub something out of your life, as though it had never been?

So Captain Taittinger told Warrant Officer Zenower – one of the few 'charmers' in the regiment – to send, as it were, an official letter to Fräulein Mizzi Schinagl care of Josephine Matzner, to say that the Captain had been given leave of absence for health reasons, and would be away from the regiment for the next six months.

Mizzi Schinagl wept long and loud when she received the letter. She felt as though her life was finished – at the very moment when it should have been beginning. She decided to fetch her son and keep him with her for the time being. He might be a source of comfort to her.

And she moved to Baden. She took out a two-year lease on a house in the Schenkgasse. Gwendl the jeweller purchased the pearls. The proceeds from the sale were administered by the solicitor Sachs. Five hundred gulden went to Old Schinagl. Five hundred went to Frau Matzner. Five hundred went to Xandl the hairdresser. Grünberg, the dressmaker on the Graben, received a thousand. Everyone was happy: everyone except for Mizzi Schinagl.

XIII

After a while it transpired that the spa town of Baden exercised no beneficial influence on Mizzi's nature. There were many reasons for this. First among them were the races. Mizzi Schinagl couldn't stay at home. She had never been to the races before in her life. Now it seemed to her she had to go to each and every one. It was as though some infernal force compelled her to keep challenging fate – the fate that had caused such a tremendous storm of good fortune to rain down on her.

Lacking all understanding of the male of the species – which was inevitable following a stint in a so-called house of ill-repute, where one learned as much about the real world as one might in a girls boarding school – Mizzi judged the men she met now by the same standards that she applied to the hourly guests at Frau Matzner's establishment. It was no surprise therefore that she took conmen and scoundrels for gentlemen from good backgrounds. She was lonely. She missed Frau Matzner's house. Every day she sent picture postcards to her father, to Frau Matzner, to each of her eighteen girls, and to Taittinger's regiment, with the instructions on the envelope: 'Please be sure he gets this. Thanks, Schinagl.'

The message was always the same: she was really enjoying herself, life was wonderful. Taittinger never replied. Frau Matzner occasionally replied with an ordinary postcard, full of sensible instructions and advice. The girls all wrote together on blue, gilt-edged letter paper, and always began: 'We're glad you're happy, and we think of you a lot.' And all their signatures at the end: Rosa, Gretl, Valli, Vicky and the rest of them, by age and seniority in Frau Matzner's house. Mizzi was eager for every item of post, and would read each one with a strange tension: it was more of a torment to her than a pleasure.

As far as men were concerned, the only reason Mizzi bothered with them was because she was quite convinced that life without them was no more possible than life without oxygen. When she'd been poor and working and not known what to do, she had accepted money. Now she could offer them love for nothing. It was good for her, to offer love for nothing. Sometimes it was she who paid men. Some of them were pleased to borrow from her for their 'business'. She didn't care for any of them. Men had been her daily, her nightly bread. She was like a poor quarry seeking its own hunters.

Her yearning for her son had once been so powerful – and now it all seemed futile and a waste. She didn't like him. He got in the way, principally because she thought she had to take him with her wherever she went: to cafés, to the races, to hotel lobbies, to the theatre, to her men friends, on outings. With large, bulging, watery eyes, the boy would take in his new surroundings with a grim and taciturn malice. He never cried. And Mizzi Schinagl, who could remember often crying as a girl, and who also had a sound instinct which told her that children who don't cry become bad people when they grow up, often hit him for no reason, just to set him off. He took his blows, the young fellow, he seemed to feel no pain at all. Although he wasn't able to say very many words, he did manage to make it perfectly clear that he didn't want anything beyond the satisfaction of his immediate wants: a piece of paper, a match, a bit of string, a toy, a pebble.

After a few weeks, Mizzi admitted that her son meant less to her than any child she could think of. That was the second disappointment of her life, following her terrifying stroke of good fortune; and more hurtful than the news that Captain Taittinger had been recalled to his regiment. Now it was as though his son had been recalled to his regiment, too.

Long before the end of the season, she hurried to Graz with the boy. She wanted to get rid of him, really. She thought she would have him brought up the way upper-class children were brought up. She had a list of addresses. She didn't go round all of them by any means, but left him at the first place she looked at. And so it was that her son, Xandl Schinagl, came to be at The Academy for Underage Boys, with Kindergarten, under the tutelage of Professor Weißbart. And as for Mizzi, once she'd begun to go south, she felt unable to stay in Graz or to return to Baden. She thought it would be mean of her to stay in Graz where her son was, without seeing him: and she didn't want to see him much: not for the moment. Nor could she return to Baden, because there waiting for her was Franz Lissauer, who had cost her so much already. God only knew why she'd been living with him for the past three weeks!

She was bothered, not only by the fact that this man was waiting for her, but that so many others were too. They were all waiting for her: all except Taittinger. He wouldn't wait!

In fact, nor did Lissauer either. Once he realized she wasn't coming back, he went to Vienna, to get Mizzi's address from Frau Matzner. He said he had some important news for her from Taittinger.

He was determined not to lose Mizzi again, instead he would try and follow her. So he left for Merano.

Mizzi Schinagl was glad to see him on the promenade. In his shiny Peiachevich trousers, blue jacket and soft ochre button-boots, he appealed to her tenderness and to a kind of remorse as well. She was scared! Scared of her own wealth, scared of the new life it enjoined on her, scared of the big wide world she had thoughtlessly gone out into and, most of all, scared of men. At Josephine Matzner's house, she had been the superior of every man, strange or familiar, exotic or local, gentleman or vagabond. It was her patch, her home. She had neither the ability nor the technique to deal with men who hadn't come to purchase her. Of course she could interpret their lustful glances and signs, make sense of their veiled expressions and their silly jokes. But on her own she was helpless and homeless, she drifted about, rudderless, without oars or sails on the world's sea, and she was scared: infinitely and indefinably scared. She was looking for something familiar, something she could at least half-recognize. She was inclined to confuse the familiar with the intimate. And so she greeted Franz Lissauer.

He must have guessed what was going on in her heart, thanks to the sure instinct some creatures have, or are able to produce in themselves, that alerts them to the presence of danger, food, pleasure or prey. He aired his sun-yellow panama hat and said coolly: 'Fancy meeting you here.'

'I'm so glad!' she replied – and threw her arms around him.

At that moment a plan formed in his head. It was the old Brussels lace scam.

At that time, Brussels lace was as highly prized as jewels – and even more coveted by women.

The celebrated lace could not fail, therefore, to inspire numerous imitations. It was in the most successful of these that Lissauer's friend, Xavier Ferrente, dealt; though a native of Trieste himself, his wares came from another foreign and fairly distant port, namely Antwerp. That was their declared 'provenance' on the forms. In fact, they came from the Schirmer haberdashery on the Wienzeile. Lissauer's job, if he could be said to work at all, was to find buyers and so-called bulk buyers for his friend Ferrente, and intermediaries, and smaller intermediaries to go between the larger ones. In return, he would earn a 'fee', though never a 'percentage'. 'The only way you'll get a percentage is if you invest capital,' said Ferrente. 'It takes some to make more,' he added. This was a current piece of wisdom among the tarot players at the Café Steidl.

Now at last, after so many years of 'sweating my guts out for Ferrente' – as Lissauer liked to put it – he saw the possibility of buying his way into the business; by using Mizzi Schinagl's capital.

Having made this decision, Lissauer went out of his way to neglect Mizzi Schinagl. He went on outings with a certain Fräulein Korngold, he sent Frau Glaeser flowers, he was seen strolling on the promenade with the Brandl girl, he either arrived late for rendezvous with Mizzi or else forgot them entirely, and altogether he gave her to understand that she meant little or nothing to him. Indeed, sometimes he even let slip that he was planning to leave quite soon.

After carrying on like this for a few days, he went to Innsbruck, and from there he telegraphed Mizzi Schinagl: 'Gone on important business, expect return tomorrow evening.'

And the following evening he appeared. Not only was he nicer to her than he'd been for a long time: he even showed her some affection. At the same time there was something excited in his manner. 'A great stroke of luck,' he said. The same breathless excitement infected his speech. At last, at last, he was on his way to becoming wealthy.

'Are you getting married?' That was the first thing that sprang to Mizzi's mind. How else would a man suddenly get rich?

'Married?' said Lissauer, 'Ha, now that's an idea!' He came over all thoughtful.

Mizzi Schinagl knew only one thing about Brussels lace, which was that it was expensive. She could hardly tell a muslin curtain from a bridal veil. She had not seen inside her own haberdashery more than four or five times. But even she understood that a piece of lace that sold for five gulden fifty and cost one gulden eighty was not to be despised. 'We'll be partners,' said Lissauer, 'fifty-fifty! Done?'

'Done,' said Mizzi Schinagl, and she put the lace from her mind. They started to extinguish the lights in the hotel lobby. An indescribable sadness emanated from the white splendour of the staircase and balustrade; the blood-red, now almost black splendour of the carpets. The huge palms in their huge pots looked like they had recently arrived from the cemetery. Their dark green leaves also looked blackish, like wizened, perished weapons from olden days. The gas lights in the candelabras buzzed a poison green, and each time she fleetingly and anxiously looked into the big reddish mirrors in their fake bronze frames, they showed her a different Mizzi Schinagl, one she didn't know and had never seen, a Mizzi Schinagl who had never been.

She became terribly sad. Her simple soul was briefly illumined, indirectly and at a lower wattage, by the light that makes older and wiser people so happy and so sad: the light of understanding. She understood the sorrow and futility of everything: not just the lace, not just Lissauer, not just her fortune, but her son and Taittinger, her longing for a home, love, a husband and the false love of her father, all of it, all of it . . . And in her own heart there blew a savage blast; a blast like the one from the icehouse back in Sievering, when she'd been a little girl and firmly believed that that was where winter and ill winds came from.

That night, Lissauer went up to her room with her, because he knew it was important now to possess her. Mizzi Schinagl could sense it. She was tired; tired and indifferent.

Laying awake that night, she decided to go back in the morning. But back where? Josephine Matzner's house had been a home of sorts. No longer. She remembered the heavy breath, the scented beard, the yellow-brown skin, the soft hands, the spooky whites of the eyes of the Shah of Persia, the founder of her fortune. She started to cry softly. It was Nature's sedative.

Just as day broke, she fell asleep.

XIV

For a long time, none of the people around Frau Matzner noticed that, as her body was changing, so was her character. They only saw she was getting old. She was aware of it herself, though she didn't look in the mirror often. It was as though she had a mirror in her head, the way some people have a clock. Only a few years had passed since she relished the odd, crude compliment from her regulars. As compliments they were meaningless. They were not intended to express any desire on the part of the client, and nor did they make any impression on the heart of Frau Matzner. There was really no reason why they could not have gone on in all perpetuity, just like certain other conventional usages that go on irrespective of age. But no, what happened? Even these notional, purely formal compliments, directed at her for so many years now, gradually dried up; and one evening they stopped altogether. It was almost as if it was something the gentlemen had tacitly agreed upon among themselves. When the last visitor had gone home, the girls had all gone to bed, and the fiddler was hanging up his tails, she took a quick peek in the mirror behind the till. Yes, it confirmed what she had known for a long time: in among her grey hair played an ugly glimmer of her younger, provocative, spicy redness. Two thick furrows crossed her brow – for no reason that she could see – down to the bridge of her nose. Her lips were dry, cracked and blueish. The eyes, under their heavily wrinkled lids, were like two tiny dried-up ponds. Her head sat squarely on her shoulders, as though she didn't have a neck. And on her breasts, under a thick layer of powder, there were flecks of orange that looked like some sort of insect.

That night, Frau Matzner realized that her life was over. She had never been much given to illusions anyway. She was minded to tackle her old age with the same courage with which she had once tackled her youth, her profession, the opposite sex and her business. In every hour of her life, she had been straight with herself. She even knew all the devils she was prey to throughout her life, and could have listed them for you. But there is one devil of old age, who often creeps into the souls of lonely old women, and hardens their hearts and fills their decaying senses with a new pleasure, whom she didn't know: and that was avarice. She couldn't feel herself becoming ever more miserly and niggardly.

Admittedly, there was a development that seemed to her to justify her avarice – or her thrift, as she thought of it – her establishment was no longer flourishing. How changeable are the fashions of the world! Frau Matzner's establishment was no longer 'in'. Two new rivals had sprung up, one near the Wollzeile, the other in the upper Zollamtsstraße. Also, the girls who were loyal to Frau Matzner were getting on – and the younger ones jumped ship. Those times were gone when Frau Matzner could talk about her 'golden girls', and when those same girls would call out to her in their twittering voices 'Auntie Fini' or 'Finerl'. They called her 'Frau Matzner' now, and the girls were not so much golden as brassy, like the coins they brought home to her. 'I have to be grateful for every penny they bring in!' she groaned.

She had sleepless nights. Each time she lay down, she had the feeling she was making herself defenceless, easy prey to her fears. So she got up again and shuffled over to her rocker. She was much given to groaning, thinking it afforded her some relief, but then she said to herself: I must be in a bad way if I, Josephine Matzner, go around groaning like this. From time to time she would take something to help her sleep, but it never seemed to work on her fears, her pains, her dread! She could picture herself in the poorhouse on the Alsergrund; at the table of the Sisters of Charity; as a skivvy, scrubbing the floors of Dvorak the dairywoman; and finally at the police station, in court, and even in prison. It seemed clear to her that eventually she would be so poor that she would be forced to steal. Then she pictured herself stealing, and already she felt the hand of the policeman on her shoulder.

She went more and more often to visit her banker, Herr Efrussi. His wealth, his cleverness, his honesty, his reputation, his age: it all soothed and comforted her. He was a quiet old man, of a calculating kindliness (the only sort that doesn't wreak destruction on this earth). Frau Josephine Matzner sat on the uncomfortable visitor's chair in his old-fashioned office, very low down (the banker Efrussi still used a high desk with a tiny backless swivelling stool attached). So, half-standing, half-sitting, he perched at his desk. He turned to face Frau Matzner. But no matter how much he lowered his seat, he remained considerably above the level of her head. There was no question of his being able to look into her face because she was wearing a large hat, and only the mild trembling of a purple ostrich feather indicated to Efrussi whether Frau Matzner was in agreement or not.

'The position is this,' he told her for the twenty-fifth time, 'you have five thousand in "Albatross", three thousand five hundred in bonds, ten thousand in the haberdashery, two thousand in Schindler's bakery, you own business is worth – I have no idea; your solicitor will know. You will know too. You are fifty-three years old.'

At which point Frau Matzner interrupted: 'Fifty-two, Herr Efrussi!'

'Even better,' he resumed, 'so if your business isn't doing too well, and you aren't ready to retire yet and live on your dividends, well, you have at least eight good years ahead of you, when you could work in your haberdashery, for instance. Or start a fashion business – buy one – you have good taste.' The purple ostrich feathers always suggested high fashion to the banker.

'Are you quite sure of all that, Imperial Councillor?' asked Josephine Matzner.

'I can prove it to you,' said Efrussi, and, as usual, he shook the little bell on his desk, at which, as usual, his bookkeeper appeared. He opened the books.

Frau Matzner looked uncomprehendingly at blue figures, red lines, green feints: how comforting it all was. She rose, nodded, and said: 'Imperial Councillor, you've taken a weight off my mind.' And, not before time, she left.

One day it occurred to her that she ought to see how things were going in Mizzi Schinagl's haberdashery. Even before she set foot in the familiar premises, something seemed somehow different. She had a sense of foreboding. There were two new gold-framed mirrors in the window, and the glass door had a sign with 'Genuine Brussels Lace' on it. And her heart stopped when she saw Herr Lissauer in the shop. She knew his type – 'clients' was the right word for them. 'It's been a long time, Herr von Lissauer!' she said. 'It's too bad, all our friends have given us up. We aren't up-to-date enough for today's gentlemen. I expect what we have to offer is pretty staid, really, compared to the upper Zollamtsstraße.'

'Oh, you know how it is,' said Lissauer. 'A man needs to settle down after a time. And, as you see, I've got a lot on my hands here.'

Yes, she could see that. With a quick look around her – of the sort that had made her such an intimidating figure in her younger years; in her own house, in the shops she frequented, in the whole district and even in the local police station, where she knew every uniformed and plain-clothes officer – she took in the entire shop. What sort of haberdashery was this? Where were the pretty little boxes of every shape and size and variety? The ornate yet dependable hooks and eyes? Where were the prize exhibits of every haberdashery, those magnificent passementerie? Where were all those trivial and unimportant little things that were really only stocked on the side, like a kind of immaterial material, an offshoot of the true, serious stock, but without which no seamstress in the locality could hope to get by? And what on earth was all this Brussels lace for? Who could afford Brussels lace, among this clientele, in this part of town? Josephine Matzner didn't need anyone to explain to her what Brussels lace was! She was unable to refrain from exclaiming to Herr Lissauer: 'You've had this shop cleared out!'

'Cleared out? Cleared out? Is that all you can say!' cried the young man. And with the eager blabber that was characteristic of him, and that had already brought him so much – inexplicable – success, he began telling Frau Matzner how much business had picked up and how much the lace had brought in already, and how much it promised to bring in in the future. And as often happens with someone who has profited from dishonesty over a long period, Lissauer's bragging led him into carelessness. Although he knew he had no right to invest Frau Matzner's share in the lace business as well, he rashly supposed that not only would she be quite happy about it, she would even see herself as his partner in crime. He suppressed the inconvenient knowledge that the books were cooked, and that he had helped himself to a third of the takings. Mizzi Schinagl had never asked for any explanation. Why should Frau Matzner want one?

Frau Matzner could not conceal a slight feeling of queasiness. She leaned against the counter, and asked for a chair and a glass of water. She took it in small sips – semi-recumbent in the chair, in spite of her corset which gripped her body like a murderous suit of armour. Gradually she felt a little better. She took a hatpin out of the impressive thatched roof on her head and, jabbing it in Lissauer's direction, she said: 'Lissauer, get me the books. I'm going to talk to my solicitor.'

Lissauer brought the books. Once again, poor Frau Matzner scanned black figures, blue figures, green strokes and red lines: but this time they did not allay her anxieties. 'Where is the capital?' she asked. And: 'Where are the profits?'

'The capital is working, Frau Matzner,' Lissauer replied very quietly. He shut the books and went on speaking. She no longer heard it all. She understood odd words and phrases like, 'different times, revolutionary business methods, no dead capital', things of that sort. She was terrified to think that her ten thousand gulden were lost.

She quickly said goodbye, ignoring Lissauer's proffered hand. She went to the post office. There was grave danger ahead. Her hatpin was still in her hand. The giant hat wobbled on her head. She overcame her fear of profligacy. She sent a wire to Mizzi Schinagl in Baden: 'Come immediately,' she wrote, then reflected a while and sucked her pencil. Mizzi Schinagl wouldn't come just like that. What use was the expensive telegram? Frau Matzner was thinking in terms of a plain post-card when one of the good fairies of falsehood that had governed her actions for such a long time whispered in her ear. 'Taittinger expects you tomorrow,' she telegraphed.

Mizzi Schinagl duly arrived early the next morning. She hadn't been to Frau Matzner's house for a long time. Everything looked unfamiliar to her. Her memories were all of glitter and splendour. But she had got used to glittering salons and houses of late. And Frau Matzner's house looked wretched, even squalid, with its blind mirrors, the candelabra missing a fair few of its crystals and resembling a half-stripped tree, the big grey moth holes in the red velveteen sofa, the peeling fake bronze mirror frame, the frayed silk cloth on the lid of the fortepiano, with its scratched polish, and the dusty curtains in the windows. But what were memories compared to expecta-tions? She was going to see Taittinger. In her little handbag she had a recent photograph of his son and his latest, admittedly rather discouraging, school reports. His moral conduct was 'insufficient', his application 'fair'. Thus far, he had had to retake every single class. Mizzi didn't care about the boy. She hadn't been to see him since Christmas. At the station he had demanded cocoa, and she went with him to the waiting room.

He drank his cocoa with enthusiasm, then opened her suitcase and took out the presents for him which were lying on top. Then he shut the suitcase and called out 'The bill!' – that was her son. But in the night, she'd made up a dozen stories that she was going to tell Taittinger: how Xandl was a promising gymnast, a good boy, a gifted singer. Once he had even saved another child from drowning. This last story wasn't an invention. Xandl really had pulled a boy out of the water; just as he liked catching frogs, fish and lizards.

Yes, Mizzi Schinagl had all this to tell, and more. She felt she was having to wait rather a long time. Frau Matzner was keeping her waiting. At last she arrived, in full armour, not in her dressing gown as was usual in the mornings, but coiffed, made-up and corseted. A hurried embrace, a cool brush of a kiss. 'Taittinger can't make it!' Frau Matzner said right away. 'Something came up!'

Mizzi Schinagl heaved a sigh and sat down. 'But, but,' she began, fell silent, and finally found some feeble solace: 'But he did want to see me?'

'Yes,' said Frau Matzner. 'But something's come up. Why don't you write to him! You know the address.'

Mizzi was still sitting there, Frau Matzner standing menacingly in front of her, like a policeman.

'I've got a bone to pick with you,' she began. 'You've cheated me, you and your Lissauer. You swindler, you robber. After I was so good to you. I was like a mother to you. Called you my golden girl. You've frittered away my money. You're coming with me now. We're going to see my solicitor. Don't even think of running away!'

Nothing living was left inside Mizzi Schinagl. Her brain seemed dead, and her heart too. Only one thing was left in her:

a great and unspecific fear. Fear sometimes sends shafts of illumination, and so Mizzi Schinagl remembered the business with the lace, and she remembered all the documents she had signed for Lissauer without reading them, and a long-forgotten sentence surfaced in her memory that Lissauer had once said to her in a tender moment; and the sentence was: 'If they catch up with me, you'll be the one they'll put away!' Well, now it was happening.

She got up and went out. Already under arrest, she walked meekly beside the grimly determined Frau Matzner.

XV

In the weeks that followed, a new vigour characterized Frau Josephine Matzner. This vigour did nothing, however, to rejuvenate her – on the contrary, it seemed to multiply the outward signs of rapidly advancing old age. She herself, though, failed to notice this, and felt light and healthy, cheerful and young. She was boosted by a deep sense of mission: that she had an important task to carry out, she had to rescue her money, or else – a version she liked even better, though it was very painful to her – she had to avenge its loss. A wonderful evil energy filled her, fuelled her, almost scalded her. She was a cauldron of boiling anger. Her days and nights were transformed; the old bland, cheerful and purposeless sloppiness of her life changed utterly. She enjoyed a deep and dreamless sleep, from which she woke refreshed and ready for action every morning. She revealed an amazing capacity for understanding and interpreting the law, for speaking with solicitors and grasping exactly what they told her. She had retained the services of two of them, just to be on the safe side: there was the Court Advocate

Dr Egon Silberer, and the secondary Dr Gollitzer, who was a kind of hedge-lawyer, and whom she needed less for the case in hand than for the pleasurable and instructive whiling away the time. Court Advocate Dr Silberer offered her half an hour three times a week, while Gollitzer was at her daily beck and call for hours on end. The real reason she retained Gollitzer as well was her distrust of Silberer. Gollitzer it was who explained to her how to deal with a great and famous lawyer. It was he who instructed her on the private lives of the judges, the opportunities afforded by the law, and various ruses and pitfalls. In his gloomy chambers at number 43 Wasagasse, 3rd floor, she gradually developed into a kind of juridical *canaille*. She experienced pleasures there the like of which she had never imagined.

In her time, she had of course known numerous forbidden pleasures, and some that were even reviled, but truly ecstatic joys she only belatedly became acquainted with now, in the Wasagasse, when she learned that those very laws she had gone in fear of all her life could be made obedient like trained hounds. All her life she had been under the misapprehension that women of her ilk were outside the law, subject to the mercy or whim of any passing police commissioner. In the depths of her soul there had always been a slumbering desire for respectability. For years she had hoped that one day, when she had money, she would be allowed to live in the protective shade of the law; in a place far away from her house, which she planned to sell advantageously, at a propitious moment: to live as Josephine Matzner, a private pensioner, with no need to work, no risk and a great deal of money. But now there was the possibility that she would have no money. No money! After a long life lived outside the law! What an appalling state to be in, for an ageing woman who had hoped finally to be allowed to enter the hallowed precincts of respectability! – Well, and now for all that, it turned out that the laws were in her favour, both her lawyers assured her of that. It was no longer as an outsider or a pariah that Frau Josephine Matzner was dealing with the law: but as their queen and, as she learned to say, their usufructuary.

As well as hedge-lawyer Gollitzer, she also had the assistance of her old friend Inspector Sedlacek. Not that her dealings with the latter were as they had been before, when she'd been open season; no, they were practically on an equal footing now. She spent many hours with Sedlacek in his office on the Schottenring while his people pursued their investigations throughout the length and breadth of the city and the Empire. Fake Brussels lace, a huge international business. Produced in Vienna, sent on from there to Trieste; thence to Antwerp; and from there back to Vienna. Sedlacek too had grown old and tired. His abrasive occupation was no longer congenial to him. His three children – all boys – were growing up very quickly. His wife was ageing very quickly. He himself – even he – was ageing very quickly. What he needed was a 'juicy case' to gain promotion, and enable him to settle down in the Commissariat in Graz, Innsbruck, Linz, Brünn, Prague or Olmütz. He had been born in Koslovitz, and even after so many years in Vienna, where he had moved in the very highest circles, it seemed to him, now that he was getting on, that the last named of these, Olmütz, was the right sort of place – big, but not too big; just right for him. He wanted to retire with the rank of Chief Inspector.

It was a business that quite a lot could be made of, and fate itself, thought Inspector Sedlacek, had set him on to it from the very beginning. What a long time ago that was! The Shah of Persia (from whom Sedlacek had received a decoration, at the suggestion of the Chief of Police, for services to the security of the noble visitor) was even now preparing for a return visit to Vienna, or so the newspapers were saying. Lazik, the crime reporter on the *Kronen-Zeitung*, and a close friend of Sedlacek's, was saying that the time had come – and this would be to his friend's advantage too – to repackage the story as a kind of scandal. It had all the elements: the milieu, the fairy-tale origins of the fortune, which one could only hint at, agreed, but that could be done quite effectively; a couple of glittering years for Mizzi Schinagl followed by her downfall; the shady Lissauer; the background to the whole Brussels lace scam; revelations about the criminal deception the Trieste-based company had been perpetrating for years; and finally the brilliance and vigilance of the Viennese police, first and foremost Inspector Sedlacek. Plenty there for crime reporter Lazik to get his teeth into!

At this time, the world was deeply and frivolously at peace. The newspapers of the monarchy were full of court and society reports, bulletins on the preparations for the forthcoming hansom-cab ball, feature articles on the Kahlenberg, the vaults of the Stephanskirche, rustic festivals in Agram, the prospects for the tobacco crop of the hard-working Swabians in the Banat, reports on army exercises around Lemberg, accounts of a children's party under the patronage of a crown prince, the annual bowling competitions among the guilds of the butchers, carpenters and cab drivers; and whatever other peaceful, happy, and inconsequential stories there might be at home or abroad. Major crimes and court cases were few and far between, and the crime reporters spent more of their time at Schopfner's up in

Grinzing than in the café next door to the police headquarters on the Schottenring. The story of the Brussels lace, brought out in small daily instalments, polished, embellished and indignantly editorialized, became a real sensation.

The trial itself was over in a couple of days. It was early September, a fine summer was fraternally giving way to a fine autumn. In the courtroom it was still sweltering. The gallery was full. Only one of the accused had been kept on remand: Franz Lissauer. His boss in Trieste had disappeared. Fräulein Mizzi Schinagl had been granted bail. She arrived in court, accompanied by her solicitor. The renowned firm of Seidmann, which had been dealing in genuine Brussels lace for many years, and felt its reputation had been harmed, was claiming damages. The company was represented by Dr Silberer, just as Frau Matzner was. It looked as though Mizzi Schinagl stood to lose what was left of her fortune. Lissauer's advocate strove to make the case that Fräulein Schinagl had used her feminine wiles to seduce his gullible client. She had come from a humble background. By a stroke of luck that had come straight out of an Oriental fairy tale, she had become a wealthy woman; then she had blown most of her fortune in a couple of years of criminal extravagance; cruelly neglected her – illegitimate, it hardly wanted saying – child, to whom she paid a short visit once a year; before finally, and there is no other explanation for it, taking advantage of a man's tender feelings for her to turn him into her accomplice and draw him into her criminal schemes.

Mizzi Schinagl was able to follow very little of the proceedings and speeches in court. At times it struck her as all rather silly, even sillier than school. Her classroom in primary school had seen similar goings on, she remembered. You got up when you were called, and you weren't able to answer all the questions, only some of them. The most difficult ones made you go quiet. You got a lump in your throat, tears came to your eyes, you needed to blow your nose, your eyelids were stung by the salt. It was all repeating itself now. She cried; often she said nothing; in her ignorance and confusion she said 'Yes!' when the prosecutor was trying to catch her out, and 'No!' when her defence was trying to rescue her. The thing that really puzzled her was the implacable cruelty of these men, and of the male sex in general, which she thought she knew by now, if experience had taught her anything. But these men wore robes, which made them look odd, sometimes like priests, but also like ceremonial hermaphrodites. They hadn't looked like that when they'd come to Frau Matzner's salon.

Lissauer's advocate asked his client: 'How often did Mizzi Schinagl come to you for sizeable sums of money?'

'Once a week, at least!' came the prompt reply.

'And why were you obliged to produce it?' Lissauer hung his head and made no reply. 'You have nothing to be ashamed of!' cried the attorney. 'Was it because otherwise Schinagl would have denied herself to you sexually?' Lissauer sighed.

'It's not true!' howled Mizzi Schinagl. But the sound of despair is never pleasant; it sounds suspiciously like lying.

It was the most important day in the life of Frau Josephine Matzner. Asked what she was and what she did, she replied: 'I'm a spinster, I work as a cashier.'

'You're registered as the madame of a brothel on the Wieden,' the judge corrected her.

She had had ingratitude to deal with, nothing but ingratitude said Frau Matzner. She had always dealt fairly with her girls. She started to cry. All she wanted from the noble court was her own money. She asked for leniency. Her purple feathers, secured to the brim of her hat by a lilac parrot, were swaying as in a strong gale. The sharp points of her hatpins glinted menacingly left and right. A hefty and engorged handbag in pale blue silk hung on her left arm. Diamonds sparkled at her ears.

'You may go!' said the judge. He had interrupted her in mid-sentence. She was still stunned by the echo of her own words. 'That's enough! You may go!' repeated the judge.

At last she understood, bowed deeply, straightened up and cried: 'I beg the court for mercy!'

She left the witness box without a backward glance.

Inspector Sedlacek was discreetly given to understand that he should draw a veil over the origins of Schinagl's wealth. He reported – and as he did, his heart warmed a little – that for a long time it had been part of his work to keep the accused under observation. He gave it as his opinion that she was foolish, rather than wicked.

The claims for damages, all told, came to twenty-four thousand gulden. Mizzi Schinagl's solicitor explained that his client offered the fifteen thousand that were all she had left. By doing so, he saved her five thousand gulden on which to live and, of course, the wherewithal to pay his own fees.

In spite of that, she received a custodial sentence. Lissauer got three years in prison. Schinagl got sixteen months.

She cried. At that moment, it was all the same to her: six months, a year, ten years, life.

Her defence lawyer promised to do everything possible to get her out early. 'I don't want to get out!' she said.

She didn't cry at all on the long drive from the district court to her place of detention. There was a smell of dirty, wet washing, dishwater and leftover soup in the corridor. In a little room she was undressed, put on a pair of scales and measured. One of the Sisters brought her a blue overall. She put it on. She watched apathetically as another one gathered up her beautiful English navy-blue tailored suit, her high-heeled button boots with patent-leather points and her pink handbag, packed them all in a cardboard box and put a metal label on it. She was made to sit down with her back to the door. She heard it open and didn't dare look round. A rattling and jangling metallic thing approached her from behind, she felt simultaneous touch of cold steel and warm hands on her head.

She screamed. The nun held her by the wrists.

Her young ash-blonde hair fell in tufts and drifts on all sides. Her scalp felt chilly. The Sister tidied away hairpins and combs.

She was brought a blue hood, which she had to put on. She looked around for a mirror. No sign of one. That surprised her. She was told to stand. She stood. She was supported on either side by nuns; her wooden clogs clattered down the stone corridor. Keys rattled. Grey light oozed from a few openings high in the walls; somewhere in the world a bird was singing.

Cell No. 23 contained two beds, both empty. 'Chose one, my child!' said the nun – it was the only comfort she had to offer, the choice between the pallet on the left and the one on the right. Mizzi Schinagl dropped on to the left-hand one. She fell asleep immediately.

An hour later she was woken up. It was her first sight of female prisoner Magdalene Kreutzer, quondam high-wire artiste, but latterly – as Mizzi Schinagl would discover soon enough – the proprietress of a merry-go-round at the Prater.

XVI

Two days after the trial, Frau Matzner still had plenty of opportunity to enjoy her sudden celebrity. Still half-stunned by the days she'd spent in the courtroom of the district court, by the questions, by her statement and by her final magnificent and magnanimous appeal to the judge for leniency, she was already beginning to bask in all sorts of confused but soothing notions of what might lie ahead. But it was only those two days after the end of the trial that were given to Frau Matzner to linger in the blissful realm of giddy dreams – just as long as the newspapers cared to run, in ever more abbreviated form, their valediction to the big story of the autumn. Frau Matzner spared no expense; she bought all the papers. But on the third day, as though by an evil spell, all talk of Brussels lace suddenly vanished, and, no matter how many newspapers Frau Matzner bought on that day too, none of them contained so much as a single word that had any bearing whatsoever on the trial. To Frau Matzner it felt as though she had entered a zone of appalling silence, the silence of catacombs or cemeteries by night. No! she hadn't entered this macabre silence of her own volition, she had been shoved into it. She felt the cruel and bitter sufferings of the betrayed and the neglected: first bewilderment and disbelief; then an uncomprehending astonishment; the illusory hope that it might all be a dream, and after that the painful understanding that it wasn't; followed by embitterment, impotence and finally vengefulness.

She hid the wretched newspapers that didn't contain anything, lest any of her girls might come across them. She went down into the street, stood at her gate for a moment to recover the composure she had displayed in all those weeks, because she thought she must look pitiful and broken. She didn't want any of that to show. She went into various shops, even though she didn't need anything. But she felt compelled to look into people's faces to see whether they too emanated the same deadly and hateful silence as the newspapers. She didn't want any pretzels – she had lost her appetite long ago and thought she wouldn't eat another bite as long as she lived. She didn't need any little hooks and eyes – it didn't occur to her to mend any of her old dresses. She didn't need any boot buttons, no new ribbon for her corsets, no Spanish comb and no hazelnuts. But she bought all these things, erecting veritable barricades of parcels about her, all wrapped in those disloyal, traitorous newspapers. Her eye was caught by the twist in which the hazelnuts were wrapped: there it was, black on white, in big type: 'Brussels Lace Storm'. Three days ago now – and already people were using it to wrap hazelnuts! Too awful to contemplate what other functions might be reserved for these papers. Bundles of them, chopped into tidy rectangles, were probably hanging from nails in café and pub toilets.

Frau Matzner was careful to speak to the shopkeepers with

her familiar loftiness and condescension. But she felt she didn't make the same splendid impression on these people as she once had. There was a certain unmistakable familiarity in their responses to her. With her chronic sensitivity, she took herself to task for it; she was afraid she might be worth even less now than she had been to start with.

'Well, you've achieved everything,' Efrussi said to her. 'Achieved everything!' the man said! He could only have been thinking of the money . . .

A fortnight later, she decided she'd had enough. Her establishment couldn't be kept going any longer. She no longer bought champagne from Weinberger the court supplier, but from Baumann's in Mariahilf. What would have been the point anyway? How the number of her good old clients had dwindled. And even they looked unrecognizable, positively withered: yellowed or bleached ghosts of their former selves. Her guests were pallid, the faces and bodies of her ageing girls were visibly crumbling, the pianist's tailcoat had a greenish hue, the wall coverings were peeling, the sofa sighed if you sat down on it, the spots of tarnish on the mirror were multiplying, and even Clementine Wastl, the char woman, was stricken with gout. There was nothing to be done about it. Frau Matzner submitted to the chilly laws of the times. She sold up. Her salon became a cut-rate branch of the fashionable house on the Zollamtsstraße.

Leaving it didn't even upset her. One evening in autumn, in the brief span between the extinguishing of the day and the lighting of the lamps, she trundled off in her hansom cab. She didn't look round. The girls weren't hers any more. They were already working for the Zollamtsstraße.

★

To begin with, Frau Matzner thought her life was over, but she was mistaken about that; and what is more, she knew, really, that she was mistaken. Because, instead of withdrawing, as had originally been her intention, into some silent and remote retirement in the provinces somewhere where no one knew her, she suddenly decided to stay in Vienna, and smack in the middle of Vienna at that. Not at all surprisingly, her natural avarice was strengthened by her fear that, away from the world, she would have nothing to do but grow old and die; and by another fear: that she would lose touch with the home of her money. She thought she would be betraying her money if she abandoned it; it would become orphaned, a helpless child. So, she wasn't leaving! On the contrary, she rented a flat in the centre of town, in the Jasomirgottgasse.

For the first few days she felt a little disorientated, and even though she knew the area very well from her childhood, she sometimes had the feeling of not being in Vienna at all. The shops were different, the street names were different. Even the animals – the dogs, the horses, the cats and birds – weren't like their counterparts on the Wieden. It was as though it would never occur to a blackbird from the 1st precinct to go to look for food in the 4th. She was also a little afraid of her two rooms, which seemed far too spacious and expensively furnished for her. Not a single item in the flat was dear or familiar to her. She couldn't look at a piece of furniture without remembering that she was paying a so-called depreciation allowance for it, and even though this had been set in advance, she continually worried she wasn't using the objects enough, and that, by some inexplicable quirk of the lease, that was causing the depreciation allowance to go up. In order to feel a little more at ease in this new environment, she withdrew five hundred gulden in cash from Efrussi's Bank, half in gold, half in notes. That way she could at least be sure something agreeable was waiting for her when she got home at night, after hours spent in purposeless wandering streets, or afternoons dozing on a bench in the Stadtpark or the Rathauspark. She rented the flat from the widow of a major who had gone to live with her son-in-law in Graz. Frau Matzner inherited some of the respect that was paid to the owner by the concierge and the other inhabitants of the building and their servants. She had put herself down as a 'Spinster', but also as 'Retired'. She looked comfortably off. Nobody knew who she was. She had friendly manners, half a dozen good dresses, three hat boxes and some good linen undergarments. The concierge did her cleaning for her. From time to time she would poke around in the drawers for letters or papers, but she didn't turn up one single photograph, or even a savings book. She finally gave up looking, and decided to take the new tenant – pending further information on her – at face value, for a rather shy, affluent, single lady.

Frau Matzner kept the money in an old trunk she had inherited from her parents: a solid, iron-bound trunk on wheels. The notes were in a wallet, the gold in a silver purse. When she got home, she took the key out of her handbag, opened the padlock, pushed the metal bar back and lifted up the heavy lid of the trunk. She opened the wallet and the silver purse, took a deep breath, then grieved that there wasn't more, whereupon she reminded herself that it was only a small part of her entire fortune, and she breathed more easily. She took off her hat, shut the trunk and locked it, and went down to the concierge who undid her dress at the back. Then, with her silk shawl covering her shoulders, she climbed back up the stairs. There, it would quite regularly occur to her that it was really rather foolish of her to leave all her money with the bank. She should keep more of it at home. She decided to call on Efrussi again in the morning. But that demanded a lot of courage. So she would turn back and go down the stairs again and order a tankard of Okocimer or Pilsner beer from the concierge – to help her sleep, she claimed: but in fact for courage for the morrow.

The following morning found her in Efrussi's office. But her Dutch courage was gone. The wise, gentle voice of Efrussi, seated high above her on his swivelling stool, drizzled mildly down on her large hat. Her suspicion was gone too. All her fear for her money. 'If you live to be a hundred and twenty, Frau Matzner,' Efrussi liked to say, 'you won't go hungry. You can have your coffin drawn by four black horses, if that's what you want, and still have something left over for a bequest.'

'Oh, thank you! Thank you so much for that information!' said Frau Matzner. 'Bye now, Imperial Councillor!' She approached his swivelling stool and dangled a hand upwards in his direction. Then, if it was fine, she went to the Stadtpark and sat down by the hut with the barometer. On such reassuring days, she would go on afterwards to the beer garden at Kriegl's on the Wipplingerstraße.

The autumn of that year remained warm, gracious and silvery. The regimental band of the Hoch-and Deutschmeisters played at the restaurant in the Volksgarten in the afternoons. The 'concert' began at five sharp. However, if you arrived a quarter of an hour before that, and ordered your coffee and whipped cream, you didn't have to pay the five kreuzer supplement for the music, only the standard thirty for coffee and fifteen for a slice of gugelhupf cake. It was a bit of an extravagance, but it was bearable. And then again the army band gave Frau Matzner pleasure that was beyond price: the pleasure of melancholy. These were, if you like, the poetical hours of Frau Josephine Matzner's life, those in which she felt the shudders of a terrible and merciful sadness, a wholesome pain, a comforting and at the same time ghastly certainty that it was all over for her. She could taste the full bitterness of her condition, revel in it. The band played long-forgotten polkas and mazurkas, tunes from Josephine Matzner's youth, when she'd been a growing lass with hopes of marrying Anger, the stationmaster. She wasn't still in love with him, of course, how could she be! But she was in love with her own youth, and even with the way she had misspent it. All the other girls she had met later on, while working for Jenny Lakatos in Budapest, had fallen by the way-side somewhere. She remembered them with a sigh. She alone had been capable of 'getting on in life'. She had 'got what it takes' and had 'come through'. What next? – Oh, the music of the Hoch-and Deutschmeisters evoked sweet and tender memories, it softened old age, it sweetened bitterness, it gilded misery, and even when it was all over, and the uniformed players had packed away their stands and scores and instruments, the music seemed to hang in the air for a long, long time afterwards, as if the players had left the melodies up in the clouds, and the trees in the Volksgarten – their leaves already dry gold – rustled in harmony with the voices inside Frau Matzner, in a kind of brotherly and comforting perplexity: What next? What next?

One afternoon, when Frau Matzner was thus treating herself to coffee, gugelhupf and music, she suddenly heard a voice: 'Grüß Gott, Auntie Fini!' Caught up in her reverie, she nevertheless recognised the confident drawl of a gentleman, someone of good breeding. She looked up. Yes, it was a gentleman – the face looked very familiar, though at first she couldn't place it.

She got up quickly – almost from memory – as though she'd been sitting in her drawing room, or at her cash desk. Yes, that's who it was: it was Baron Taittinger – but he was not in uniform. He hadn't even taken off his little green huntsman's hat. He just smiled. He still had dazzling teeth. But their steady dazzle made Frau Matzner realize that something about him was different, and a moment later she had it: the Captain's moustache was almost grey, pepper and salt you'd have to call it . . .

Frau Matzner remained standing – partly out of her, as it were, long-standing respect for the Captain of Horse, but partly in awe of his altered moustache. The Baron quickly looked around, and seeing no one he knew, he said: 'May I, Frau Matzner?' and he sat down. He took off his jaunty little hat, and now Frau Matzner could see that the Baron's head was as grey as his moustache – or more so, it had gone almost completely white. Still she didn't sit down – less out of respect than sheer bewilderment. Had the years gone by so fast? Or did one person's time go faster than another's? Or was it that the Baron was unhappy or unwell? 'Do sit down!' he said, and she perched stiffly and cautiously on the edge of her chair, resting her elbow on the little table. Which, she thought, looked lady-like and suited the circumstances.

'Well, and are things still going with a swing in your house?' began the Captain of Horse.

'In my house? The house is sold, Baron, haven't you heard? I'm not the Auntie Fini of old. I'm not even Frau Matzner. It seems I'm back to being Fräulein Matzner, just as I was twenty years ago! I'm living in the Jasomirgottgasse, I'm a retired spinster, and no one's interested in me. Ah, Baron, the old times! Eh? And now the loneliness!'

She stopped and sighed.

'Go on, go on!' the Captain said cheerily, as though a string of amusing anecdotes would unfailingly follow this mournful introduction.

Frau Matzner related what had happened, in exact sequence. It was as though she were giving a military briefing. When she got to the part about the lace, she stalled once or twice. 'Mizzi Schinagl, the Baron may have heard –,' she said, and then stopped again.

Indeed, the name Mizzi Schinagl aroused various uneasy feelings in the Captain.

'I even petitioned the noble court for clemency,' Frau Matzner resumed. She expected some admiration for this, some recognition, even a paltry word or two, just a look of approval. But evidently the Captain of Horse hadn't heard that weighty sentence. He seemed to be staring up at the treetops. As if he had fetched it down with his look, a broad chestnut leaf of beaten gold slowly fluttered down and came to rest on the broad brim of Frau Matzner's hat. He studied the yellow leaf on the purple velvet. What prompted him to think of Kagran? Why Kagran?

'And now she's inside!' Frau Matzner said, with another sigh.

Yes, he remembered now. It was a couple of weeks ago, he had been given a piece of paper to sign in the regimental office. It was a registered letter, a familiar hand, and a red stamp on the envelope said: 'Passed by the censor!' Even more than the handwriting, that stamp had a whiff of 'tedious business' about it. It was a cheap and ugly envelope, blue-green in colour, redolent both of poverty and the law. The Captain of Horse had signed for it, absent-mindedly opened the envelope, and then glanced at the letterhead. 'Female Penitentiary, Kagran' it read. That exhausted his curiosity. He had never been particularly inquisitive. Such a letter, with such a ridiculous, pathetic and boring heading, ranked with the other inexplicable phenomena that occasionally dogged Baron Taittinger, like the letters from his steward Brandl, the bills from the head waiter Reitmayer, and all the unnecessary communications from the Mayor of Oberndorf, where he had his estate. To him these were like occult phenomena. They were not about love, or Viennese society, or the cavalry, or horses. And that made them not just irksome: they were *'ennuyeux'*! – the utmost in tedium.

'Go on, go on!' he said, having finally resolved not to listen any more. After many weeks, he had finally got a grip on himself and gone to Vienna again. And again, as had happened so many times since the awful business with the Shah and his abrupt transfer back to his regiment, he felt himself seized by that powerful, dangerous and mysterious hurt that he had no name for. It was a peculiar mixture of pain, shame, longing, love and forlornness. When it was upon him, the Captain of Horse had a keen sense of his own shallowness, and remorse plagued him in such a way that he could physically feel its sharp teeth. He futilely asked himself why he had done one thing instead of another in his life. Everything that had happened to him since his graduation from cadet school seemed pointless. He strove to direct his memory back to those days, to mother and father and military academy, but it wouldn't obey him, and it ran on and dwelt instead on Countess W., the Shah, the charming Kirilida Pajidzani and the awful Sedlacek with his topper. First it stopped and then it circled round and round these four people. That miserable episode was long buried, no one had heard about it, neither the Colonel nor his comrades.

But how did that help Taittinger himself? His life harboured an incident he could never tell anyone about. It circulated like a foreign body in his bloodstream, every so often it came up to his heart and squeezed it and pricked it and drilled into it. At moments like that, there were three possibilities: to flee to Vienna, the pinnacle of glory and the birthplace of shame; to get drunk; or – or: to shoot himself. War would have been a way out. But wherever you looked, the world was plumply, contentedly, frivolously at peace . . .

So now he knew: it was Mizzi who had written to him from prison – to him – from prison – it was like that knowing greeting from that vile detective Sedlacek. Such an embarrassment might happen again at any time. How to prevent it? However little poor Taittinger understood of the laws of the civilian world, he understood this much: that it was a prisoner's right to send letters out into the free world. They were read by the prison governor. He would have read Mizzi Schinagl's latest letter to him too. Taittinger was still looking at the golden leaf that had spiralled down on to the brim of Frau Matzner's purple hat. Not that he harboured any poetical inclinations. But in that instant he began to feel a peculiar, ridiculous affection for that wretched little leaf. It was a harbinger of autumn, clearly! How many times in his life had he seen such harbingers! But this particular leaf was a harbinger to him, Taittinger, of his own individual autumn. He shuddered.

Just then he heard the jingling of sabres. So, worried that some comrades of his might see him sitting at Frau Matzner's table, he pulled out his watch and, interrupting her indefatigable, sighing speech, he announced: 'I'm going. I'll see you this time tomorrow – where shall we meet?' He thought for a moment – where was a quiet and discreet place? – Aha, it came to him, and he said: 'At Grützner's! That suit you, Frau Matzner?'

'Whatever you suggest, Baron,' she replied.

He called out: 'Bill!' and put his little hat on. He paid for both of them, and Frau Matzner saw with shock and pain that the waiter had charged the extra five kreuzers, though she'd been there a full fifteen minutes before the music had begun!

Taittinger casually held out four fingertips. She rose and bowed; the leaf slipped from her hat on to the table.

Then the Baron disappeared into the now dark Volksgarten.

XVII

For the first time in his life, Baron Taittinger was to learn the meaning of the expression 'to take steps'. In the army, you didn't take steps. Everything was done by the book. There were no complications, and if ever there were, they were the outcome of certain instructions and decrees that had the power to set them aside no sooner than they had arisen. In civilian life, though, a man quite regularly had 'to take steps'. Every so often you had to sort something out for yourself, because the laws, so it seemed, weren't there to regulate people's lives, but rather to plunge them into chaos. Such thoughts kept the Captain of Horse awake all night. He got up early, as the autumn dawn was just breaking. Only yesterday he had thought of police surgeon Dr Stiasny, who joined Taittinger's regiment on manoeuvres every years as a medic with the reserves. Taittinger would have found it quite impossible to look up, for instance, Chief Commissar Baron Handl, who was a distant acquaintance, for the simple reason that he'd never yet met him in uniform. With Dr Stiasny at least he'd been to the officers mess, and played dominoes.

The police headquarters troubled poor Taittinger. He was in civilian dress and so inevitably the two officers on duty looked him up and down, and the spies swarming in the corridors shot swift, penetrating glances his way. He felt he might run into detective Sedlacek at any moment. It was 'embarrassing' and 'tedious'. He was made to spend a traumatic quarter of an hour on a brown bench with some people he thought were probably supplicants. 'The Doctor will see you now!' the official finally said.

'Ah, Baron!' said the police surgeon, and got to his feet. He trotted over to him on his short legs, a roly-poly figure.

Taittinger had remembered him differently. He couldn't square the man in front of him with the man he'd dreamed up. Out of uniform, Dr Stiasny wore a pince-nez on a black ribbon – which bothered the Captain of Horse. '*Servus*, Doctor!' he said, in a strangulated voice. The doctor had just come from hospital, and he smelled like a chemist's shop – of iodine and chloroform. The sharp mercury tip of a thermometer glinted in his top waistcoat pocket. In confusion, Taittinger sat down. The doctor asked after his regimental comrades, to which the Captain of Horse kept replying: 'Very well, thanks!' And: 'What a memory you have, Doctor!' He himself forgot most of the names as soon as he set foot on the garrison station to go on furlough.

It was a torment to have to wait such a long time to present his request. And how to frame it? 'You see, Doctor, there's this girl, from the wrong side of the tracks, and your lot are looking after her now,' he began, and Dr Stiasny – not unnaturally – jumped to the conclusion that what was at issue here was what was known as a 'confidential' or even a forbidden 'midwifery case', as he would put it. It was only after a lengthy interrogation that Dr Stiasny was able to piece together the story from Taittinger's clipped utterances. It was like having to tie lots of short pieces of thread together. When he finally grasped it, he was a little surprised, but on the whole relieved, and offered to go out to Kagran with the Captain later that very morning, if he liked. 'No, no, dear Doctor, it has to be right away!' said Taittinger. He couldn't have waited another half an hour. All at once, facing the tedious prospect of Kagran, he seemed to feel all its terrors in advance. Him! Visiting a prison! It was ghastly! How could Dr Stiasny talk about it so casually! Then again, the man was a police surgeon and went into prisons every day of his life. Best get the whole thing over with a.s.a.p.

During the drive out to Kagran, Taittinger was silently fretful, even though they were almost doing a gallop. When they arrived, boredom, worry and apprehension had taken it out of him to such an extent that he felt almost indifferent.

The prison governor, Government Councillor Smekal, wore gold-rimmed glasses – but not even that could shock the unhappy Taittinger. He was introduced. He shook hands. He did all there was to be done, and had only a dim notion of what was going on either in or around him.

As if from a great distance, he heard the prison governor say that it was impossible for him to prevent the inmates from writing letters. Impossible! Quite! He appreciated the 'difficulties' of the Herr Baron – but, to repeat: 'The regulations!' . . . He would try to influence the inmate Schinagl to desist from writing, except to her father in Sievering and her son in Graz. But surely the simplest thing would be for the Baron to have a word with her himself. Nothing in the regulations against that. Government Councillor Smekal can have the prisoner Schinagl sent for right away, and brought here to his office, why not, he was just off on his rounds now for half an hour. Before Taittinger understood what was happening, Dr Stiasny said:

'Excellent!', and as a strange, unprecedented feeling of fatigue descended on poor Taittinger, compounded of lead and sorrow, the Government Councillor was already on the case, ringing, giving instructions, taking his hat off its hook, and saying: 'Well, I'll be back in half an hour, Baron!' and Dr Stiasny for his part was saying: 'I'm just going to take a turn in the yard myself!' – and the pair of them were gone. He hadn't even heard the door.

And there was Taittinger on his own in the prison governor's office, surrounded by strange graphs and charts on the walls, peaceful green stacks of files, and face to face with a steel inkwell, whose hellish black muzzle gaped hellishly up at him.

A warder came in, saluted, and left again. Mizzi Schinagl walked in through the open door. She gave a start. At first she turned as though to go back out into the passage, then she stopped and seemed to reconsider, and finally she stood in the doorway with her head in her hands. All she had been told was that she was to see the governor. When she saw Taittinger, her initial impulse had been to run, as from a catastrophe, but this was followed by the terrible certainty that she couldn't escape. A hot joy flooded her, and then an equally burning shame. She stood like that for a long moment, with her hands shielding her eyes. She had the idea that if she dropped them, she wouldn't be able to see Taittinger any more: he would have disappeared. And so with her hands and her eyelids she was keeping him safely there. At last she did drop her hands, but her eyes were still closed. She felt she would cry in a moment, and fretted about it, but longed for it at the same time.

Taittinger was as confused as he had ever been in his life. He stood up and headed, not in the direction of Mizzi Schinagl, but for the wall, where he stared at some meaningless graphs. He fiddled with his green hat and his grey gloves. It took him a couple of minutes to recover his usual unbothered serenity, his equable indifference.

'So there you are, young Mizzi! Let's have a look at you! How're you doing?' he said in his old, tender, cheerful drawl. It sounded sweet to Mizzi's ears, and to hear it better she opened her eyes as well. 'Sit you down, Mizzi!' said Taittinger, and she did as she was told and sat there on the edge of her chair, with her hands folded like a schoolgirl's. He thought a little compliment was probably in order now, but he couldn't think of one that fitted these particular circumstances. 'You're looking well,' for instance, certainly couldn't be said.

'Thank you,' stammered Mizzi, 'for coming to see me, Your Lordship, I'm sorry about my letter.'

Yes, of course, the letter, that was what he was here for, but it had to be done delicately.

'It's so nice,' Mizzi went on almost tonelessly, 'that you came when I asked, when I was in trouble. It's so, so − noble of you!' She found the word with some difficulty, and it seemed to unblock a stream of sobs from her heart.

Taittinger leapt towards her − through the wash of her tears she saw him coming − an angel in a grey lounge suit hovering close. When he stood in front of her, he still didn't know what to say. An unfamiliar voice suddenly started speaking through him, a voice he had never heard before. It said: 'I'm pleased when I get a nice letter. Read it right away, in the office. You know, I'm a decent enough fellow at heart.' He wanted to say more, he wanted to say that he'd like many more letters from her, but suddenly his tongue went on strike, and he remembered that he had actually meant to say exactly the opposite. And so it seemed right to begin the next sentence with the word 'but'. 'But you see, it's like this,' he went on, 'Zenower, our Warrant Officer, he gets a stack of mail to deal with every day, so I'm thinking he might open a letter from you by mistake, and so I've asked all my friends and acquaintances not to write to me, er, except – except' – he stalled, and the unfamiliar voice suddenly became very loud, it dictated to him, and he repeated after it: 'except to H. v. T., poste restante!'

'H. v. T.,' Mizzi repeated, 'poste restante.'

Now he took in her dark blue hood, he stood in front of her, his knees brushed against her long, striped robe. The hood bothered him, it was made of the same coarse, fibrous stuff that sacks are made of, and he remembered Countess Helene W. and the hair of both women and, suddenly, with an abrupt movement of finger and thumb, he pulled her hood back. At the same instant, Mizzi Schinagl covered her head with both hands. Her bitter sobbing started up again. Mizzi's hair stood out in stiff, irregular, spiky tufts, and Taittinger found it hard not to recoil. He was filled – flooded – with pity and alarm. Yes, pity! It was the first time in his life he had felt pity. He felt like someone frightened by his own good fortune. He awkwardly put out his hand, and stroked the spiky head, and was surprised at himself as he did so. He was no longer the Taittinger of old, he was losing himself, he was falling, and falling gave him a new sensation of bliss, it felt like floating.

'When do you get out?' he asked, pulling the horrid hood back over Mizzi's poor head.

'I don't know,' she sobbed. 'I wish I could stay here!'

'I'll see what I can do!' said Taittinger.

'Thank you, Baron, Sir!' said Mizzi.

He was no longer capable of looking at her. All of a sudden it seemed to him that it was all his fault, though he couldn't say why. Maybe she sensed it. She got to her feet with a sudden movement. 'May I go, Baron?' she asked, and her look and her voice were full of dignity and beauty.

'H. v. T., poste restante,' Taittinger repeated. Her clogs clattered off, first on the wooden floor of the office, then louder and harder on the stone-flagged passage. Taittinger didn't look around. He stood facing the wall, staring at the meaningless graphs.

Only now did it occur to him that he should have asked about the boy. Where was he now? – Not that he had any sense of obligation! It merely pained him that he had committed a breach of manners. At the same time, he had a vague memory that Lieutenant Wander had an illegitimate child, and had to pay a fixed sum every month towards its upkeep. Why he, Taittinger, had so far not had to pay anything for his boy, he couldn't presently account for. It was something to do with those baffling 'laws'. But something, he didn't know quite what, pained him. He felt he would never forget Mizzi Schinagl's cropped head. His right hand seemed to have acquired the faculty of memory. The palm of his hand would always remember the rough, prickly tufts of Mizzi Schinagl's hair.

Once he was in the cab, heading back towards town with Dr Stiasny, he began, in spite of himself, to talk about *n'importe quoi* – all sorts of silly, jolly, light-hearted things, scrapes from his boyhood. He could hear himself saying these things, and thought he must be old already, and he felt the absurdity of it all, and he was lenient with himself; and he contained two Taittingers: one who was young and foolish and one who was older and wiser.

He went along to his appointment with Frau Matzner in the afternoon in a sorry state of confusion. He heard the full story of the lace and the trial. To his own astonishment, he could even follow the business details.

He was a little disgusted by Frau Matzner. (He had never previously grasped the distinction between disgust and boredom.) He even wondered at Frau Matzner's peace of mind, recognizing as he did that it was her avarice that was responsible for the whole court case. In a peculiar way, he felt simultaneously repelled and attracted, helplessly entangled in 'someone else's business'. When, in the course of her narrative, Frau Matzner let drop the name of Sedlacek, the Captain also felt a little afraid. He paid quickly and walked off, leaving Frau Matzner behind, somewhat bewildered. 'Baron, my address,' she called out and quickly wrote it down on the back of an envelope she pulled out of her handbag.

The Captain of Horse politely put it away in his wallet.

Frau Matzner stayed there till late in the evening. The autumn air was clear, bitter and strong. When she got up to walk to the horse-drawn tram, she felt a little giddiness in her head and a frosty shiver in her heart. She put it down to the wine that she wasn't used to, and the excitement of being with the Baron. On the way to the tram, she decided to stop for a glass of camomile tea.

XVIII

And the following day Frau Matzner resumed her familiar life. She woke up feeling reasonably alert. She no longer read the paper, not since the day she finally understood that the world was no longer interested in her. Her two meetings with the Baron still gave her a little sustenance today. She got the most important news from the *Kronen-Zeitung* and the *Neuigkeits-Weltblatt* from the concierge, who came up at about nine to clean and tidy. Although her tips were not generous and she was registered as a spinster, the concierge still addressed her as 'Gnädige Frau'. (Generally, she avoided addressing her as anything.)

So this day had not as yet distinguished itself from its predecessors. The weather continued bright, kindly, autumnal. Frau Matzner planned her day as the concierge buttoned her dress. First of all, she would go to Efrussi's Bank, then to her solicitor, and after that to the police headquarters to see Inspector Sedlacek again. It was important, so she thought, to inform Sedlacek that she'd been in contact with Baron Taittinger again.

However, once she was out in the mild, silvery and optimistic breath of the clement autumn, Sedlacek took on more and more importance. More compelling, too, became her desire to be able to boast of her meetings with the Baron in front of someone who could appreciate such a thing. So she directed her resolute strides to the Café Wirzl on the Schottenring, where Inspector Sedlacek regularly played tarot with the crime reporters between eleven and one. Who knows? Anything's possible. Perhaps the Baron had come to Vienna on some important business: in civilian dress – why was he in civilian dress? Perhaps Sedlacek could shed a little light. Or perhaps her information would be of use to him. He used to come to her house often enough, enquiring which gentlemen had been there the previous night. All the editors would be in the café, too, including Lazik. Maybe their newspapers would be interested in what Frau Matzner had to say.

At the Café Wirzl they were just between games. Sedlacek and his companions were tucking into frankfurters with horseradish and drinking mugs of beer. Frau Matzner was greeted with a boisterous chorus of 'Long time, no see, Auntie Fini!'

She was brought a dish of coffee with a poppy-seed biscuit and, crunching the biscuit with audible pleasure, she began her story: 'Now then, Herr Sedlacek, you'll be amazed! There I am, minding my own business in the Volksgarten, when who should walk up? The band are just playing: "Up over the clouds" – and who do you suppose it was? . . .'

'Well, well,' the Inspector kept saying. Editor Lazik scribbled the date of Taittinger's departure on his shirt-cuff, just in case. 'I'm much obliged to you!' said Sedlacek. Frau Matzner got up. She was like a balloon that had just dropped its ballast and was now rising proud and free into the higher reaches of the ether. She floated out of the door, and set off for Efrussi's.

But today, for the first time in thirty years, the Imperial Councillor was not in his bank. His bookkeeper, a changed man, almost unrecognizable today, received Frau Matzner. He told her that the Imperial Councillor had suddenly been taken to hospital the previous night, and was even now being operated on, it was his appendix, and his life hung in the balance.

'And what about the money?' cried Frau Matzner.

'What money?' asked the bookkeeper.

'Mine, mine!' she screamed and fell heavily back into a chair, as though her weight had suddenly doubled.

'There's nothing to worry about, Madam,' said the bookkeeper. 'The bank will remain the bank, even if, God forbid, the worst happens! Your money will still be your money!'

'I prefer to visit the hospital myself,' she said. 'I'll find out what's going on.' Already there were tears in her voice, and a clutching at her heart. Her eyes swam. 'The address, the address!' she cried. She was given it. Then, with trembling feet and pounding heart, she was suddenly, miraculously outside, hailing a cab. 'Klinik Haselmeyer,' she shouted as shrilly as if she was crying 'Fire!'

She arrived barely a quarter of an hour after Imperial Councillor Efrussi had died of complications following his successful appendectomy. So she was told, in the cold and businesslike manner of all hospitals everywhere.

She fainted. She came round in the examination room, in the acrid whiff of sal volatile. She staggered downstairs, supported by a nurse. She could feel the floor underfoot, the umbrella handle in her right hand and the handbag in her left, but her thoughts were all over the place. Like a swarm of wild birds, they scattered in a kind of silent commotion, heads and wing-tips brushing and colliding, disappearing and suddenly returning, in renewed confusion. Her heart had stopped beating, it was heaving and lurching back and forth, back and forth. Someone asked Frau Matzner where she lived. Someone put her in a cab. Someone delivered her into the care of the concierge. She was taken up to her flat, and made to lie down on the sofa. She still had sufficient presence of mind to say: 'Leave me now, I want to sleep!' She was left on her own. She went to her trunk and checked up on her money. She took possession of it; her wallet and her silver purse. She tucked them both inside her stocking. The little silver purse felt agreeable as it slipped from her calf down to her ankle like a clinging pet. She collapsed into the rocking chair. She fell asleep with the profound desire to sleep for a week, a month, an entire year.

But she awoke the same evening – the sun still hadn't gone down. Her brow was burning, her temples felt leaden and numb. Her body shook from one convulsion after another. She got up, wheezed over to the door, opened it and with all her remaining strength, called: 'Frau Smelik, Frau Smelik!' surprised that she still had a voice at all. The concierge came up, undid her laces, and soon Frau Matzner's body turned into a brimming shapeless mass of some indefinable substance, swaddled in white linen. She wouldn't let her touch her stockings.

Frau Smelik thought it was high time to send for the doctor. She said as much to Frau Matzner, even though she had the impression that the invalid didn't really understand what was put to her. She was wrong about this. Frau Matzner's question came back: 'What does he charge for a home visit?'

'Half a gulden!' said the concierge, 'I remember that from the last time he came, to see the Major's widow.'

'Go on then, send for him!' said Frau Matzner. All she could think about was pulling off her stockings without anyone seeing, and hiding them and the money, under the pillows.

The doctor arrived. Frau Matzner was lying undressed in bed, she could barely feel the stocking with the money under the pillow. She felt like she'd been lying there for an eternity, waiting for something to happen. Her face was burning, at times she felt her head was no longer connected to her body, which was as cold as a block of ice. At last she heard the sound of the key in the door, she tried to remember if she was expecting anyone and who it might be, and couldn't remember. She saw the concierge come in with a man she didn't know – and she knew it was the concierge and a man she didn't know, but at the same time she half-believed it was Mizzi Schinagl coming in, followed by Baron Taittinger. How the world had changed! People turning up in twos and threes, and you no longer knew who anyone was. The doctor – or was it Baron Taittinger? – waved away the concierge – or was it Mizzi? – went up to the bed, and pulled a gleaming thing out of his waistcoat pocket. Frau Matzner screamed. She quickly calmed down again, soothed by the doctor's fragrance of cigars and carbolic soap.

He palpated, listened and tapped, took her pulse. His touch was in equal parts embarrassing and calming, pleasant and shaming; it disquieted and soothed Frau Matzner's feelings at one and the same time. The doctor went away. Like a bank of fog he loomed over the basin, splashing about childishly in the water. The door opened again, the concierge reappeared, and this time it really was her, not some phantom transfiguration of Mizzi. And the doctor was truly the doctor, and nothing to do with Baron Taittinger. And Frau Matzner could clearly hear what the doctor said to the concierge, namely: 'Pleurisy! She has a high temperature. I'll send a nurse over. She'll be here in half an hour or so. Will you sit with her till then?'

'Of course, Doctor!' said the concierge. She stayed. She drew up a chair and sat down very close to the bed. The concierge's face melted, dissolved, ran into a grey paste. By the time the nurse arrived, Frau Matzner had lost all idea of where she was. She was babbling about her childhood.

The following morning, she felt better. She left the doctor in no doubt about that, asking him right away what he charged for a visit. 'Half a gulden!' he said.

Well – she said – if he expected to make many further visits, perhaps they could agree on a rate reduction here and now. And to soften his resistance she added that the sudden death of her banker Efrussi meant that she was in danger of losing her 'last farthing'. Yes, the doctor replied mildly, he would need to call on her a few more times, and there was no need to send for the priest just yet either. It would be easier to come to an agreement on money once she'd fully recovered.

For as long as the doctor was in the room with her, Frau Matzner remained serene. But once he'd left, she couldn't remember anything he'd said to her except something about getting a priest. And suddenly the good doctor seemed to her deceitful and dishonest, slyly announcing her imminent death. A cleric! She hadn't thought about that for many, many years. A cleric! She remembered her first communion. 'Jesus!' she'd often exclaimed in the course of her life, and sometimes: 'Jesus Mary and Joseph!' – without thinking anything of it. Why had the doctor brought up a priest? Why had he said there was no need to think about that yet? and if he'd said that, wasn't it proof of the very opposite, that it *was* time to think about it? – Death! Was death at hand? – What was death? – It was like communion, but probably black instead of white.

Frau Matzner managed a little barley broth, fell asleep, dreamed of her first communion, her parents, and then of the trial, the judge, the prosecutor, the attorneys, the jury. Once or twice she cried out aloud: 'I ask for leniency!' At night her fever rose again. Shortly before midnight she asked for the priest. He was a simple man. Roused from his bed, he was even simpler than he was by day. It was a long time since he'd last attended to the dying, especially the delirious dying. He didn't understand everything that Frau Matzner said to him.

For instance, she asked him if he thought the profession she'd pursued all her life would condemn her to hellfire. And when he asked what profession it was she had followed, she said she had been the proprietress of the Matzner house on the Wieden. He didn't understand, and said owning property wasn't a mortal sin. She told him she was unmarried. That too, according to him, was no sin. She grew tired and closed her eyes, and the priest thought she had fallen asleep.

She was awake, though, and thinking clearly in spite of her fever. Her immense fear of death chased away her confusions. Her fear of the beyond cleared her brain and lifted her spirits. In the pathetic and cheerless notion she had had all her life of the burden of guilt, and the possibility of shifting it or reducing it a little, she had always thought of money as being among the prime means. So, with her eyes tightly shut, she was coolly considering the possibility of absolving sins by charity. Sins: the whole of her sinful existence, the brothel and the trial that had put Mizzi Schinagl behind bars, the little deceitful and unjustified deductions she slapped on her girls from time to time, and whatever other sins that there were listed in the catechism, straightforward sins, for example, like defamation and blasphemy, that her life was crawling with. She had already decided to tell the Reverend that she wanted to leave her money to charitable and religious purposes, and part of it, by way of reparation, to Mizzi Schinagl, who must have lost everything. Yes, all her money! Even though Efrussi her banker had died – she thought she would look him up in the afterlife somewhere – and despite her distrust of that double-dealing bookkeeper, she must have something left in the bank! Not a lot, but something! And some needed to be set aside for the burial. It will be a nice funeral, she thought, and she sat up in her pillows. Very quickly and volubly, as though reciting something she'd learned by heart a long time ago, she told the Reverend Father that she wanted to leave a third of her money to the poor, a third to the Church and a third to Mizzi Schinagl. She wanted the notary to come round first thing in the morning. The priest nodded. She asked him, with a hint of suspicion in her voice, what he thought a first-class funeral with four black horses would cost. That, said the Reverend Father, was something the undertaking firm Pietas would know, and it would be easy enough to find out. He himself was paid just one gulden for saying the mass, that was a standard rate. And now she felt she was ready to die, and the priest went to work. 'Humbly and sorrowfully I confess my sins,' said Frau Matzner, sonorously as a schoolgirl.

She lapsed back into her pillows and fell asleep right away. She slept a peaceful and untroubled sleep all night. In the morning she woke with only a slight fever, feeling alert and energetic and fully restored. She sent for the notary right away, no expense should be spared, the concierge was even allowed to take a cab. It was as though Frau Matzner saw death as a business to be transacted. She asked for a blue nightcap and the camisole with the pale blue trim, and thus attired she received the notary.

She asked him first if anything would have happened to her money that was in the late Efrussi's Bank – and the notary set her mind at ease: there was no danger whatsoever. The money was perfectly secure. Then Frau Matzner asked the notary to draw up a will, and she made a list of all her assets, true to the promise she had made to the priest the previous night. The notary took down the details on a piece of paper, then got pen and ink from his leather case, and sat down at a table. First he wrote out the usual phrases with his slow, methodical and pellucid writing. When he got to the figures, he turned to Frau Matzner and asked: 'Do you have any idea of the size of your fortune?" She did not. 'You have,' said the notary, leafing in his papers once more, 'exactly thirty-two thousand gulden and eighty-five kreuzer. And the one thousand gulden you withdrew only a fortnight ago from Efrussi!'

'How much?' asked Frau Matzner.

'Thirty-two thousand and eighty-five kreuzer!' repeated the notary.

All that money – and she had to die! Why did she have to get ill? Wasn't this whole illness just a bad dream? What do doctors know anyway? Was it not just her fright following Efrussi's death? Who said she was going to die anyway? Where was it written? And if she had another twenty years to live, or say another ten – was that not time enough to make a will? 'Are you sure, Notary?' she asked.

'Quite sure,' he affirmed.

She leaned back in her pillows, and paused for thought – a

very, very long pause – while the notary sat with his pen poised an inch above the paper.

Finally her mind was made up. Propping herself up, she said, a little shamefacedly: 'For now, I just want to bequeath the thousand gulden I have at home. If the need should arise, I'll have you sent for again. I want it divided in three, Notary! Three hundred for the poor, three hundred for the Church and three hundred for Mizzi Schinagl. The other hundred to cover various expenses.' She had no idea what 'various expenses' might be, she just said it. She thought it sounded rather airily magnanimous.

'Various expenses!' said the notary. 'We need to be a bit more precise than that.'

And he proposed: 'For funeral and tombstone!' Two words that to Frau Matzner, who only a moment ago had been ready to die, sounded rather upsetting.

And, slowly and implacably, the notary wrote. His body, his face, his head, they were all inscrutable. He might have a lot of thoughts – or then again, he might not have any at all. He had taken an official oath of confidentiality, it was as though he were behind a locked door. Who could tell what went on behind a locked door inside a 'k. und k.' notary's head?

Frau Matzner held her breath. She relished the formality of the proceedings, particularly in the light of her secret conviction that she had a lot longer to live. This was just a dress rehearsal. The whole world – including yesterday's Reverend – was looking forward to it already. She alone knew that she was going to prolong her life. And what a life it would be! The life of a newborn, the life of someone just back from the dead!

'What about the rest of your fortune?' asked the notary.

'We'll talk about that when the time comes!' said Frau

126

Matzner. She signed with the pen the notary held out to her. He fussily stuffed the paper into a heavy cloth-lined envelope. Then he sealed it. He took candle and sealing wax from his case. The burning candle suggested death to Frau Matzner, who promptly shut her eyes and didn't open them again until she heard the notary blowing it out. 'Goodbye!' he said. She gave him a smile.

She took some barley broth with a keen appetite, wishing it were something more substantial. She had a craving for some goulash and a mug of Okocimer. She wasn't ill, not ill at all. She thought she might play the invalid for another day or two. But in the evening, when the doctor came, she failed to recognize him. Thick drops of sweat stood out on her brow. Her nightcap pressed down with its taut elastic. She felt she was wearing a crown, and she begged pathetically: 'Won't you take my crown off!' – and in a muzzy recollection of yesterday's absolution, she added 'My crown of thorns!' – But they paid little attention to what she was saying. The mercury showed forty degrees.

Suddenly she screamed. She felt a slicing pain in her back, as though a double-edged sword had been pushed right through her ribs. Her mouth gaped open, she couldn't breathe, she wanted to cry out: air or window – but she forgot the words. She felt terrible heat, a huge fear, her fingers drummed on the covers. She rolled her eyes. The doctor sent the nurse to the chemist's shop for oxygen, he prepared a syringe of morphine. The nurse arrived with the balloon. At that moment, Frau Matzner sat up in bed and fell back. Her eyelids twitched faintly, and her fingers fluttered on the covers. Then her right hand flopped down over the side of the bed. Josephine Matzner had found peace.

She was buried on one of the first rainy days of that autumn. It was a third-class funeral – two horses and no attendants in crêpe. In accordance with practice, the notary published the usual announcement in the newspapers: 'Heirs sought!'

A couple of months later, a nephew of Frau Matzner's came forward, a hop farmer in Zǎtec, comfortably off and with no feelings of gratitude towards either fortune or his aunt.

The female penitentiary in Kagran was notified that prisoner Mizzi Schinagl had been mentioned in the will of the late Josephine Matzner, spinster, and had come into a legacy of three hundred gulden.

The crime reporter Lazik saw the announcement in the newspapers. A definite plan formed in his fertile brain.

He discussed it with his friend, Inspector Sedlacek, in the Café Wirzl on the Schottenring.

XIX

Far and wide, the world was deeply – horribly deeply – at peace, and the official police records, which included even the most trifling incidents, ran to barely two and a half pages a day. The group of crime reporters sat in a depressive huddle in the Café Wirzl, exhausted by the never-ending tranquillity, lamed by the uneventful peace, and without the remotest hope of a sensation. Each time the door opened, the men looked up from their cards. When it was one of the detectives who were forever popping in and out of Wirzl's, they looked at him expectantly, as though their eyes could pick up what their ears could not yet hear. 'Any news?' five or six men asked all at once. The detective kept his hat on; an indication that he wasn't staying and had nothing to relate. The heads drooped back over the cards once more, in lethargic resignation. Only the reporter Lazik was quietly following a particular idea. He didn't let it show at all. He was careful to look just as fatigued as the others by the hopelessness of these miserably tranquil times. But all the while he was spinning thread after thread, weaving them into webs and breaking them up again, trying to coax apparently unrelated matters into a brotherly knot, but also cutting apart things that did go together, because he needed all the individual members of a family of thought for different links, chains and relations. He alone intuited a connection between the death of the banker Efrussi and that of Josephine Matzner. Unless his memory deceived him, it was Efrussi who had advanced money on the surety of Mizzi Schinagl's famous pearls, and probably sold the same pearls on to Antwerp. It wasn't possible to establish any direct connections between the pearls, Persia, the Shah, Frau Matzner, Efrussi and Mizzi Schinagl, but the indirect ones looked rather promising. Beyond that, the unattractive deception that had been practised on the foolish Mussulman had involved Baron Taittinger as well. A good thing that the late Frau Matzner had found time to drop in on the Café Wirzl so soon before her sudden death! 'Material' was plentiful. Lazik, prick up your ears! said Lazik to himself.

One morning, while they were all slumped over their dejected game of tarot, Lazik heaved a deep sigh. 'What's the matter?' asked Keiler, 'has the Muse returned to you?' This ranked as an insult in that circle. There were still a couple of hacks who remembered a slim volume of Lazik's.

'It makes a man melancholy,' said Lazik, 'to be reminded of death. It seems like only yesterday that Frau Matzner, God rest her soul, was sitting over there, and now she's food for the worms. All the money she left!' The others merely nodded.

'It was time for her to die,' said Sedlacek. 'Things have moved on. She didn't belong any more. The new house on the Zollamtsstraße did it for her.'

'The high point of her life,' said Lazik, 'was the Shah's visit.

Do you remember the pearls? Where did they wind up in the end?'

'With Efrussi,' replied Sedlacek. 'And he's gone as well!'

'Now if only we had a story like that,' said Lazik. 'Will the Shah not come back? I think there was some muttering about that in the *Fremdenblatt* – Dr Auspitzer mentioned it in the office.'

'That would be news to us,' remarked Sedlacek. The 'us' was rather emphasized, and sounded formal.

'But Efrussi must have sold the pearls?' Lazik asked casually, and the very next moment cried out 'King! Jack!' and smacked the cards down on the table, to mask how important the question was to him.

'He gave them to Gwendl on commission. They were in the window there for months. I used to go and look at them a lot, with our gem specialist, Inspector Farkas. Then one day they weren't there!' replied Sedlacek.

The conversation died again. They played on. The customary apathy descended on the café once more, just like in summer when the mugginess returns following a short-lived and inconsequential breath of wind.

Lazik lost twenty-five kreuzer to Keiler. He'd meant to. His was a superstitious nature. In advance of every difficult task, he always sacrificed to the gods. Suddenly he stood up. 'I've been asked out,' he said. And he was gone, without saying goodbye.

First he headed down the Wasagasse, to throw his friends off the scent, as he knew it was in their nature – as indeed it was in his own – to go to the door after someone had left their company, to at least know which direction he had taken. Then he turned down the Währinger Straße, jumped on to a horse-drawn tram, and rode as far as the Opernring. He walked down the Kärntner Straße to the great jeweller Gwendl.

He asked to speak to Herr Gwendl in person. Herr Gwendl knew him well. He sat at the back of his shop, in a narrow, green-walled office, over an array of little black cassettes and cases, opening their sweet blue velvet throats for him and displaying the glittering, sparkling, gleeful splendour they had swallowed. He closed all his cases and cassettes, put down his magnifying glass, and went over to greet Editor Lazik.

'Greetings, Commercial Councillor!' said Lazik.

'Editor!' said Commercial Councillor Gwendl. 'What can I do for you? Care for a cigar? Take a seat, please,' and as the Commercial Councillor reached down to get the Virginias out of the bottom drawer – the Trabucos for better customers were kept in the upper drawers, for business friends and noble clients for example – he kept a watchful eye on Lazik's hands. And he sighed when the cigar box was finally on the table.

They spoke first about the news, of which in these quiet times there was little. Although in the *Fremdenblatt*, they were speculating about a possible return visit of the Shah of Persia.

The mention of this sovereign awakened distinctly pleasurable associations in the bosom of Commercial Councillor Gwendl. They revolved around Mizzi Schinagl's string of pearls, which Efrussi had given to Gwendl on commission. They had been in the shop a long time. Finally, Commissioner Heilpern from Antwerp had taken them. The purchaser was the jeweller Perlester. Gwendl and Heilpern netted a thousand each for the sale. The pearls had been valued at fifty thousand gulden. Perlester had later sold them – according to rumours in the profession – for sixty thousand. Still, one thousand gulden was not to be sniffed at. And now the Shah of Persia was coming back. So there might be more money to be made. Commercial Councillor Gwendl's mood lifted. 'Would the Commercial Councillor know,' Lazik began – he liked to begin in the third person – 'Surely the Commercial Councillor knows the present whereabouts of these celebrated pearls?'

The Commercial Councillor related as much as he knew. But he promised to ask his colleague Perlester what had become of them subsequently. Within a week, he would have more information for Lazik.

They went on to talk about the weather, about Court society, the sluggish state of business, even in the festive season, whereas in past years, as Gwendl said, it usually 'blossomed'.

'Well, it'll be Christmas soon!' said Lazik.

And with that consolation he left the jeweller, who slowly formulated the hope that the Muslim potentate's visit might coincide with the Christian holiday. His open eyes beheld a visionary land, an Orient stuffed with Christmas trees.

A few days later, Lazik was in a position to say what had become of the Shah's pearls. But he decided not to share his knowledge immediately, and baldly, with the readers of the *Kronen-Zeitung*, as his unimaginative colleague Keiler would have done. No: this story demanded to be carefully set out; artistically composed is what it demanded to be.

He announced a series of articles, to be entitled: 'The Pearls of Teheran. Behind the scenes of the *grand-monde* and the *demi-monde*'. He started off with a lapidary statement of fact of the sort that important novelists often like to begin with: namely with the news that Josephine Matzner – 'a certain Josephine

Matzner', wrote Lazik – had lately died. Then, following the obligatory rhetorical question 'Who was this Josephine Matzner?' he gave a full description of the house: its opening in 1857, its girls, its visitors and its regulars from the smart set – not naming them but offering unmistakable identification to anyone in the know. This series of articles was simultaneously offered for sale in the form of separate little booklets, mere off-prints admittedly, but supplied with eye-catching covers, on which an appealing half-naked girl was depicted sprawling on a garish green *chaise longue*. She lay there, all colour and expection, at once vulnerable and ready. The booklets went on sale in *Trafik* shops and news-stands. Schoolboys, seamstresses, wash-erwomen and janitors bought them, even if they had already read the articles in the *Kronen-Zeitung*. For a long time there was no further mention of the pearls, though they continued to be alluded to in the title every day.

During these weeks, Lazik rationed his daily visits to the Café Wirzl to a minute or two. He wasn't getting on at all well with his colleagues or the detectives. He felt that they were rather jealous of him, but also that they had stopped treating him as one of themselves. They were no 'writers'. They had no 'imaginative vision' to unfold. They offered 'news items', big, small or sensational, but never 'stories'. In meagre times like these, they scraped together the meagre offerings of the day, here a stabbing, there the birth of triplets, somewhere else a fall from a fourth-storey window. Lazik had betrayed their guild. He wasn't even welcome to spectate at their tarot games.

He had often dreamed of making a lot of money quickly, and throwing in his job. He was approaching fifty-six, and he had lost his hair and most of his teeth. His wife had died young, his daughter was living with his sister in Podiebrad. He had no major money worries, but small troubles, minor debts, troublesome creditors, interest payments that were swelling menacingly, waiters who no longer let him run up a tab. Oh, and his soul had a taste for the luxuries that the *crème de la crème* enjoyed. He loved the high life, races, quiet restaurants where proud waiters served and proud gentlemen with impassive faces ate and drank with refinement and pleasure, before going home in sealed carriages to their yet more sealed and impassive dwellings. Each time Lazik left the Café Wirzl, his colleagues and the detectives, the grimy playing cards and the smell of coffee, Okocimer beer, cheap cigars and bread sticks, it seemed to him that he had compromised himself, somehow lowered himself. That much was clear: he had been going steadily downhill – from the poet who had once even submitted a play to the Burgtheater, via the court stenographer, to the crime reporter known in professional circles as 'Scuttlebutt'. Now for the first time in thirty years he saw his name – Bernhard Lazik – in print, and not just in the paper either, but on the cover of the eye-catching little booklets. Lazik sent copies of them to Podiebrad, to his sister and daughter. What else would he leave behind? An announcement in six point type in the *Kronen-Zeitung*: 'Yesterday our long-serving colleague . . .' and finis. And a few ells of graveyard space out in Währing. The 'studio' he lived in in the Rembrandtstraße wasn't much bigger than that. Nor was it much lighter than a grave, seeing that it 'gave' on to the corridor. He had never been able to economize. He spent his paltry income at the races and at gaming tables. He was paid two kreuzers per line. A 'coup' he sometimes said to himself – a 'coup', Lazik, just once in your life!

After a few days of feeling very lonely and even slightly embittered, because it seemed to him not that he had begun to avoid his acquaintances, but rather the other way round – that they were cutting him – he began to study the list of new hotel arrivals in the *sûreté* every morning. Of all the 'top ten thousand' who had frequented Frau Matzner's establishment, the only one of interest to him was Baron Taittinger. Lazik didn't know under what pretext he would approach the Captain of Horse; nor even what he would propose to him. All he knew was that he would have to speak to Taittinger; and that on 15th November the three hundred gulden he owed Brociner, the 'Bloodsucker', fell due. During these days, Lazik had a sense of being at a crossroads in his life. A vague megalomania fogged his brain, making him think it was now or never.

And one day in the *sûreté* he duly came across a registration form with the Captain's name on it. He was staying, as ever, at the Imperial. Lazik set off immediately before he knew what he was going to say to the Baron – indeed, before he had even grasped that he was on his way to the Hotel Imperial. He had a couple of his eye-catching booklets in his pocket and kept pulling them out along the way, gazing at his name on the cover. There it was, big and bold, just under the virulent green sofa with the reclining girl. And he thought about the three hundred gulden that were due on 15th November. And the 'Bloodsucker' Brociner appeared to him even uglier and more dangerous than usual, in spite of the fact that he'd known him well for two years, and knew how to appease him – 'to knock out his poisonous fangs', as he put it.

Baron Taittinger found it exceptionally disagreeable to receive visitors. He had no particular fondness for the people he knew, they were mostly boring. Even the ones that weren't boring might 'pall' if one wasn't properly prepared. When Lazik's card was brought to him, his immediate response was horror. The mere sound of the name 'Lazik' was offensive to him. Under the name Bernhard Lazik was the designation 'Editor'. That was one of the professions that Baron Taittinger thought of as 'squalid'. Except for the army paper, Taittinger didn't read newspapers. Yes, and when he went into *Trafik* to buy cigarettes, as he occasionally did, he had to avert his gaze from the hateful piles of them, with their piercing smell of printer's ink. He didn't exactly know what they contained or what the point of them was. In a café, when he saw a gentleman sitting with a pile of newspapers in holders in front of him, he would be gripped by something like rage. And now he was to make the acquaintance of an actual editor! Whatever next! He put the card down on the metal tray, and told the waiter: 'I am not receiving!' And he heaved a sigh.

But barely three minutes later, there stood in front of him a man, bald and ashen-faced and with a sadly drooping ashen moustache. 'I am Editor Bernhard Lazik,' the stranger said. His voice was thin and whiny, and put the Captain in mind of a melancholy, out of tune spinet – the kind that he might once have played in his childhood.

'What d'you want?' asked Taittinger.

'I'd be grateful if the Baron would listen to what I have to say,' replied Lazik. 'It's in your interest,' he added, in very low tones, and almost miserably.

'Yes, well?' said Taittinger, fully determined not to listen.

'If the Baron will allow,' Lazik began, 'it's not a straightforward story. Speaking in confidence, it's a police matter –'

'I don't want any confidences,' the Captain interrupted. Even though he'd resolved not to listen to the man at all, he was forced to take in every last mournful syllable. It was a disconcertingly effective voice.

'I didn't mean confidence like that,' the man resumed.

'A while ago, you see, a certain Josephine Matzner died.'

The name struck Taittinger's ear with some force, it felt more like a blow on the temple. 'Ah, she's died, has she?' he asked.

A small joy lit up in Lazik's eye. 'Died,' he went on, 'just like that! And she left a small sum of money to the Schinagl girl, who's doing time. Nothing like enough if you ask me – I mean the money – seeing as she was worth a fortune.' Lazik was silent for a moment. He waited. The Captain of Horse didn't speak, but his interest was so obviously engaged, that Lazik positively drew encouragement from the silence. His voice became more confident. He was still standing in front of the little table in the hall, looking like a porter, but he had dared to grip the leather back of an armchair with both hands. It was as though his hands had been allowed to sit down.

Taittinger observed this, with displeasure to begin with, and in the next moment with a measure of tolerance. He did not yet admit to himself that the 'squalid' man interested him, however annoying he might be. But he did think it might attract attention if the man remained standing for much longer. So he said: 'Sit down!' Lazik was already sitting. He had sat down so swiftly that Taittinger regretted having asked him. His silver cigarette case was open on the table. He felt like lighting up a cigarette, but now there was this fellow sitting down – wasn't he obliged to offer him one too? Taittinger knew exactly how to treat equals, superiors, subalterns and servants; with editors he wasn't so sure. He decided, after giving it some thought, to light a cigarette himself, and then offer one to the editor.

Lazik smoked slowly and respectfully, as though the 'Egyptian' were a particularly delectable brand. He pulled his booklets out of his pocket, and laid them on the table. 'Here's what I'm publishing now, Baron!' he said. 'Please, just take a look at the beginning!'

'I don't read books!' said Taittinger.

'Then would you object to me reading to you from one?' asked Lazik. And before he could receive a reply, he began to read aloud. Nothing matters now, Taittinger thought to himself. But lo, straight after the sentence: 'Who was this Josephine Matzner?' he was full of childish curiosity. With unconcealed pleasure, he leaned forward. He heard the story of the early days of Madam Matzner's establishment, and, by some distinguishing features that the author had provided, to go with the initials of the habituees, he recognized to his great glee some of his former friends and comrades, the 'bores', the 'so-so' and the 'charmers'. When Lazik paused and modestly, almost anxiously asked: 'Is it all right to carry on?' Taittinger urged him: 'Carry on, Sir, carry on'

'That was the first instalment!' observed the author, once he had read the whole of the first booklet.

'Will you sell 'em to me!' asked the Captain of Horse.

'Permit me to offer them to the Baron gratis,' said Lazik, and he tapped on the metal table rim with a pencil and called to the waiter: 'Pen and ink!' They were brought, and Lazik dipped the pen and wrote in each of the three booklets: 'Respectfully dedicated to Captain Baron Taittinger, by the author, Bernhard Lazik.'

'Thank you very much!' said the Baron. 'Send me the next instalment. I'll be interested to see 'em!'

'Baron, you flatter me,' replied the author. 'But I have a problem – I don't know how I'm going to go on with the books.'

'What do you mean!' exclaimed Taittinger. 'You're wonderfully well informed, almost like an insider!'

'Indeed, Baron, indeed,' replied Lazik. 'But it all costs

money! and I'm looking for backers! I'm looking for a sum to enable me to continue the work I've embarked on. Life's so hard for the likes of us!' And here Lazik sighed. His head hung down to his left shoulder. Taittinger felt sorry for him, and offered him a cigarette. The fellow's really not at all boring, he thought to himself. 'How much do you need for your little booklets?' he asked.

Lazik's first thought had been a thousand gulden, and a sudden spasm of joy squeezed his heart. Three hundred for the 'Bloodsucker' Brociner, and then seven hundred left over – that was it! That was a 'coup', that was *his* 'coup'! Immediately his greedy imagination doubled the sum. Two thousand! said his imagination. He saw the amount in figures and written out, cursive and printed, and then as cash in the form of twenty blue hundred-gulden notes. He felt his hands growing hot and clammy, and at the same time a shiver went down his spine like an icy thread. He pulled out his handkerchief – a movement Taittinger took against, and at which he wished he had covered his eyes – dried his hands under the table, and breathed: 'Two thousand, Baron!'

'They cost two thousand gulden?' asked Taittinger. He had rather vague ideas about money, except that he knew the price of a horse, a uniform, a barrel of burgundy, a flask of Napoléon. Years before, he had once lost a thousand gulden in Monte Carlo. But these skinny little booklets! – Still, the fellow certainly wasn't boring; not at all. And if he went on to name names! Wouldn't that be something!

'Well, why don't you call people by their names, instead of their initials?' asked the Captain of Horse.

'Because then, Baron – the Baron would have to appear in them himself!' Lazik whispered.

'Not me, of course!' said Taittinger.

Not once in his life – which at that moment seemed to him particularly very long and rich in incident – had he felt hatred. But suddenly, at that moment, he relished the idea that one or other of the 'bores' he hated might appear, with name and rank, in one of those pretty, eye-catching booklets; he felt some resentment against the 'bores' too, because of his precipitate transfer back to barracks from Vienna. It was an innocent, childish resentment – a mood, a tantrum, rather than hatred.

'I can name names, if the Baron would like me to!' said Lazik.

'Good!' said the Baron. 'Excellent!'

Lazik didn't move. His heart pounded, his limbs felt leaden, and at the same time he felt how his thoughts, confused flocks of birds, fluttered round his poor head. They fluttered around, two thousand thoughts, one gulden each one, two thousand gulden in all.

'Two thousand, eh?' Baron Taittinger asked.

'Yes, Baron!' breathed Lazik.

'You can pick them up tomorrow!' said Taittinger.

Lazik stood up with difficulty. He bowed deeply and murmured: 'Eternally grateful to you, Baron!'

'*Grüß Gott!*' said Taittinger. He put the three booklets in his pocket.

In the usual way, as he had done many times before, he wired his 'boring' steward: '2000 Imperial'.

They duly came, but with an accompanying wire: 'Money coming, urgent letter follows.'

The Baron tore up the wire, out of irrepressible disgust at the expression: 'urgent letter'. He put the money in an envelope, told the porter to give it to 'the fellow yesterday', and got into a carriage. He hadn't been up to Grinzing for some time. And tomorrow he was expected back at the barracks.

XX

Usually Taittinger fell asleep the moment he boarded a train. Today, though, he stayed awake and read Lazik's booklets, including the first one, which the author had already read aloud to him. He imagined the whole world must read these pamphlets with the same relish and enthusiasm. The next day he wanted to tell the regiment all about his new literary discovery, and maybe treat the mess to a sample chapter – so long as the Colonel wasn't there, of course. With these cheery thoughts he passed the time till he arrived at the garrison town.

It was evening when he got in. A thin, chilly, boring drizzle was coming down gently and persistently, giving the dismal yellow oil lamps on the platform a damp halo. Even the first-class waiting room harboured an oppressive gloom, and the potted palm on the buffet let its heavy slender leaves droop as though it too were standing out in the autumn rain. Two gas lights, the newly acquired pride of the station, had something wrong with their mantles, and gave out a flickering greenish glow. They emitted, what's more, a plaintive buzz, a lamentation. The white shirt-front of Ottokar, the head waiter, bore sorry stains of unknown provenance. The metallic glitter of the Captain of Horse made a victorious entrance into all this gloom. Ottokar brought a Hennessy 'to take the chill off' and a menu. 'We have soup with liver dumplings today, Baron!'

'Pipe down!' Taittinger replied happily. Whenever he spoke like that, he really meant the opposite, as Ottokar well knew. He therefore went on to recommend the boiled beef with horseradish sauce and plum dumplings fresh today. 'Pipe down and dish up!' said Taittinger . The cognac improved his mood further, and whetted his appetite. He stood up and took off his coat, which he'd kept on till now. Ottokar ran up to help him with it. The eye-catching corner of Lazik's oeuvre peeped out of one of the pockets, and Ottokar's avid eye spotted it right away.

'Tales from the *grand monde* and the *demi-monde*,' the waiter ventured. Once the Captain had told him to 'Pipe down!' it was permissible to talk to him about absolutely anything.

'Ah, so you're a reader too, Ottokar?' asked Taittinger.

'The *Kronen-Zeitung* every morning, Baron, beg to report, sir! That's got the stories in, even fresher, like getting them still warm from the baker!'

'I see,' said Taittinger. He ate with healthy enjoyment, found the beef 'distinguished' and the plum dumplings 'not uninteresting', drank a slivowitz with his black coffee, and decided to stay where he was until the late train from Vienna got in – which wasn't till quarter to midnight; sometimes one or other of his comrades travelled on it, cutting it fine, though usually it brought officers from the reserve regiment with which the dragoons shared the garrison. He had these moods sometimes, these evenings. As long as you were still at the station, in a sense, you weren't quite back in the garrison. Anyway the rain was still lashing down. The cabs in the town weren't up to much, and the paving was pretty wretched. Best sit tight. Ottokar knew how to play patience. Taittinger didn't think it appropriate for himself. Therefore Ottokar played for him, standing facing him, leaning forward, pensive, the napkin swinging on his shoulder. And Ottokar talked. He was still young, he wanted to 'better himself', he had learned how to wait tables in Vienna, and wanted to go back there. Things still happened in Vienna, the kind of things you read about in the booklets and the *Kronen-Zeitung*. Yes, and some of the characters were so skilfully described, you could even identify them.

'Is that right!' exclaimed Taittinger. 'You can identify them!'

'Yes,' said Ottokar. Herr Hanfl – who ran the first-, second- and third-class station restaurants – knew it all. Back when the Shah had visited Vienna, he'd run a restaurant on the Wieden. He knew the house, the story of the pearls; it had been the talk of the whole district. 'And the Baron as well,' said Ottokar without thinking, then bit his tongue and pretended he suddenly had to think very hard about the patience.

'What was that you said?' asked Taittinger.

There was nothing for it, Ottokar had to confess. So that was how it was, Taittinger's story was widely known. Ottokar even had to get the restaurant manager out of his office. Herr Hanfl recounted one or two particulars, though nothing specifically about the Baron. He talked with the airy cheerfulness of someone who has waited a long time to relate something that only he knows.

'How d'you come to hear of the story?' Taittinger asked at the end.

The manager leaned forward – rather too close for Taittinger's liking – and whispered almost as one might whisper to an accomplice: 'Inspector Sedlacek is a close personal friend of mine, Baron!'

All of a sudden, the world seemed a changed place to the Captain of Horse, or, more accurately, it seemed to be beginning to reveal itself to him in its full, true ghastliness. His whole life had contained one awkward episode. For many years he had been choking on it – a tough, hideous mouthful it was impossible to swallow or spit out. There was nobody in the world he could talk to about it. Now the episode was clutching at him, it was known to the managers of station restaurants. His comrades were probably talking about it, particularly those two-faced reservists. In his mind's eye, Taittinger saw the hideous form of the detective Sedlacek, and he relived the moment on the stairs: the upraised hat over the coarse physiognomy; the bright eyes like pale blue lamps; the turned-up moustache full of mild, golden-brown effrontery, with the long, yellow horsy teeth visible below it.

The restaurateur was still speaking, but Taittinger had stopped listening. Suddenly he heard what he had previously been unaware of, the miserable drumming of the rain on the glass platform roof, and the lamenting buzz of the acid-green gas jets. Even while Hanfl was still reminiscing away, Taittinger got up, was helped into his coat, put on his cap, asked to have his travelling bag and the bill forwarded to him at the Black Elephant, and went out, almost like a condemned man. Had it not been for his jangling spurs, one might have thought he had slunk out in shame.

The Kaiser-Josef-Straße, which led from the station to the Town Hall and the centre, was quiet, only the cold rain was abroad. Captain Taittinger was all alone with the rain and the road.

Grave, or even half-serious, forebodings or premonitions were completely unknown to him. He had no patience with difficult, or as he would put it, boring moods. This time, though, he abandoned himself to them, along with the rain and the night and the Kaiser-Josef-Straße. Before, each time he returned from Vienna, it had always been his custom to drop into the mess to 'reacclimatize'. Today he almost fled to the Black Elephant Hotel. Two first lieutenants, Stockinger and Felch, stayed there too. Taittinger wanted to avoid running into them at all costs. He made straight for his room. He did not perform the usual elaborate ablutions, his nightly ritual for fifteen years now. 'Don't bother with that stuff!' he said to his valet, who, as usual, had begun to lay out brush and comb, toothpaste, hair pomade and hairnet, vaseline and cocoa butter. The Captain merely had him pull his boots off. 'Now go to bed!' he said. He lay down in his socks and trousers. He didn't dare undress. He couldn't understand why, for the first time in his life, he was afraid of the night. It was as though he wanted to prolong the day, the evening. He was afraid of the night ahead. I won't be able to sleep, he thought to himself. But he fell asleep right away. He collapsed into it, as though he'd been knocked out.

And yet, his fear of the night had been justified, because for the first time in a long time he had vivid dreams that were part terrible, part ineffably sad. He saw himself going down the red carpeted marble steps, and saw Sedlacek coming towards him and lifting his hat; but at the same time, he himself, Taittinger, was Sedlacek; it was him lifting his hat; him coming towards himself. He was going up the stairs and at the same time going down them. Suddenly he was standing in the director's office in the penitentiary in Kagran, and the police surgeon was asking him: 'What's the matter with you? Why can't you tell me how my regiment is getting on?' He was unable to answer, poor Taittinger. He was afraid too that the police chief might come in at any moment and say: 'I don't know any Baron Taittinger.' Then Countess Helene W. appeared, with a shaven head, just like Mizzi Schinagl, and wanted all her letters returned. He could only say that there had been some terrible mistake, that he had never received any letters from the Countess, least of all any registered ones. 'Please, Countess,' he said, 'ask Warrant Officer Zenower.'

'Too late, too late!' she cried, and he awoke. His valet was shaking him.

It was late, a quarter to seven, there wasn't time to be shaved. He had asked two corporals, Leschak and Kaniuk, to report to him today for turning out unshaven on the parade ground a couple of days ago. His official, soldierly conscience troubled the Captain of Horse. Never mind, he had to go – boots, jacket, schako, and off to the barracks. The whole squadron was already mounted. No time even to do roll-call. It was raining gently and incessantly, just as it had been the previous night. The rain stitched yesterday and today together, it was as if there hadn't been a separate dawn, as if no day would ever dawn again! . . .

The regiment formed up, the broad black and yellow striped double gates opened, and they rode out. It wasn't until he was

148

in the saddle that Taittinger began to feel reality returning. It had taken him until now to understand that all that horror last night had just been a dream. Through the saddle and through the shafts of his boots, he felt the blood-warmth of his horse. He was sitting well today on his mare. Valli was her name. A chestnut, he loved her, even though she was nothing like as intelligent as his grey, Pylades. He had called him that under the misapprehension that Pylades was a Greek philosopher. Valli was slow, and could be mulish at times – she needed a lot of talking to. Gentle pressure of the thighs alone didn't do it. She had her moods, she wasn't female for nothing, she could be slothful one minute and exuberant the next. But he loved her for all that.

When he dismounted in the meadow, he was almost the familiar, the old Taittinger again. He took the report, he punished the two unshaven corporals very harshly, each with three days in solitary confinement. 'It's a disgrace for a non-commissioned officer to be unshaven!' he said. He couldn't help rubbing his own prickly chin as he spoke. The duty officer Prokurak couldn't have helped but notice. So what! There followed gymnastic exercises, riding exercises, weapon exercises. Captain of Horse Taittinger was extremely pernickety that day.

But then, four hours later, after they had returned to barracks, he was standing awkwardly, almost apologetically, in the warrant office again. There was a registered letter for him. Another one. He had to sign a piece of paper. Warrant Officer Zenower had such a frightfully serious expression on his face today, it wasn't the way he usually looked when there were registered letters. And this letter was very heavy and thick. If he'd tossed it into the wastepaper basket, it would certainly have made a loud and disagreeable noise. On the yellow envelope he read 'Town Hall, Oberndorf'. Rather now than later, Baron Taittinger told himself. He tore it open and started reading.

Accompanying an official letter from the Mayor – who was informing Taittinger that a juvenile minor by the name of Alexander Alois Schinagl had reported to the Town Hall, and, claiming to be the illegitimate son of Captain of Horse Baron Taittinger, had asked for the address of his natural father and of his mother, the unmarried Mizzi Schinagl – was a letter from his steward. Actually, it wasn't so much a letter as a bit of maths homework of the kind that the cadets at the military academy at Mährisch-Weißkirchen were so unreasonably expected to do. It was only the final sentence that Taittinger could make any sense of at all. It read: 'In view of the above, I humbly and respectfully permit myself to inform the Baron that only by his prompt arrival here is there any prospect of alleviating the situation.' Taittinger decided to show both letters to good, clever Zenower. He had known for a long time that he would be needing Zenower. 'My dear Zenower!' he said. 'You must have some civilian clothes!'

'Yes, indeed, Baron!'

'Well, would you do me the kindness of putting them on, and meeting me in the small lounge of the Black Elephant at about six tonight, after evening orders? And then will you tell me what these people want from me?'

XXI

In the evening, after orders, Zenower walked into the small lounge in his civilian suit. He looked even more serious in it than he did in uniform. It was the first time Taittinger had seen him in his own clothes. He was no longer Warrant Officer Zenower, he was no subaltern and no superior officer, yet nor was he a civilian, he was a being between worlds, between breeds – curious, unfathomable, but certainly ominous and intimidating. Taittinger would need a stiff drink, then things wouldn't look so bad. 'Zenower, my dear fellow!' he began. 'Do you drink cognac?' Taittinger felt as though his entire fate depended on Zenower's willingness to drink cognac.

'Oh, indeed, Baron!' said Zenower. He even said it with a smile. Curious, how people changed. Zenower was not at all boring, not at all subordinate, not at all indifferent. Had Taittinger not had such strict standards, he might even have called him 'charming'. They drank.

'Well, now,' said Taittinger, and he distinctly felt that the cognac had not yet done its work, 'how can you cheer me up,

Zenower?' Suddenly he could see Zenower's true face. It was hard and cold, and harder and colder in a civilian's white collar and tie than in the high-necked green uniform tunic. The lofty brow was deeply furrowed, and there were more wrinkles under the eyes and at the temples. Yes, even his hair suddenly seemed to have become greyer. He was an elderly, severe and thoughtful gentleman.

'Baron,' said the thoughtful gentleman, 'I am afraid there is nothing cheerful in what I have to say. Will you listen to me carefully?'

'Of course, of course!' said Taittinger.

'Right. The first thing is to do with the Mayor. He writes that, having run away from the institution in Graz and having been picked up by the police, Alexander Alois Schinagl has turned up on his doorstep. He is fourteen years old. He was brought to the Mayor by a police sergeant in Eichholz. The institution in Graz has not been paid for the last six months. The head of the institution has learned that the mother, Fräulein Schinagl, is currently in the female penitentiary in Kagran. When he applied to her, she wrote back saying that you are the boy's natural father, had been to visit her in prison, and would certainly look after him. The boy must have stolen this letter. It was found in his clothes. He denied it, and asked for the whereabouts of his mother. His legal guardian is Fräulein Schinagl's father. He is now in the old people's home in Lainz. He is a paraplegic, and his shop in Sievering has been sequestrated. He tells the Mayor that Baron Taittinger, the boy's father, has to date not contributed to his upkeep in any way. Now, in light of the circumstances and to minimize the scandal, the Mayor has left the boy with your steward. They are all waiting for your decision, Baron!'

'Mizzi never asked me for money,' said Taittinger. 'Pity! – so what'll I do, Zenower?'

'If I might advise – have the boy returned to Graz, and settle the outstanding debt. It stands at about three hundred gulden.'

'I'll do that, my dear Zenower.'

'Now on to the other matter, Baron,' said Zenower. He waited a moment. 'The other matter is extremely disagreeable. Your steward begs your forgiveness, but he thinks it's his duty to inform you that, following the most recent wiring of two thousand gulden to you in Vienna, any further withdrawals are not advisable. In the course of the last four years, you have spent approximately twenty-five thousand gulden. The remaining cash comes to about five thousand. Thirteen thousand have been paid out for the bills of exchange presented by your cousin, Baron Zernutti.'

'Zernutti, now there's a boring man!' said Taittinger.

'That might be one way of putting it,' replied Zenower. He took the Captain as he was, and was fond of him, with his cheery heartlessness, his incapacity to think beyond a couple of thoughts, for which his skull was far too roomy, his insignificant love affairs and childish infatuations, and the pointless and unconnected remarks that came out of his mouth, seemingly at random. He was a mediocre officer, who didn't care about his comrades, his men, his career. Zenower had no understanding of the machinery that drove a being like the Baron to perpetuate a series of such pointless, fatuous and even self-destructive actions. To Zenower, who expended more thought on man and the world than the rest of the regiment – plus Colonel – put together, Taittinger was an enigma of Nature. If only he had been exceptionally stupid! Exceptionally wicked! An impassioned gambler or lover! If only he had visibly suffered as a result of being jilted! And for all that, Zenower said to himself, he must be unhappy. Perhaps he has experienced such a monumental misfortune that it's left him incapable of human thought or feeling! Or maybe some such misfortune is waiting for him, and he knows it and can't do anything about it. How otherwise could a man remain impassive on receiving news like this? To be telling a grown man that he has no more money – and all he can say by way of reply is: 'Zernutti, now there's a boring man!'

'Your estate is in bad shape,' Zenower continued. 'The mortgage on it is thirty thousand – that's my understanding – again, partly due to your cousin. I'm sure he must have long since exceeded his share. Your late uncle obviously stipulated that your cousin shouldn't be allowed to withdraw cash from the estate, much less take out a loan against it without your agreement. Is that not right, Baron?'

'Yes, I expect so!' said Taittinger. 'I always said yes, he was always too boring. It all goes on boys. Now tell me, Zenower, do you understand what pleasure there is to be had from boys?'

'No, Baron,' Zenower replied curtly, 'but that's not at issue. What is at issue is that your estate hasn't made any money for three years now. Two years ago you had the small pine wood logged. The logger declared bankruptcy, so you only got the first part of what was owing to you. Last year there was the big snowfall in May, which ruined the seed. This year's harvest is awful. The house is dilapidated, no one's lived in it for ten years. The condition of the livestock defies description. Two horses are needed, and there is no money.'

'No luck, eh?' said Taittinger; clapped his hands and ordered two more cognacs.

He drank his down in two large gulps. He was silent. Already a quiet resentment against Zenower began to rise in him. But he also felt a great sense of abandonment, and a trace of gratitude. Here was someone who agreed to read letters and reflect and ponder. He was a clever fellow, Zenower. He was probably doing what all clever people had always done with Taittinger, starting with Captain Jellinek the maths teacher at cadet school: first they softened him up – frightened him with a lot of boring stuff – and after that they picked him up again with good, healthy advice. He didn't actually have to *be* softened up, often enough just looking the part would do.

On this occasion, though, Taittinger had miscalculated. For, when he followed the script which on previous occasions had always helped him in his dealings with clever people, and asked:

'So what shall I do?'

Zenower replied: 'There's no helping you, Baron!' Must be a queer new kind of clever, that Zenower.

For a long time, neither of them spoke. Then Taittinger ordered a bottle of white bordeaux. He looked at the clock, there was an hour to go till dinner.

When he had taken his first sip of wine, Zenower said: 'Baron, may I be entirely open with you?' Taittinger nodded. 'Well: to begin with, you could sell your grey!'

'What? My Pylades!' cried Taittinger, 'I'd rather sell Valli!'

'No, that wouldn't raise enough, and you'd only have to sell the grey later anyway. You need money for two farm horses. You should take a furlough, go out to your estate, get the house repaired, talk to the mortgagers, the Mayor, get a new guardian appointed for young Schinagl. Three months might be enough, Baron! Don't sign any more loan papers for your cousin, that goes without saying. Unless you do all this, I see a bleak future for you. You'll have to transfer to the infantry!'

'Join the reserves, you think?! My dear Zenower, I don't know how to march!'

'Exactly,' said Zenower. He too looked at the clock. 'Now if you'll allow me, I'll take my leave, Baron!'

'No, Zenower, stay!' said Taittinger, with the desperate look of a little boy about to be pushed into a dark room.

'Very well!' said Zenower.

The Captain walked over to the rack where his coat was hanging, and pulled out some of Lazik's eye-catching booklets. 'Ever come across these, Zenower?'

Zenower flicked through the booklets, read a little here and there, clapped them shut and said: 'Hideous, Baron!'

'Not at all!' cried Taittinger. And he explained how all the people in them 'were marvellously well done'. He himself had met Lazik, the author. And that's who he had given those last two thousand gulden to.

'That's worse than everything else put together!' said Zenower.

The title alone was enough to tell him what it was all about. He too had heard the stories that had been circulating about Taittinger, almost from the day of his return to the regiment. As an experienced and long-serving Warrant Officer, he was well acquainted with the penchant of some members of the officer corps for malicious gossip. Long before Taittinger had been transferred back, some ill-disposed members of the regiment had told unbelievable stories about him. They were envious of his posting to Vienna. But later, when he was a soldier again like everyone else, people began asking themselves why his special secondment had so suddenly come to an end. The station restaurant manager had a few tales to tell. Ottokar the waiter hinted darkly at this or that, since the articles in the *Kronen-Zeitung* had begun to appear. 'Did you give him money so that he didn't mention you by name?' asked Zenower.

'No,' replied Taittinger, 'what does he know about me anyway?'

'Is there anything he might find out about you that might harm you, Baron?'

Taittinger didn't reply. This was even worse than yesterday's experience in the waiting room. During the course of the day, he had forgotten the previous evening, in spite of the two letters. He wished he hadn't asked Zenower for advice now. It would have been better, and in accordance with years of practice, to have ignored the letters. But something had changed of late – he couldn't quite put his finger on it. It was all he could do to remember when things had begun to change: but suddenly he knew exactly when it had been: from the moment Taittinger had seen the cropped head of Mizzi Schinagl. Yes, that was it.

It was all so hopelessly tangled and difficult. Even if he'd had the strength to tell Zenower everything – even about the 'shameful episode' – he couldn't have done it at that moment, as he felt incapable of stringing two sentences together

'If you'll permit me, Baron – I ought to go now,' he heard Zenower say.

'No!' he cried. 'For God's sake stay! I can't speak at the moment, that's all, I need to think, Zenower!' But he didn't think. His eyes were vacant, two blue marbles. Even not thinking took it out of a man. He drank, smoked, attempted once or twice to smile, racked his brain for a joke, an amusing expression, an anecdote, and none of it was any use, and all the while

he felt ashamed of his obdurate silence. You see, in the officers
mess, with his own sort, he always had the right word for every
occasion. With his own sort! He clung to those words – they
provided him with a simple explanation for his present difficulties, namely that Zenower wasn't really 'his sort'. For a
moment he thought he'd recovered his balance, firmness, composure, and with the friendly hauteur with which he spoke to
subalterns, he said: 'Now, my dear Zenower, why don't you tell
me something about yourself for a change!'

'I'm completely uninteresting, Baron!' said Zenower. 'I've
been with the army for the past twelve years. I was a goldsmith
before that. A long time ago, now. I'm single. I joined up when
I was twenty-two, because the girl I loved married someone
else.'

'That's not nice!' interjected Taittinger.

'No, Baron, it was the only hurt in my life, and it will be the
last.'

'Impressive!' exclaimed the Captain. 'Are your parents still
alive?'

'I have none! My mother died young. She was a cook. I don't
know anything about my father. I was an illegitimate child.'

'Interesting,' Taittinger said, 'and you grew up all alone?'

'In the town orphanage in Müglitz, then at sixteen I was
apprenticed.'

'You're a clever fellow, Zenower,' said the Captain, 'why
don't you take the accountancy exams?'

'I intend to,' said Zenower, 'even though I couldn't be promoted any higher than Paymaster, Captain. Even then there are
difficulties because of my being illegitimate. But I know someone who's in the Accountancy Department in the War
Ministry.'

'I'm sure they'll sort it out for you!' Taittinger said encouragingly. 'You have had an interesting life! One would have to call you, what's the expression: "a child of the people"! I never took you for that.'

'If you say so,' said Zenower, 'but "child of the people" doesn't mean much to me. I'm the child of a cook!'

Taittinger remembered the old cook in his father's house. Karoline, she was called. She was old, and she always cried – three times a year – when Taittinger came home: at Easter, in the summer holidays, and for Christmas. Suddenly, unaware that he was speaking aloud, he said: 'My dear Zenower, just now I thought, I couldn't really speak to you openly. Now I know why that is: I'm ashamed in front of you, I envy you, I wouldn't mind changing places with you!' His own sentence shocked him – his honesty, but above all the speed with which he had managed to give an account of his thoughts. He had caught himself telling the truth; and for the first time in many years he blushed, the way he had once blushed as a boy when he'd been caught telling a lie.

Zenower said: 'Baron, you've no cause to envy anyone, or to change places with anyone, so long as you're always honest with yourself. And, just for today, with me too!' he added.

'Ah, Zenower,' said the Captain. He felt a powerful sadness and a great merriment at the same time.

'I'll meet you after dinner – at Sedlak's, my usual place, do you know it? Will you come? I'll leave the mess in two hours.' He pressed Zenower's large hand, which seemed like a single warm and intensely alive muscle. He felt goodness and strength coming from that hand, and honesty. He could almost hear it. It was as though Zenower's hand had said something good.

XXII

Sedlak's bar was on the wrong side of town, opposite what were known as the sandhills, some half an hour from the centre. It was a meeting place for small farmers, grain merchants, horse breeders; and, of the better class of person, occasionally for the two vets. There was no possibility of meeting anyone in uniform there. It started to snow gently as Taittinger left the officers mess. 'Sorry, I've got an appointment,' he said, running into First Lieutenant Zschoch in the doorway.

'What's her name?' Zschoch asked, but Taittinger didn't hear him. It was the first snow of the year. Taittinger, never otherwise impressed by natural phenomena, whether routine or unexpected, now for the first time in his life took a boyish pleasure in the soft, gentle, charitable flakes that fell dreamily and casually on his cap and his shoulders, and across the whole breadth of the road that led up to the sandhills. It seemed somehow significant to him that the first snow was falling today. He walked briskly through the thick white veil. The level crossing gate was down; he had to wait a long time. On any other day he would have called the railway 'boring'. Today, however, he waited with relish. He felt as if he were becoming snowed further in even as he stood there. An endless freight train rumbled past. What was in the silent wagons? Was it animals, or logs, or crates of eggs; bags of grain or barrels of beer? The thoughts that are occurring to me today! Taittinger said to himself. The world is full of things I had no idea of! People like Zenower, whose mother was a cook and who grew up in an orphanage, they know a lot of things. The train was still taking its time. Or perhaps the freight train was carrying luggage, like all the suitcases that belonged to the Persian monarch, that had arrived so late. Taittinger remembered the charming Kirilida Pajidzani. What could he be up to now in Teheran? Maybe it was snowing there too. That Pajidzani was a lucky fellow. He had no guilty episode on his conscience, no Mizzi Schinagl, no boring cousin Zernutti, no registered letters, no trustee, no steward! Finally the train had passed, the gate lifted, as though fighting slowly and with difficulty against the gentle weight of the snow. I'll tell him about it, Taittinger decided, the moment he saw the two illuminated windows through the snow.

Zenower was already there, sitting reading some of the eye-catching booklets – Taittinger spotted them from the doorway. He reached automatically into his coat pocket, supposing the booklets that Zenower had spread out in front of him on the table were his. But no! Zenower must be reading different ones. 'Aha, you've come round to them?' said Taittinger. 'Are they the ones I have?'

'No, Baron, I'm afraid they aren't! In the short while since you've been back, two new booklets have appeared. Unfortunately!'

162

'Let's have a look, then,' said Taittinger.

'Later, Baron,' said Zenower, 'but it's bad news. Bad news for you!'

They drank Vöslauer wine; how quickly Zenower changed. Even that afternoon he'd looked different. It wasn't the civilian clothes that had changed him – after all he was wearing the same brown suit. He was a few years younger than the Captain, but his thin fair hair had a greyish sheen in the light of the big gas lamp, and the bright soldierly gleam was gone from his grey eyes, left behind in the barracks, along with sabre, cap and uniform. The eyes that were now looking at the Captain were sad, troubled and searching. He couldn't bear them. He couldn't quite bring himself to call them 'boring'. In fact he didn't know how to classify Zenower. He seemed not to fit into any of his categories: not 'charming', not 'so-so'. Whatever was inside that Zenower was as hard to gauge as what had been inside all those sealed-up goods wagons. But it still felt good to be sitting with him, he had a way of making the most hair-raising things sound almost comforting.

'You're the first person,' the Baron began, 'that I feel I can talk about the "affair" to.'

'That's not necessary, Baron,' said Zenower, 'I know all about it. It's there in that booklet, for all to see. You've not been named, but it's obviously you.'

Taittinger turned pale. He stood up, sat down again. He worked his finger inside his collar.

'Calm yourself, Baron,' said Zenower. 'I've managed to buy up all the stocks of booklets in the local *Trafik* shops.' And he pulled a large bundle out of a bag. 'We need to think. But I don't really see any solution. One thing is perfectly clear: Lazik's not exactly shy. He's capable of writing "high-class pimp", for instance. To listen to him, one would think certain very distinguished personalities, yourself among them, Baron, were nothing but profiteers. It's terrible.'

For a long time Taittinger didn't say anything. He drank in hurried little sips. He felt he had to keep his hands busy at least. He wanted to say something, to find the words to escape something that was still remote. But quite against his own volition he spoke the terrible words that were trapped inside his brain: 'I'm finished, Zenower!'

He could now bear Zenower's sad eyes quite effortlessly. They were his only comfort. 'Not finished, Baron, that's not right. You don't know what finished is. The world you live in, forgive me, isn't the world where a man is actually finished. The real world is very big, and it contains quite different destructive possibilities. As yet, nothing is "finished", as you would have it. I would say you're in danger. That journalist is certainly very dangerous, but he's very stupid. It must be an easy matter to put him out of commission. I'm sure these booklets have no circulation in good society. In themselves they are of no danger to you. But there is the risk that the author may approach others in person – as he approached you. I don't think anyone else will give him money. But he must hope they will. He can always appeal to your example.'

'What shall I do, my dear Zenower?'

The Captain looked like a little boy with grey hair. He chewed his lip. He looked at his fingers as though wondering whether they still belonged to him, or were already those of a condemned man.

'Let me have a word with Lazik,' said Zenower. 'I'll ask for three days' furlough tomorrow.'

Yes, everything would be sorted out. Taittinger recovered

his habitual cheerfulness. That good, clever Zenower will go and talk to people and fix everything. The other things too. The young Schinagl boy will be packed off back to Graz. The estate will be put to rights. Pylades will be sold off. Tomorrow, right after morning exercises, a trip to the post office, where there'll possibly be a letter waiting in poste restante from Mizzi in Kagran. From now on there's no need to be afraid of letters, of signatures, of all the dreadful events that happened outside the charmed circle of the barracks, the mess, the Imperial Hotel in Vienna, and 'society'. Taittinger was by now 'honestly' convinced that since yesterday he'd aged by many years, was the richer by much bitter experience and had overcome many obstacles; and all of it thanks to Zenower. And to think that he was a child of the people!

'The people are good!' Taittinger said aloud.

'What do you know about it?' said Zenower, 'The people! The people is made up of individuals. An individual is good and bad.' With that he stood up so resolutely that Taittinger had no time to ask him for another half an hour. Now that Zenower was standing there in his civilian coat, with its black velvet collar, with his top hat and gloves in his left hand, and his cane hooked over his arm, for the third time he looked nothing like Zenower. He was once again altered, unfamiliar, stern and dear and – it's true – also a bit boring. But his hand was as warm and strong and eloquent as it had been earlier, and after he was gone, Taittinger missed him. It bothered him to be left on his own. He drank another bottle, watched the last of the customers leave, and hope and good cheer blossomed in his heart once more. Everything will be sorted out, he thought. It was still snowing, more heavily now, what was the date? November. The snow put him in mind of Christmas;

and so Taittinger thought: By Christmas everything will be sorted out!

His sleep that night was deep, untroubled and dreamless.

By morning, the snow lay thick and firm and frozen. The hooves of Pylades, whom he was riding that day out of sentiment and the pain of imminent separation, slipped precariously on the swept cobbles. The sound of the cornets was muted, veiled and stunned. 'Pylades,' said the Captain of Horse, as he dismounted on the parade ground, 'Pylades, this is the last time!' He patted the grey on the neck, took a sugar lump out of his ammunition pouch, pushed it between the horse's teeth and held his hollow hand against the warm soft muzzle and the big, grateful hot-and-cool tongue for a long time. He felt he wouldn't have the fortitude to ride Pylades back to the barracks later. He ordered the sergeant to have him sent back. Then he handed over charge of the squadron to First Lieutenant Zschoch. He left during the ten o'clock break, signed off with Major Festetics and strode briskly into town, faster and faster and making more and more noise to numb his melancholy and also his slight fear of whatever letters there might be waiting for him at the poste restante counter.

There was only one letter, already three weeks old, and with that vile Kagran stamp. It read:

Respected Baron, sir! It was an extraordinary honour for me and a great joy in my heart to know that the Baron was thinking of me. I am doing fine, the Sisters are good to me, and I'm working in the sewing shop, where I am allowed to sing. I will be released soon, and it's already October.

Most respectfully and with a full heart,
Mizzi Schinagl

Taittinger had to read the letter through twice in the post office, because it was written on the same soggy grey paper as paper bags, and the writing was punctuated and disfigured by great blotches. He was moved – by the letter, and still more by his own perseverance in collecting it and reading it twice, though most of all by having taken leave of Pylades. In Tartakower's Breakfast Bar he tucked into herring and slivowitz. He still had to go to the office to catch Zenower before he set off for Vienna. He decided not to have lunch in the officers mess, but out at Sedlak's instead. The air was crystal clear, and a pleasing chill blew over the sweet melancholy of the Captain of Horse. The sun warmed his back, he could feel it through his thick litevka. All was well with the world. There were no more surprises. It was as though he and Zenower hadn't merely talked about everything, but sorted it out too. It was the way he felt after he'd done an exam.

XXIII

Alas, misfortune hit poor Taittinger with such devastating abruptness that he had no time to switch from the state of cheeriness he now felt quite at home with, to despair. He had no time even to be shocked. Speechless and uncomprehending, under a kind of spell, he heard Zenower report to him in the office. He was the old Warrant Officer Zenower again, in uniform. He stood to attention when the Captain walked in, he had the old bright, soldierly, disciplined gleam in his eye, and in his normal soldierly voice he said: 'Captain, beg leave to report that the Colonel has allowed me three days' furlough; further beg leave to report that the Colonel wants to see you in his office immediately; he is waiting!'

'At ease!' ordered Taittinger. 'Sit down, Zenower!' He himself sat down on a corner of the desk. 'What's he want then, the old fellow?'

For a second, a distant resemblance to yesterday's civilian look flickered into the eye of Zenower: 'Baron, the Colonel's quite beside himself. A registered letter arrived this morning from the War Ministry, I saw it lying on the staff sergeant's desk. Baron –' Warrant Officer Zenower stalled.

'Come on, man, out with it!' said Taittinger.

Once again, Zenower leapt to attention: 'Captain, beg leave to report that the Colonel left orders for the Captain to see him in his office immediately.'

'Ah, I understand!' muttered Taittinger, who still didn't. He went out and crossed the yard. The old chap sometimes liked to lurk behind the curtains. He liked his officers to cross the yard with swift strides, and to respond, as per regulations, to the salutes of any soldiers that might be around. Maybe – Taittinger said to himself – he's got wind of the fact that I'm having to give up Pylades. He always had a soft spot for the grey.

He stepped inside the office He barely recognised Colonel Kovac. Normally he was a short, plump man with a round skull, a reddish nose, a bristly grey moustache and tiny black eyes that seemed to be all pupil. His little arms – that always seemed to be too long for his sleeves – had meaty red hands at the end of them that looked like hammers encased in skin. Now, though, Colonel Kovacs looked positively lean. His nose was a livid blue, his hands almost white. Right across his low forehead, divided by the bristly grey widow's peak, was a thick, swollen, blue vein – visible evidence of barely suppressed rage. The Colonel walked round in front of his desk, put his hand on his hip, and studied the Captain, who was as motionless as a statue. The old fellow failed to say: At ease, much less: 'Servus!'. Taittinger began to feel uneasy. He couldn't think. The little sparks that were the Colonel's eyes ran up and down Taittinger, up and down. One, two, three minutes passed in this way. The silence was such that he could hear the ticking of two watches, his own and the Colonel's.

Finally – and his voice was eerily soft – the Colonel spoke: 'Captain, do you know Count W., the head of section in the Finance Ministry?' Taittinger felt a frost penetrate his kneecaps; at the tops of his boots were no longer knees, but only ice. It was hard to remain standing, with his thighs resting on lumps of ice.

'Yes, Colonel!'

'And do you know a . . . a . . . a certain Bernhard Lazik, Editor?'

'Yes, sir!'

'Do you know why you're standing here, then?'

'Yes, sir!'

'At ease!' ordered the Colonel. The Captain slid his right foot forward and to the side. 'You may sit!' said Kovac, pointing to a bare wooden chair.

'Thank you very much, sir!' said Taittinger. He hesitated.

'I said, sit down!' screamed Kovac. The Captain sat down. The Colonel walked back and forth across the big carpet. From time to time he crossed his arms, then he uncrossed them again, he clenched his fists, shoved them in his pockets, jingled his keys, took his keys out, twirled them round his thumb, put them back in his pocket. He seemed to be getting thinner and paler and more unreal by the minute. Outside in the yard, the November afternoon was beginning to fade, and only the reflected light off the snow opposed the gathering gloom.

'Say something, damn you!' shouted the Colonel. It was a half roar, half scream. 'Explain yourself, Captain!'

'Sir!' said Taittinger, 'it's the unfortunate business that brought about my return to the regiment.'

'Unfortunate, unfortunate!' cried the Colonel. 'It's frightful, it's atrocious, it's –' at last the word came to him: 'a scandal!

That's what it is, not ghastly, it's a scandal! And you did it to me! To our own ninth dragoons, Captain – no, not ours, mine! Not yours, oh no! I will not, will not, will not stand such men here. I'm a simple front officer, got that, a simple front officer! I've never been on secondment. I've got no fancy chums in Vienna. I don't hobnob with any Excellencies! As my name is Colonel Joseph Maria Kovac, plain Colonel, you understand Captain, you will regret this! Here, letters like this!' The Colonel disappeared behind his desk and returned brandishing the letter from the War Ministry in his fist. 'Do you know what it says?'

'No, sir!' said Taittinger. He could feel the sweat on his brow. His feet were cooking in his boots, but from the knees up all was ice. His heart was beating so hard he thought it was probably visible through his thick tunic.

'Well, listen, Captain! When you returned from your special assignment to the regiment, I knew of course that you'd committed some *faux pas*. The episode was swept under the carpet. But you! You can't stay away from these sex scandals, you . . . you . . . so you go to this individual, this specimen, and you pay him two thousand gulden, and you get involved in his filth – that's right his filth – and the man goes to Head of Section W. and asks him for money, and he tells him how much you've already paid, and it happens that the Head of Section is paralyzed – he had a stroke, you know, a couple of months ago – and his wife appears in these shitty books, and he can't fight you, and he wouldn't have done you so much honour even if he'd been hale and hearty, and he writes a letter to his friend, the War Minister, yes, His Excellency in person, got that, and me, and me! Not in the history of our army – words fail me. I'm at your disposal, Captain!'

Taittinger leapt to his feet. 'Colonel!' he cried.

'Attention!' roared Kovac. And then 'Stand easy! Sit down!' Taittinger sat down again.

The Colonel had shouted so loudly that his voice could be heard all the way down the left wing of the building. The adjutant, First Lieutenant von Dengl, stood at the door for a time, clutching a couple of files and the day's orders, all set to claim – if the door had just then happened to open – that he'd been 'just about to' knock. Sergeant Steiner and his two secretaries could hear every word through the connecting doors, although all three of them pretended to be engrossed in registry entries, desertion warrants, reports from the military police and conduct lists. Even in the yard, and in the mess, the noise of the junior officers' card games died. The icy pellucid air of that November evening carried every sound of the Colonel's roaring voice. It was the voice of an irate barracks god, a natural phenomenon of the first order. Everyone knew right away that it concerned Taittinger; and not only because he had been seen going into the Colonel's office, oh no! They had read Lazik's booklets – Zenower hadn't been able to buy up all the stocks in all the *Trafik* shops! A terrible shock and a great depression descended upon everyone, even though they hadn't much cared for Baron Taittinger. He didn't fit in with the regiment, he didn't fit in at the barracks. All the rural types in the regiment – those from Bukovina, from Slovakia and the Bacska, and who had never seen inside a Viennese drawing room – had only to look at Baron Taittinger to be convinced that the drawing room was the place for him. Even so, they could imagine his suffering, thanks to the solidarity between soldiers that turns squadrons and regiments into families, makes fathers or older brothers out of commanding officers, sons of subalterns, grandsons out of recruits, and uncles and cousins out of sergeants and corporals.

The Colonel suddenly fell silent, and that silence was still more terrifying than his yelling had been before. He had exhausted his voice and his vocabulary. He too felt his knees freezing and quaking; he needed to sit down. He buried his head in his hands and said, more to the papers on his desk than to Taittinger: 'Resign! Resign, Captain! I don't want a court martial! Listen! I'll put it about that you've handed in your resignation. I've had a word with the regimental medic Dr Kallir and he knows you're in bad shape. Your nerves are shot, your mind is impaired. Resign! I don't want you transferring anywhere else with a conduct sheet like yours, do you understand, Captain?'

Captain Taittinger got to his feet: 'Yes, sir! I will hand in my resignation tomorrow.'

The Colonel felt a pain in his heart. He also tried to stand, but felt too weak. He shook hands with Taittinger across the table and said: 'Farewell, Taittinger!'

XXIV

They were up all night at Sedlak's, Taittinger and warrant officer Zenower. Zenower, too, was numbed by the speed of fate. He too, though the child of a cook, was a child of the army. He too, although he knew of the real misery in the world beyond the barracks, did not underestimate Taittinger's pain: and he too was downcast, along with everyone else that day, from the Colonel to the new recruits. Of course there was plenty of misfortune in the world. But here was a visible and palpable misfortune in the barracks – where they all lived and ate and slept. As recently as yesterday he had been able to speak to Taittinger, to offer advice and counsel. Today he was dumb. Taittinger was dumb. From time to time he said: 'But think, Zenower . . .' Although he didn't know what Zenower was supposed to think. The clock ticked on, its black hands turning indefatigably, slipping smoothly past the numerals as though they were just minutes. Often the two men looked up at the clock at the same time and as they did so both felt with the same clarity the powerlessness of men against the unalterable laws of time, and against all other laws too, known and unknown. The hours passed, little portions of life. One or two or three or ten hours of his life were lost to Taittinger or abandoned by him: there was nothing to be done about them, or anything else.

The last of the customers left, the oil in the glass oil lamp was getting low. They called for candles and wine, and stayed. When the lamp went out, they saw the silvery gleam of the snow at the windows. The icy wind whistled thinly and keenly through the night, and the window panes rattled faintly. Although they hadn't said anything to that effect, they both knew they were sitting there until dawn. One couldn't abandon the other in the middle of the night. They sat tight.

'I'll go with you, Baron,' Zenower finally said. 'You're going on furlough tomorrow. I'll accompany you to Vienna. I owe my friend in the Accounts Department a visit anyway. I think I'll be allowed to take the exam in January.'

'I'm sure!' said Taittinger

Sedlak the landlord was asleep behind the bar. He muttered indistinctly in his sleep from time to time. Zenower said: 'He's sleeping soundly!'

To which Taittinger, not having listened, replied: 'Yes, his Vöslauer's not at all bad!'

'I'm a beer drinker myself really!' said Zenower. Silence fell again. They made sporadic efforts at small talk. They didn't think about what they were saying, they just talked so as not to hear the clock – uttering pious wishes, unconnected phrases, foolish little white lies. Their candles were already two-thirds burnt down when they noticed the snow outside beginning to turn blue, the singing of the frost becoming keener, the sky paling. Zenower walked over to the bar, woke Sedlak and paid.

They walked slowly back to town, to the barracks. 'Starting

tomorrow, I'll be in civilian clothes for ever!' said Taittinger as they entered the barracks and the sentry saluted them. 'That's the last time he'll salute me!' he added. What does that matter! thought Zenower, not being saluted any more! But at the same time he could feel he was being unfair. This was the end of some sort of life. A soldier takes off his uniform as a dying man takes leave of his body. Civilian dress, no more uniform: it was the unfamiliar, and quite possibly terrible.

At nine o'clock there was the officers' report. Taittinger was immediately given indefinite leave 'on grounds of health'. His note from the regimental medic, Dr Kallir, diagnosed a severe nervous breakdown. It excused Taittinger from having to take leave of the regiment. At twenty to three in the afternoon he boarded the train, in civilian clothes, with Zenower. At six o'clock they arrived in Vienna. Zenower composed his resignation letter for him. Taittinger copied it out in the library of the Prinz Eugen Hotel, in his sloping, official hand, with four finger's space at the top and three at the margin. He signed it, very slowly: 'Alois Franz Baron von Taittinger, Captain of Horse'. He formed the letters so slowly and carefully it looked nothing like his normal signature. He felt as if it weren't his name. He had signed under a strange name.

Zenower was waiting in the lobby. He took the letter, looked at it for a long time, making it seem as though he had to study it carefully, just so as to put off the moment when he would have to look at the Captain. At last he folded it up.

Taittinger said: 'Now I'm not your superior officer any more, Zenower!'

He took his watch out of his waistcoat pocket, a gold watch from the jeweller and watchmaker Commercial Councillor Gwendl, with Taittinger's initials and his uncle's engraved on the back. It was a present from his uncle on the occasion of his graduation from Mährisch-Weißkirchen. 'Take it!' said Taittinger. It was the first time he had ever given anyone a present: apart from money and flowers, he had never given anyone anything.

Zenower looked at it long and hard, then pulled out his own large silver watch and said: 'Take this one, Baron!'

Then, when he saw that Taittinger was waiting, with the silver watch lying in the palm of his hand, he added: 'If you ever need a friend – '

'I'm going on to my estate today!' said Taittinger. He slipped the watch into his waistcoat pocket. He adopted an air of bustling activity. 'All right? You'll hand in my letter. Sell the horses for me. I don't care for them any more. Drop me a line. Thanks for everything, my dear Zenower! You've got my address!'

'*Bon voyage!*' said Zenower, and stood up.

'My bags!' called the Baron. He headed for the Eastern Station.

XXV

Taittinger's estate was not easy to get to. It was in the Ceterymentar district, buried deep in the snowy Carpathian mountains. He had to change trains twice. From the station at Ceterymentar, there was a drive of another four miles up to the estate, and then another mile to the house itself. It was called Zamky, but Taittinger had always called it the Mousetrap, even as a boy, when his uncle had invited him to stay in the holidays. The Mayor – Wenk – was a German, one of a scattering of Saxon colonists who lived in the area. The steward was from Moravia, the peasants were Carpathian Russians, the now-deaf footman was a Hungarian, who had completely forgotten where he had come from and when and why. The most recent events in his memory were the Uprising in Budapest and the death of his old master, the previous Baron. The forester was a Ruthenian from Galicia, the police sergeant came from Bratislava – and he was the only person for miles around with whom Taittinger could have any sort of conversation in the bar.

It was early December. The snow had moved down from the peaks and was occupying the estate. Ravens sat black and motionless in the snowy pines. Except when they suddenly flew up with an almighty croaking, it was possible to take them for an odd fruit of some description. It had only been possible to repair the main house cursorily (Taittinger had given very little notice of coming, and there was still less money available for repairs). The steward only paid the workmen half the agreed sum – and they knew him well enough to be certain that the rest would not be coming 'after Christmas'. There were, in any case, two Christmases, one for Roman Catholics and one for Russian Orthodox! The roof got a few new tiles here and there, but by and large it kept its old holes.

When the place was heated again for the first time in years, the old door jambs and window frames warped, none of the locks and fastenings fitted, and there were wheezings and creakings in the massive wardrobes, where the shelves and struts twisted out of true. In the study the gloomy old ancestral portraits of the Zernuttis hung crookedly on half-loosened picture hooks. There was rampant mould in the unmanageably large dining room. Big brown, white and blue pieces of cardboard had been put in the empty frames of the balcony windows. The kitchen harboured a couple of ancient toads which Joszi the footman fed on the few winter flies that crept out when the stove was lit, and which even Joszi had no trouble catching. The Baron's unexpected arrival created difficulties for everyone. They had thought he would stay a week or so at the most, pack off his bastard son, have a look around, and go away again. But when the police sergeant told them Taittinger's intention was to stay there for good, and that he had actually left the army, they began to hate the Baron with that particular hatred that's born of fear. They didn't really know him. He had been rather fool-ish thus far: he had frittered away his corn and his wheat and his little woods and his money. But now that he knew how poor he really was, wouldn't that make him more circumspect? Wasn't that why he had left the army? Once he got started, there was so much to be accounted for. What had become of the wine cellar? Who was it who had made up a plague of locusts one year, a bad harvest the next, and then the bank-ruptcy of the man who'd bought the wood?

It's his very first evening back, supposedly the bedroom isn't ready yet, so Taittinger has to sleep in a room over the pub. A few peasants are still sitting at the big wide brown table, beside the big bare clay stove. Janko the landlord keeps tiptoeing round the Baron, even though he knows Taittinger isn't going to speak and isn't curious to hear anything either. The peasants are accustomed to speaking noisily or to being silent. They don't know how to speak quietly. They daren't speak loudly, on account of the Baron. All they can do is knock out their pipes from time to time, though not on the edge of the big table, as they like to do, but under it, against the heels of their boots. When the police sergeant walks in and stands to attention in front of the Baron, who asks him to sit with him, shakes his hand, and even touches glasses with him, the peasants lapse into complete silence. Their heads drop, and they only shoot the occasional covert glance in the direction of the master's table. The Baron and the sergeant are speaking German, of which they understand about one word in ten, but even if the pair of them had been speaking Slovak or Ruthenian, they would have been afraid to listen. To Taittinger it seems only natural that the peasants should be this quiet. In the time he's had his estate, and even before that – he's been here maybe ten times – the peasants have always been this quiet. But the sergeant knows they like to make a racket really, and he tells the Baron: 'They're being so quiet because they're scared of you, Baron!'

Scared of me! thinks Taittinger. 'I'm not going to gobble them up!' he says.

'That's why, Baron!' says the sergeant.

'That's deuced awkward!' says Taittinger. The sergeant goes across and tells the peasants in Slovak that the Baron desires them not to be silent on his account. It's practically an order. Two or three of them start speaking at once, saying things they hadn't meant to say at all. Then they are silent again. The land-lord brings beer and plates of goulash. Taittinger and the policeman eat.

The door flies open, and in comes a young man who makes straight for Taittinger. The Baron, still holding knife and fork, stops eating, and looks at the young man, who doesn't look familiar. '*Servus*, Xandl!' says the sergeant. All the peasants know it's the Baron's bastard son, and they look up. The ones who have been sitting with their backs to Taittinger turn round. It doesn't make the Baron any less strange to them, but their curiosity is greater than their fear; and malice is a great lure. All it would take now would be for one of the creditors to walk in too. The peasants know the landowner is in debt.

'Your son?' Taittinger asks the sergeant.

'No,' says the young man, 'your son, Baron!'

'Aha,' says Taittinger, 'so you're young Schinagl!'

'That's right!' says the youth. Taittinger has a good look at him. He's wearing a green velvet suit whose sleeves are too short for him, and his raw, red hands are much too large, and have upsetting fingernails. The head's bearable – Taittinger is endeavouring to find some trace of a resemblance between the youth and himself. There's nothing there – try as he may, he can't find one. The boy has red-rimmed eyes of china blue, he keeps twisting his mouth, his ears are burning red, his head is shaven so he can't tell what colour the hair might be, he keeps maltreating his blue ink-stained cap and its wretched plastic, crumpled visor with his ugly fists. He can't keep still for a second. He shifts from foot to foot; sometimes he gets up on the balls of his feet. Taittinger has never seen such a creature in all his life. He thinks he might leave the next morning.

'Well, now, Herr Schinagl,' he says, 'and what do you want?' It's his old Baronial Captain's voice, very slow and drawly, and with a clipped metal edge to it.

The lad lurches back a step. 'I'd like to know how Mum's doin'!' His voice is very loud, in fact it sounds – so Taittinger thinks – red, every bit as red as the lad's fists and ears. The young man is absolutely grotesque, he thinks, and he pushes away his goulash and drinks some beer.

'What do you want?' the baron repeats.

'Wanna know how Mum's doin'!' Xandl says again. The Baron ponders awhile, not about the state of Mizzi Schinagl's health, but as to whether it was correct to say: Your *Frau* Mama or your *Fräulein* Mama! It doesn't occur to him just to say your mother.

'It's been some time since I last heard from Fräulein Schinagl,' he finally says.

'But her address?' asks the boy.

'Don't you go to school in Graz?' asks the Baron.

'Yes, but they've gone an' chucked me out. Mum couldn't pay the bills. I did some stuff too, and I don't wanna go back!'

The sergeant, meanwhile, has quietly finished his goulash, and drunk his beer. Now he orders another, takes a great swig from it, suddenly turns purple, and wipes his moustache on a similarly purple handkerchief. Then he gets up, puts the handkerchief in his pocket, and smacks Xandl across the face. The boy staggers. The sergeant sits down and says quite calmly: 'Xandl, you will speak to the Baron properly, or I'll have you taken down and you'll spend the next two years in prison. Don't you know how to behave?'

'Yes, Sergeant!'

'Well, apologise to the Baron!'

'I'm sorry, Baron,' says Xandl.

The peasants laugh uproariously and smack their thighs.

'Now, Landlord,' calls the Baron, 'give the young man something to eat. Over there!' he adds. 'When you've eaten, I want you to go home to the steward and tell him you're going back to Graz tomorrow!'

'Thank you very much, Baron, c'n I ask another favour?'

'Yes?'

'Can I come back 'ere for Christmas?'

'Yes!' says the Baron.

'If you don't mind my saying so, Baron,' says the sergeant, 'that boy's a bad lot.'

'It's not his fault!' replied the Baron.

'I know,' says the sergeant, 'gentlemen like yourself are always far too lenient with such riff-raff. When I bring in the lists of political subversives, our District Commissioner always says it can't really be that bad.'

'He's a child of the people!' says Taittinger, thinking of Zenower, himself an illegitimate child, perhaps fathered by some Taittinger or other. It's all so confusing – who knows?

Xandl has eaten, rises to go, stops, says 'Please excuse me!' and hands the Baron an envelope, makes an appalling botch of a bow and leaves. Taittinger hands the envelope to the sergeant: 'What's he want?'

The sergeant reads aloud:

Esteemed Baron, the steward is a crook, and the Mayor knows it. The steward's wife has got all the tablecloths, napkins and sheets marked with a crown, and the big fish tureen with the portrait of an empress on it. It is gratitude what prompts me to tell your Lordship about it,
    With respect,
    Xandl Schinagl

'It happens to be true!' says the sergeant.

Taittinger says: 'There's nothing to be done about it!' He stares into space. He knows he's not really cut out for this world.

Ever since that first encounter with his son, Taittinger has known that he hates his estate, the whole region, the house, the memory of his late uncle Zernutti, and his son – Taittinger's tedious cousin – the mountains, winter, the steward, the stolen crockery, even deaf old Joszi.

The house wasn't heated properly. In the middle of the night, when the fire went out in the bedroom, it abruptly became icy and damp, the pillows and sheets were clammy to the touch and smelled of rotten hay. Christmas was drawing near, a disagreeable festival, full of the deceitful desires of evil men everywhere, of greedily outstretched grasping hands, of peasant lads in fancy dress and paper angels – and, thanks to the Russian calendar, Christmas in these parts went on for about three weeks. And young Schinagl had invited himself on top of that. Alone, without the presence of the sergeant, it was impossible to look at the boy. Both the horses had been sold now, Schinagl's bill for next term had been paid, Baron Taittinger had enough money, really, to hole up in Vienna for a few weeks. On a more modest footing, admittedly, not at the Imperial. Every night when Taittinger left Janko's pub on the bitterly cold Via Dolorosa home, he had drunk enough slivowitz to feel sure he could pack his things that very night, and get saddled up and drive off first thing in the morning. But when he entered his house, lit a candle and then a lamp, he was seized by fear and disgust at the nocturnal shadows of the furniture, at the mould on the walls, the creaking of the doors and windows. He quickly lay down, while the fire in the stove was still going, fell into an unquiet sleep, woke late, drank some chicory coffee and a glass of straw-coloured local wine, got dressed, prowled around aimlessly and thoughtlessly, longed for evening to come, went to the pub, waited for the sergeant, exchanged barely a word with the Mayor and the steward who sometimes came in, and drank himself enough courage to last a couple of hours and enable him to face the walk home again. Baron Taittinger was one of the not uncommon sort, who, accustomed to military discipline, look to fate as much as to their superior officers, for orders and instructions.

And one day one such instruction arrived. Captain Taittinger was to present himself to the Super Arbitration Committee in the Second Viennese Military Hospital at half past nine on the morning of 14th December. This was the response to his request for indefinite leave on grounds of health. They were evidently in a tearing rush to be rid of their Captain. Normally medical certificates didn't go up to the

Commission anything like as fast! Taittinger felt offended by their haste. He felt melancholy, pain, self-contempt. He left on the 10th. Before leaving he told his steward: 'Well, I'll be back in February! Then everything will be different!' As he said goodbye to the police sergeant at the station, he said: 'I'm relying on you to send the Schinagl boy back to Graz. He can spend a week with the steward's household if he likes!' When the stationmaster gave the signal for departure, Taittinger gave him a friendly wave, with gratitude in his heart, as though the official had allowed the train to leave as a personal favour to the Baron.

I'll be back in February, he thought – and buoyed up by a totally unfounded conviction, he said to himself: by February I'll be a different person, and: February is almost spring anyway.

He thought it would be good to see good old Zenower while he was in Vienna, so he wired him from Bratislava where he changed trains: 'Expect see you Vienna, Prinz Eugen'. He went blithely towards the Super Arbitration.

His medical condition, according to the certificate, was: cardiac dilatation, advanced neurasthenia, unfit for active duty for the foreseeable future. They didn't even examine him. The major general of the medical corps at the Second Garrison Hospital in Vienna merely said '*Servus!*' and signed the paper.

'All the best, Captain!' he added. It sounded like a condolence.

That was it then. He was out of the army. Baron Taittinger walked down the Währinger Straße. He walked in complete indifference through the dirty slush, no longer a soldier, for the first time he could think no longer a soldier. So what was he? A civilian. The streets are full of civilians, but they've had practice at it. He, though, so to speak, is a newly recruited civilian. His discharge papers are folded up in his wallet.

It's not easy to become a civilian just like that. A civilian may have a boss, but that's not the same as a commanding officer. A civilian may go where he pleases when he pleases. A civilian is not obliged to defend his honour with sword in hand. A civilian is capable of getting up without a valet: a civilian uses an alarm clock instead. Taittinger walks through the dirty slush, as though to make himself still more of a civilian, not caring; he makes a left at the Schottenring to sit in a café somewhere. He doesn't look in the window first to see whether the place is compatible with his rank and status. As a civilian he doesn't have to worry about things like that.

So Taittinger finds a café on the Schottenring, near the police headquarters, and goes in. It's a small, so-called popular café. Six men in hats are sitting round one of the few tables. Top hats, all of them. They're playing tarot. Nothing to do with me, thinks Taittinger, and he looks out at the dismal winter day, and sips coffee with whipped cream.

Another customer walks in. Taittinger is aware of someone entering, but no more than if it had been, say, a fly.

This man doesn't take his hat off either, he touches his finger to its brim, sits down with the tarot players and watches. Just at the moment when Taittinger calls, 'Bill, please!' the man jumps up and looks around. He looks half familiar to Taittinger. Then he takes his hat off. He approaches Taittinger and says: 'Fancy seeing the Baron here! Oh, the Baron doesn't remember me?'

Yes, it's the man with the booklets, now Taittinger remembers. 'Do you mind if I join you?' asks Lazik, and he's already sitting down. And talking away. 'What a world we live in! But I've got their number, those cowards, those crooks! Those so-called gentlemen! Every one of them has at least one life on his conscience – they're murderers, blue-blooded murderers. Look at their medals and their money and their honours. And then look at me, Baron, look at the pitiful state I'm in.' And Lazik stood up, plucked at his trousers, turned up his coat to show the ragged lining, lifted up his shoe and pointed at the hole in the leather upper, touched his shirt collar and said: 'I've worn this all week.'

'That's bad!' said Taittinger.

'Baron, you're an angel. Baron, you're the only one who showed me any kindness,' said Lazik. 'I want to kiss your hands, Baron. Let me kiss your hands.' Lazik leaned forward, Taittinger kept his hands firmly in his pockets. 'No, I understand, I am not worthy,' said Lazik. 'But let me tell you about an injustice that cries out to high heaven. Yes?'

'Yes!' said the Baron.

'Well, I went round to Count W. to show him my booklets, he's paralyzed now, thank God, there is some justice in the world after all. And I start talking to him in the same vein I talked to the Baron, remember? But unfortunately the Count still has the use of one of his arms, and he reaches out with it and rings a bell, and the servant comes, and the Count says: "My secretary!" – and the secretary comes, and the Count says: "Will you please deal with this gentleman." And I go on talking to the secretary, all innocent, like a babe in arms – and when I get home – there's Rothbucher from the flying squad, and he says: "Lazik, I'm afraid I'm going to have to arrest you!" Well, and the upshot is the booklets have been confiscated and banned, I've been sacked by the paper, and I'm only living by the grace of the fellows over there, who are from the squad as well!'

'It's too bad, Editor!' said Taittinger.

'The Baron is so kind as still to give me my title,' said Lazik, audibly swallowing tears of gratitude. 'If I may reciprocate, I'm working as a rep for a pharmaceutical business now.' He took out an array of little tubes and powders from his pockets. 'A man can't help the odd bout of sleeplessness, I know, Baron, and you won't get these on prescription!'

At that moment, the six men all stood up, tipped their grave top hats, and the last of them said: 'Excuse us!', pocketed the tubes and sachets and ordered Lazik: 'You come with us!' Lazik got up, bowed, and trotted out after them.

The waiter came up to the table. 'Pardon me, Baron, Chief Inspector Sedlacek – he says you didn't recognise him – says to tell you that Editor Lazik's dealing in cocaine and the police are using him and the Baron should take care not to support him!'

'Thanks!' said Taittinger. He left, flagged down a cab, and said: 'Kagran!'

When he entered the prison and had himself announced to the director, he had the feeling he'd come to have himself locked up. The director was still the same man, he recognized Taittinger right away: 'I'll leave you here alone, shall I, Baron?' he said as he had before.

'No, please!' said Taittinger, so decisively that the director didn't get out of his chair. 'I don't want a tête-à-tête with Fräulein Schinagl.'

The door opened and Mizzi Schinagl appeared. As before, she stopped in the doorway and covered her face with her hands. Taittinger walked up to her. '*Grüß Gott*, Mizzi!' he said. Mizzi saw the director seated at his desk, panicked, and curt-seyed awkwardly.

'Come in, Mizzi!' said the director – and to the Baron: 'She's been terribly well behaved! We're letting her go in March!'

'What will you do?' asked Taittinger.

'Oh, Baron, you're so kind!' said Mizzi. She seemed different to Taittinger than before. He pushed back her hood, and the hair was growing thick and blonde. The director quipped: 'We really don't like to be heartless, Baron!'

'Thank you, Councillor!' said Mizzi with another bungled curtsey. She took a handkerchief out of her blue overall and dabbed her eyes. Even though, the Baron saw quite clearly, her eyes were dry. Nothing stirred in his heart. It wasn't like last time. He wanted to be generous, maybe it was the presence of the director that accounted for the difference in Mizzi, or the fact that her hair was beginning to grow back.

'Your son's been to see me!' said Taittinger. 'I sent him back to Graz!'

'Xandl!' exclaimed Mizzi. 'How does he look?'

It was on the tip of Taittinger's tongue to say: Unfortunately nothing like me, but he replied: 'Not so bad, not so bad at all!' Now Mizzi really did begin to cry, but this time she dried her eyes on her wrists. She didn't cry for very long anyway. In a hard, indifferent, metallic-sounding voice, she asked if she might leave now. 'Of course!' said Taittinger. She was led away.

'She's quite happy here with us, Baron!' said the pleasant director.

'I'm sure – you can tell she is,' said Taittinger. 'You're very good to her.'

'Always eager to be of assistance, Baron!' The director stood up. 'Always eager to be of assistance!' he repeated.

The cab was waiting. Taittinger had the distinct feeling that something had broken. At the same time, though, it seemed to him that the world was such a bewildering place that he could not, and never would be able to, understand it. It was just as it had been with the maths exam at the academy in Mährisch-Weißkirchen. He was no longer a soldier, and not yet a civilian. Did it have something to do with that? He couldn't tell whether someone was good or not. If asked, he wouldn't have been able to say whether Lazik was good or weak or crooked, if Mizzi was decent, spoiled or bad, nor even if her son – his son, rather – was a rascal or had some good in him. If only Zenower was there already.

It was certainly an eventful day, the expression 'date with destiny' sprang to mind, he remembered reading it somewhere. They told him at the hotel that Lieutenant Zenower had just arrived.

He found Zenower in his new officer's uniform, now changed for the fourth time, and even stranger than he'd been in civilian clothes. Now that he no longer wore his sergeant's stripes, but the budding pips of the lieutenant, he seemed old – much older than he really was. He probably sensed it himself. His bearing was no longer military, there was a touch of the reserves about him: a suggestion of dressing up. It wasn't civilian dress, nor was it working clothes either. A Lieutenant in the Pay Corps doesn't wear spurs. So, after he's worn spurs for thirteen years, a man either thinks he must be out of uniform or failing that, that he's not walking at all. It's almost like having no feet! All this Zenower explained with almost deadly seriousness. Taittinger understood completely. You weren't given a schako as part of your dress uniform but a tricorn hat, like a district commissioner. Taittinger felt for him. It was a long time before they had finished condemning the deep injustice that a ridiculous set of rules foists on the Pay Corps. All his inborn cleverness was of no use to Zenower whatsoever. Thirteen years in the cavalry were second nature to him.

And now he was a Pay Lieutenant. An elderly lieutenant.

It was inevitable that they should drink in brotherhood that night. They returned to the hotel arm in arm. Pay Lieutenant Zenower was leaving in the morning for his distant new posting, somewhere they happened to need a Pay Lieutenant. He was joining the 14th Jägers, in Brody, on the Russian border at the end of the world.

They got up late, barely had time left to talk at all, much less to recover the intimacy of the 'Du' form of address they had broached the previous night. 'Who knows when I'll see you again!' said the Baron.

'Who knows if I'll ever see you again!' said Zenower. They embraced and kissed each other on both cheeks.

The Baron was left behind, like an orphan. He let himself go. In time his indifference acquired a rhythm and purpose of its own. He stopped seeing old friends. He enjoyed hours of utter blankness, walks with no destination, food without appetite, drink without pleasure, women without desire, meaningless solitude in the midst of bustling people, and occasionally intoxication without cheer.

Sometimes his thoughts turned to Mizzi Schinagl, and to March. One night he wrote to the prison director. He was told that she was being released on 15th March. Neither Mizzi nor the fifteenth moved him in any particular way. Still, it was a date, a point on the calendar, a line. His restless thoughts stopped there, as before a barrier.

XXVI

Spring came early that year. March already brought the warming sun of May. The laburnum – abrupt and glutted – burst into flower in the gardens. The blackbirds drowned out all the other noise of the city. The pale green leaves of the chestnuts grew bigger and broader while you watched, and their candles had a tart, proud, white and soaring aroma. Even the darting swallows seemed more fearless that year. They fizzed over the heads of passersby, peaceful arrows from heaven. A steady, mild breeze blew into the city from the heights of the Kahlenberg. The walls and paving stones responded gratefully with their own particular breath. And when evening came, from all over the city you could see the gentle red sun caressing the steeple of the Stephanskirche. There was a smell of waking elderflower, of fresh bread from the bakers who left their doors open, of the oats in the nosebags of the cab horses, of spring onions and radishes in the street markets.

On one such day, at twenty to ten in the morning, Mizzi Schinagl was released from the female penitentiary. For weeks her approaching release had given Taittinger an excuse to put off the date of his return to his estate.

Sometimes, while he sat all alone in one of the early blooming gardens of the Vienna suburbs, melancholy with wine and drunk on the air, he would talk silently to himself. He asked himself questions he was unable to answer. It wasn't that his conscience pricked him! Whether it had been his fault that Mizzi had come to be in Frau Matzner's house or not, didn't bother him because he saw nothing distressing in the fate of a lost woman. He knew only cheerful, unworried girls who got a lot more out of life than, say, the wives of ministerial councillors and heads of section, than soured and peevish owners of *Trafik* shops, or teary cooks, or daughters from good middle-class homes abandoned by their husbands. Besides, his squalid 'episode' had given Mizzi a couple of splendid, fairy-tale years; and the same 'episode' had cost him his allure, his ease of manner, and almost his good name and his honour as well. So why did he still think of Mizzi? Did he love her? It wasn't that. Taittinger's heart was among his atrophied organs. He didn't know why. He just felt some baffling and inexplicable connection with Mizzi, and with the 'affair'. Baffling it might be, but it was also final and indissoluble. There was nothing to be done about final and indissoluble things.

He couldn't suppress a certain sense of occasion when he drove out to Kagran on the morning of 15th March. He had forgotten that collecting Mizzi had been his own idea. It was his impression that some ceremonial or other had dictated this foolish act. In any case, the cab ride through the lavish triumph of the morning was quite enough to dispel Taittinger's reservations with a cheerful intoxication.

And so, as if it were the most natural thing in the world, he turned up in the office of the prison director to collect Mizzi. Consequently, she was brought down from her cell half an hour early. She wore the brown coat in which she had been sent down the previous autumn. She held her broad hat with glass cherries in her hand, afraid that it might have become unfashionable in the meantime. Her still-short, but beautiful and abundant hair shone with a fresh luminosity, and her pale features looked fine, almost noble. She really does have something of Helene about her! thought Taittinger.

'I can see there's no need for the usual moral lecture,' the director said with a smile. 'Mizzi Schinagl, the Baron has so nobly concerned himself with you that I have no doubt that I'll never see you here again. Baron, I'll always be at your disposal!'

The cab was waiting for Taittinger outside. 'Where can I take you?' he asked. Mizzi was looking around anxiously – evidently she was looking for someone.

'I have to wait,' she said, 'Leni's not here yet. You got me out too early!' It was a reproach. Her liberty, the spring, the waiting coach and the Baron weren't enough to make Mizzi happy.

'Who's Leni?' asked Taittinger.

'She's my special friend, Baron! We shared a cell. Leni was in for aiding and abetting an infanticide. She's a lovely girl, Leni, we got to be very close – she was let out four weeks ago. I'm sure she's coming, she keeps her word.'

Just then the Baron saw something garish and substantial waving and coming nearer. The phenomenon acquired definition. It was shouting something in a piercing voice. It became clear after a time that it was the name 'Mizzi' that was being broadcast, and that this, almost incredibly, was a female of the species – dressed in a yellow outfit of raw silk, yellow button boots, topped off by a bright green hat roughly the size of a cartwheel, with unruly black curls spilling out from under it, and complete with an umbrella, feather boa and reticule. Behold Magdalene Kreutzer, concessionaire and merry-go-round proprietress at the Prater. The women exchanged fervent kisses.

'You're the Baron, aintcha, say no more, Mizzi's already told me everyfink. And 'ere's the cab, so let's get in it wivvout furver ado, and first off we'll see your Da, who's paralyzed, else he'd a bin 'ere hisself!' And before Taittinger knew what was happening to him, he was sitting in the back of the cab opposite the two ladies, feeling shy and extremely uncomfortable, with his knees pushed up against his chest. His head drooped. Incomprehensible argot, flashing exclamations like bolts of lightning, crashing laughter like joyful cloudbursts whizzed over him in a dialect he had never experienced so intensely or at such close quarters, and which seemed to be compounded of the noise of trundling wheels, brass bands and miaowing all rolled into one. Eventually they reached Sievering.

This was where Mizzi had once driven up in her pomp, as the 'concubine' of the Shah of Persia. The concierge was still alive, Xandl the hairdresser had married and moved to Brünn. The shop had reopened (it now belonged to a young man). Old Schinagl had been released for the day from his nursing home in Lainz, because he didn't want his daughter to know about his 'disgrace'. Old and paralyzed, he was sitting just inside the open door. Behind him in the dark interior of the shop, the white meerschaum pipes glimmered like old bones. The shop awakened memories in Taittinger as well. This was where he had seen Mizzi for the first time. Old Schinagl was only able to move his arms. His tongue was crippled too; he stammered and groaned, and finally blew his nose with unexpected vigour.

Out of embarrassment, Taittinger bought five pipes. The concierge asked whether he wanted tobacco as well. Out of embarrassment, he said: 'Yes, please, thank you very much!'

Did Mizzi want to stay here? the old fellow mouthed.

'No!' determined Magdalene Kreutzer. That had been decided some time ago. To 'recoup' herself a bit, Mizzi was going to stay *chez* Kreutzer for the foreseeable future, on the Klosterneuburger Straße. She had brought some printed calling cards in her reticule, pulled one of them out, gave it to Taittinger, and said: 'Don't lose this now, Baron, we'll expect you tomorrow, Sunday, it's the third storey on the left-hand side, number 21, we'll see you at five o'clock. Don't be late, Baron!' He was dismissed. He bowed, gave the driver Kreutzer's address, paid the bill in advance, and disappeared round the corner, where he caught sight of a soothing café terrace.

Nor did he lose the address or forget the time – he kept the appointment, as he always did. Sunday found him feeling rather apprehensive, standing at the door of number 21, where he smelt sauerkraut, cats and nappies, heard the sounds of voices from various rooms, above, below, next door – among them the voice of Mizzi. He pulled the bell resolutely, and walked into a room put together from red velvet, a green tablecloth, yellow vases, gâteaux, oranges, coffee cups and an enormous gugelhupf cake. The woman sat side by side in white summer dresses with black polka dots; two sisters. One dark, the other golden blonde. He did all that was asked of him: he ate sponge, sampled preserves, drank coffee followed by raspberry liqueur, smoked a Trabuco, although he normally only smoked cigarettes, listened, couldn't follow, couldn't think, and got indigestion. He plucked up courage to ask for the toilet, was conducted to an indeterminate space beyond the kitchen where he was shut in, contented himself with pouring water from a can into the bowl, and walked out again. No sooner had he sat down again than the bell rang. In walked a monster, a creature from another world. A cross between a coachman, a butcher, and a statue in modern dress. This was Ignaz Trummer, boyfriend of Magdalene Kreutzer. That was how he introduced himself, and among all the other things he uttered in the next few moments, at a speed that seemed at variance with his physical bulk and his gravelly voice, Taittinger was able to understand only that he felt deeply honoured by his presence. He ate, drank, talked, smoked, drank, ate and talked. 'Wassup wi' you?' he asked finally. 'When are we going?' 'Bleedin' Ada!' he exclaimed at intervals, seemingly for no reason, and: 'Strike a light!' This was no longer mere Vienna dialect. It was as if a bear had attempted to speak Italian.

The horse-drawn omnibus was crowded, so Trummer, strike a light, insisted that they walk to the Prater, to see the 'premises' – meaning the merry-go-round. Taittinger duly walked along beside Trummer, while the ladies went on ahead. As he got accustomed to the dialect, he found himself able to understand a little of what Trummer was saying to him. Trummer, apparently, had been around, he had indeed once been a coachman, for Count Zamborski. Following the old fellow's death, he had become a horse trader. Then he had done something foolish – he had tried to hoodwink a military horse-examining committee, for the sake of a friend, by sending them a different animal than the one examined and bought. Well, the Baron must have come across a few misdeeds like that in his time, and anyway he wound up buying a share in Magdalene Kreutzer's merry-go-round, and a good business it was too; and now he'd heard there was a chance of getting the waxworks on the cheap and all. There's a fine thing, more aesthetic, kindalike art if you know what I mean . . .

The merry-go-round – consisting of horses, carriages, sleighs and boats – was indeed impressive. It revolved around a large papier mâché statue of a lady with two wheat-coloured braids, enormous arms, a towering coiffure, and a gigantic crinoline. This lady revolved too, on her own axis. The sounds of a hurdy-gurdy emerged from her insides. The merry-go-round was mounted on a round wooden base. There was a little wooden door let into the side of it – the women went in, and so Taittinger was obliged to follow; even the monster somehow managed to squeeze his bulk through it. Now they were standing at the bottom, with all the noise – from the people, the organ music, the rattling of the chains on which the individual conveyances were suspended – above them. It was damp and dark. A donkey, blending into the gloom, trudged round and round in a circle, in vain pursuit of a bag of oats that dangled for-ever out of reach. The animal kept the merry-go-round going, sometimes Schani drove it on, till it nearly raised a gallop, like a horse. 'We're not inhuman,' explained Magdalene Kreutzer, 'we keep a spare donkey so the two can take turns!' They all squeezed out through the little door, and found themselves in the open.

On Trummer's orders, they made for the 'Second Café'. A band was playing, and people were laughing – white, sweating and jolly, all part of a collective stupor. And yet the air was light and fresh, almost elegant, a civilized air, and the people, though boisterous, were still themselves. Their cries sounded like exhortations to others to put aside their gloom, the wish of the merry to see more merriment about them. Taittinger bright-ened up.

Magdalene Kreutzer asked him if he'd ever seen a panopticum. 'Oh yes,' he said, and he animatedly listed everything he remembered seeing. There was Bluebeard, the criminal Zingerl, Krasnik the brigand leader from Transylvania, the Bosnian partisans, the Komitadjis, and a pair of Siamese twins.

'The Baron,' pronounced Trummer, 'has a prodigious memory!'

Taittinger had never been complimented like that. When would he next appear in uniform, Mizzi asked him. On the Emperor's birthday, Taittinger replied. He knew it was a lie. But he wanted to make everyone happy. Everyone here was 'the people' really. They were so charming, these 'children of the people', even the monstrous Trummer.

In order to rebuild Mizzi's shattered life, it was necessary to take advantage of the one favourable opportunity on offer, which meant the panopticum. Frau Kreutzer was sure the Baron would have no objection. Taittinger murmured: 'Not in the least!' That made it simple, they just had to be sure they weren't diddled, and pay a sensible price.

'It's too much!' cried Trummer.

Not if the Baron was going to contribute, so to speak in lieu of his parental contribution, seeing as Mizzi had brought the boy up by herself, and in fine style at that, as befitted the child of such a father.

I see, thought Taittinger. This way I'll finally be shot of that tedious upkeep business. 'But of course!' he said. 'I should like to do whatever's feasible,' he said, not out of caution but because it sounded weighty, 'to help Mizzi!' Unfortunately, just then something extremely embarrassing happened. First Lieutenant Teuffenstein of the 11th Uhlan Regiment walked by, arm in arm with his fiancée, Fräulein

Hoffmann from Nagyföteg, and exclaimed: 'There he is! It's Taittinger!'

It was a frightful situation, or, to be precise, 'dashed inconvenient'. 'I'm at the Prinz Eugen!' he told the company at the table. 'Look me up tomorrow.' In his haste he forgot to pay, he got up, hurried over to Teuffenstein, was dragged over to another table nearby, drank wine, was forced to laugh, listen to stories, explain that he had retired to his estate. 'You know,' he said, 'it's worth a fortune, and if I wasn't there to run it, it would be ruined very quickly.'

Late that night he walked through the Prater all alone. Dust was still swirling in the air. Down the main avenue came the delicate clopping of the elegant horses' hooves in front of the soundless rubber-tyred cabs. 'Ir-re-deem-ab-ly, ir-re-deem-ab-ly, ir-re-deem-ab-ly-lost' clopped the hooves. From the bushes along the avenue came the heated whisperings of lovers. A flower lady came offering violets. Taittinger bought five bunches, and held on to them unthinkingly. He gave them to the first girl he saw, and went with her to the station hotel. He was afraid to spend the night alone.

XXVII

In the morning the Prater combined the civilized prettiness of a park, the mysterious silence of a forest, and the bustle and commotion of the eve of a holiday.

Baron Taittinger was often to be seen walking on the main avenue at that time. Many years before – it was another world then – it had been his habit to go riding out there, on Pylades.

Sometimes the Baron walked along the edge of the bridle path. The riders came trotting or galloping past him. Some he recognized without even looking, by the rhythm and step of their mounts, by the rider's seat, his way with reins and whip, the uprightness or otherwise of his posture. Here was the mare Glans-Ei-re-pasz. That was Tibor von Daniel riding. Over there Emilio Casabona was stopping to greet his countryman Count Pogaccio. Von Goldschmid the banker was mounted on a chestnut from the stables of Count Khun-Hedervary, worth every kreuzer of its two thousand gulden. By contrast, that Seilern and Aspang woman was riding an ugly mare with a coarse gait and fat hindquarters. Every morning Taittinger compiled his observations with the utmost seriousness. He no longer went out in society, but he still knew everyone. He somehow felt it was his job to be *au courant* with what they were doing. Sometimes he got upset at the absence of a rider he hadn't seen for a couple of days. Then he walked up to the Spitz and sat in the restaurant where a number of the riders liked to stop by. Many of them remembered him. What had he been up to, they asked, and he always replied with the same lie: 'I'm looking for the farmer in me!' or so he said. Life on his estate was grisly, but his presence there was indispensable. He had become a bit of a recluse. He didn't show himself much in drawing rooms any more. And life had lost all meaning for him.

'Time to think about getting married, my boy!' said old Baron Wilmowsky, a member of the upper house and for years passionately committed to pairing off elderly gentlemen with young girls from impoverished families. He freely admitted that this was the sum total of his political vision, too.

'I should have married Helene back then!' said Taittinger.

'She's very unhappy!' replied Wilmowsky. 'Count W. is paralyzed. Young Tschirschky is courting her. Her husband always was a bit of a dry old stick.'

The Baron's mornings were generally devoted to the aristocracy. His afternoons, though, also within the confines of the Prater, were given to the service of 'the people'. He often looked in on the merry-go-round, conversed with Mizzi and Fräulein Kreutzer and Herr Trummer, listened to the band with them in the 'Second Café', and was kept informed of the state of the negotiations for waxworks. He was keen on the idea of the panopticum. There was something attractive about wax figures; more than a merry-go-round at any rate. Trummer said it cost a fair bit of money and all to do the thing in style. Then again, the potential earnings were colossal. On occasion, Mizzi Schinagl, as though suddenly remembering a long-neglected duty, would swap places with Fräulein Kreutzer or Trummer, and sit pressed against the Baron, quietly stroking his hand. The first time this happened, he was shocked and suddenly became very quiet. Then he got used to his explanation: it doesn't matter really. Mizzi's a good girl; they're all good people. These are just her 'folk ways'. By and by he took a liking to these ways. On cool spring evenings, a friendly warmth emanated from Mizzi Schinagl. Fond memories were awakened in him, memories of her body, its secret places, its quiet abandon and its gifts of pleasure. Of course Mizzi did many things that bothered him. But she was quick to notice them herself, and gradually dropped them from her repertoire. She reined in her vivacity, no longer clapped her hands in front of her face when she laughed, and no longer screeched when she was startled. She managed to drop all these things, comforting herself with the same thought she had used to get herself through the school day: it'll all be over in four hours anyway.

Weird and wonderful things went through her mind. She had felt punished in prison, as she had at school, but never humiliated. But now that she was at liberty again, she felt there was, unjustly, a stain on her. But it was unjust! What was she guilty of? She thought hard, and went over her previous life, year by year, action by action, with the precision that only people who have suffered hurt or scorn are capable of. At the beginning was Taittinger. Before that there had been only the vague twilight of her father's shop. Then a glorious figure strode in. He had stars on his collar, suns on his jacket, and a silver shaft of lightning at his hip. She would have duly married Xandl the hairdresser if the shining one had not come! She wouldn't have gone to Frau Matzner! She wouldn't have become a concubine, dripping with pearls. Pearls are unlucky! It was all Taittinger's fault.

Incapable as she was of keeping her own counsel, she confided in Magdalene Kreutzer, who backed her up. Magdalene Kreutzer raised the matter of her bastard. It was Taittinger's responsibility to look after mother and child. Ignaz Trummer came along. He was of the same opinion. 'All people is equals' – that was his starting-point. 'The likes of us gets a summonses if he don't pay upkeep – and blow me if that ain't just the beginning! You get the full majesty of the law on yer like a ton of bricks!' Trummer had his own three illegitimate children in mind. No end of trouble they were. Their mothers had of course taken him to court. In two cases, he'd managed to deny paternity successfully. The third, a little girl, he had put with his old aunt in Krieglach. There, she had fallen into a copper and been scalded to death. Of course if you're a haristocrat it's all different. It was only right that the Baron should give Mizzi the waxworks as a present! And even that was only modest compensation in view of all she'd been through.

'But I still love him!' confessed Mizzi. It was true. Sometimes she thought she could do it all over again for him, leave her father for the Herrengasse, and then to Frau Matzner's house, and have a child, and be given unlucky pearls, and get locked up again. She didn't regret any of it. She missed him too; his hands, his smell, nights spent together with him, his love. She longed for him; and it struck her as curious, in her moments of clarity and insight, that she was driven by desire for revenge as well as desire. She wanted to retaliate against him. She belonged to him. So why was Taittinger keeping his distance?

She knew that he liked to go for a morning stroll in the Prater; one day she took it upon herself to meet him there. She spotted him in the distance, she recognized his back and his walk. He seemed so thin and frail, surrounded by all those tall trees, it moved her to tears; she felt like crying just seeing him walk. It was lovely actually, walking after him like her master, to see and to love his back and his shadow, when he left the avenue from time to time and walked in the sun. Even in the privacy of her own heart, she didn't dare think of him as Franz – she was too afraid. When she thought 'Franz', she felt a dagger in her heart.

It was just as well that she hadn't bumped into him by chance; that might have been more than she could bear. She was on the point of turning back anyway, so that he didn't see her today, not today; but she kept putting off the moment. Without realizing it, she walked faster and faster. Now she could hear his footfall ahead of her. Suddenly he stopped and turned round and saw her. He had sensed he was being followed.

He let her draw near. 'You know I'm not keen on surprises, Mizzi!' That was true, he really hated surprises. He hated Christmas presents that he hadn't asked for – practically ordered – and he lost or destroyed them right away. To him, surprises were vulgar, like a shriek of alarm, a woman crying aloud, a noisy game of tarot in a café, two men quarrelling in the street.

'It was an accident, Baron, I'm sorry!' lied Mizzi. 'I thought the Baron liked to ride?'

'I don't have a horse now, Mizzi, and I won't ride on a hired animal! Where are you off to?' It was almost suspicion.

'Nowhere, just walking,' said Mizzi.

'Well, just you turn round, go and sit in the garden at Steinacker's and order a beer. I'll be along in an hour!' He turned and walked off.

But he no longer had any desire to walk. He kept out of the way of the riders. He started back. He felt a little sorry for Mizzi. And then he felt ashamed of feeling sorry for her. Everything would be fine, if she hadn't had that wretched son of hers! Then he remembered it was his son too. Not that he felt responsible for him – not at all. But it was a fact: undeniably Xandl was his son, and Mizzi could do nothing about it – or very little. By the time he reached Steinacker's, his expression was almost benign. The Baron's afternoon was beginning a little early – that was all. Mizzi was ushering in the 'popular' part of his day at eleven o'clock.

Automatically, Taittinger turned his interest to the wax figures. A lot of money was needed. How much? Trummer had the figures. And how much of it did she have herself, asked Taittinger. Mizzi owned up to the three hundred gulden she'd inherited from the late Frau Matzner, but nothing more. She kept quiet about what was left of the haberdashery. Back in their shared cell, Magdalene Kreutzer had advised her not to breathe a word of that 'nest egg' to anyone, not even Trummer. And least of all to her son. But it wasn't Leni's good advice that she was following now, so much as the promptings of her own heart. Ever since her imprisonment she'd been terribly worried about old age and poverty. It was as though all the irresponsibility in her character had been used up, or had melted away, along with her money; her entire stock of optimism, trustfulness, exuberance and generosity had been spent. What was left, deposited at the bottom of her heart, was her natural fear of the mutability of life – only eclipsed previously by her youth – her yearning for security, her deep hankering for property, her jealous affection for what had been set aside and saved, tucked and salted away; in short the innate faith in savings and insurance held by any woman of her sort. She felt no shame on account of it. Her discretion was a moral duty. And it was her moral duty to let Taittinger pay. The money he spent on her strengthened her love for him. Her two thousand gulden was in the post office, and her savings book was lying, wrapped in a handkerchief, at the bottom of her trunk. And the key to the trunk was round her neck, along with her crucifix and the medallion of St Teresa. 'I'm sure three hundred won't be enough,' said Taittinger, who had scant regard for money, and was rather in awe of the wax figures. Wax figures like that certainly would not come cheap. Yes, yes, he understood. 'I'll permit myself to help you out a bit,' he said.

'Oh, thank you! That's so sweet, so refined, that's just you all over, Baron!' And she reached for his hand with both of hers, and before he could refuse she was bending over it, kissing it fervently. He was shocked, puzzled, helpless.

Suddenly, Mizzi burst into tears. This heightened Taittinger's displeasure, but it also touched his heart, almost as much as when Mizzi had started crying in the prison director's office. 'You are still a bid fond of me, aren't you?' asked Mizzi.

'Yes, of course I am,' said Taittinger, confidently expecting her tears to dry up. But in fact the opposite happened: they flowed hotter and faster than ever. Though, admittedly, not for all that long. Mizzi lifted her face. Her dishevelled hair, her crumpled hat, her crushed handkerchief and the forget-me-not blue of her eyes, which looked positively childlike between her tear-swollen lids, all pleased the Baron, and made him warm towards Mizzi. She sensed it straight away, and with the speed of an eagle, after circling for a long time suddenly swooping on its prey, she asked, 'Can I come to you – tonight?'

'Not tonight,' said Taittinger. He disliked improvisation.

'Then tomorrow? The day after tomorrow? When?'

'Tomorrow!' said Taittinger, 'unless something crops up!'

XXVIII

He did vaguely hope that something might crop up, but nothing did, and Mizzi Schinagl came to visit him as arranged. He quickly got used to her, as he generally did to things, whether good or bad, 'charming' or 'tedious'. He rediscovered Mizzi's familiar warmth, and reacquainted himself with her well-remembered secrets. Mizzi came to visit more often. She fed the reawakened habit eagerly. Her love was as passionate as it had been when it first began. And, as before, she sometimes surrendered to her dangerous dreams, knowing full well how foolish they were, and how bleak and bitter it was to wake from them. Ridiculous dreams, fleetingly kind and beatific, for all the misery of waking from them. The Baron will grow old, and perhaps a little infirm. Not badly, oh no! Maybe a very mild seizure that will need plenty of attention. Then she will nurse him, devote herself entirely to him – instead of just in that way – sacrifice herself to his well-being. Then he'll get older still, and become more and more dependent on Mizzi – and then he'll make her his wife. For one night of her life she's played a Countess. Why shouldn't she be a Baroness for the last ten years of it?

On one of these days, old Schinagl – still officially his grandson's guardian – was notified by the director of the institution in Graz that they no longer saw themselves as being in a position to keep Xandl; either he should join his mother in Vienna right away or other arrangements should be made. But neither his moral conduct nor his industry nor his gifts were of a standard to allow him to attend another institution in Graz, or in Styria. The old man forwarded the letter to his daughter. Magdalene Kreutzer and Trummer both agreed that a child's place was with its mother, and no bastard should be in an institution. He should learn a trade, and then something could be made of him. Besides, it was a sign from Heaven, a pointer from Almighty God, as is written in the Bible, and as the catechist always says. The father is at hand too. Not a word to him, of course. Get the boy to come, and just send him to the Baron one day, preferably in the morning. Here I am, what do I do? Here I am, Dad! Maybe he'll send him away to his estate, who knows? The Baron is impulsive like that, lord yes!

One morning the following week, just as Taittinger was leaving the hotel, the young man, Schinagl, was announced to him. The hideous youth had left a strong impression on poor Taittinger. He knew right away who it was – which was most uncharacteristic of him. 'Bring him to me!' he ordered. 'But if he shows his face again, throw him out!'

Yes, there was the hideous fellow again, he had grown since last time, his eyelids were redder and his mouth more twisted. His son! His son looked as though Nature had played a joke on the Baron. The brow was similar, the hairline, the chin, the eyebrows, the shape of the eyes.

214

'Good morning!' said the boy. He had his cap in his hand. He had changed – he had become considerably uglier – but even so, it was as though he'd seen him only yesterday.

'Herr Schinagl?' said Taittinger.

'Mum said I was to say g'morning to you!'

'Thank you, and give my regards to Fräulein Schinagl!' said Taittinger, and waved for a cab. What a terrible start to the day. Now where to? 'To Baden!' cried Taittinger, but while still on the Kärntner Straße he changed his mind, and said: 'No, the police headquarters!' He got out, paid, and found he didn't have the courage to go and see the police surgeon and discuss the Schinagl business with him.

Instead, he wandered aimlessly through the streets. As the clocks were striking twelve, he was just passing the Hofburg, a moment before the changing of the guard. The lieutenant of the Deutschmeisters ordered 'Shorten your strides!' because the clock in the palace yard hadn't yet begun striking. The drum major raised his baton, the last sounds of the Radetzky March died away sadly, with a feeble echo in the vaulted arch of the Palace gate. Now the clock struck, now there was a soft drumming of velvet paws on calfskin, now a command came from within: 'Present arms!' Now the Emperor himself was peeping out from behind a curtain somewhere. Taittinger was gripped by an indescribable melancholy. For the first time in many weeks, he felt a nostalgia for uniform, and grief for the army. The band played 'Blue Danube'. The crowd in the Palace yard thought they had caught a glimpse of the Emperor at one of the windows. Hats and hands flew up. The huzzah almost buried the music. The mild spring sun lay over the palace and smiled: a young mother. 'God Save the King' was intoned, Taittinger felt the familiar patriotic gooseflesh of soldiery and anthems. He stood there, hat in hand; everything in him yearned to have been allowed to salute instead.

As he made his way to the Deutsches Haus, where he planned to have his lunch, he seriously wondered whether he shouldn't rejoin the army. He had no more money. Fine! The reserves were all right. They could revise the medical opinion. His friend Kalergi was in the War Ministry. For an hour or two the decommissioned Captain surveyed the futility of his life. His estate, Mizzi, the people at the Prater, the Kreutzer woman, that Trummer fellow! . . . Even the wax figurines left him cold. Once, he had bought a haberdashery, now he would have to acquire a panopticum; and that's it, *sela*, end of story. Sell off the pathetic remains of his estate! And then back where he belonged! To the bosom of the army! He wanted to have another think in the hotel. He went back, and sat down in the lobby.

The porter came over to him and announced that the young man who'd called in the morning had shown up again, but in the company of the lady who visited every day, so they weren't sure what to do. Have the pair of them come, said Taittinger. They came. Taittinger had planned to remain seated, but he stood up: he was brought to his feet. He was incapable of remaining seated in the presence of any creature in female garb. (If he had been approached by a shop-window dummy in a dress, he would have stood up as well.) He even smiled. He asked them to sit down. Mizzi Schinagl took the school director's letter from her handbag, and showed it to Taittinger. She took out her handkerchief at the same time. She was all primed to cry. Taittinger read a couple of lines, and laid the letter on the table. Mizzi was poking at her eyes with her handkerchief. With a great sob in her voice, she blurted out: 'You see, the boy's gone to the dogs!' It was a clear reproach. Taittinger's work was botched.

'Dear Fräulein Schinagl,' said Taittinger, 'how old is your son?'

'He's eighteen, tomorrow!'

'Congratulations!' said Taittinger to Xandl.

'What are you planning to do with him now?' Taittinger asked.

'I think, and this is what Herr Trummer says too, that he should go to my father and help in the shop, then he might inherit the shop, because my father's not well!'

'Not tomorrow,' said Xandl, 'it's my birthday!'

'Then let me give you something,' said Taittinger, 'that way you needn't trouble to come here again!' He took a hundred-gulden note from his wallet. Xandl folded it up and held it clenched in his fist.

'Ta!' he said.

'Say: Thank you very much, Baron!' cried Mizzi.

'O.K.,' said Xandl, 'thank you very much, Baron!' There was silence for a moment. Then Xandl abruptly said: 'Come on, Mizzi, let's go!' and stood up.

'I must go too!' said Taittinger; he looked at his watch and got up. He picked up his hat, and was the first one through the door.

'Give me the money!' Mizzi said to her son once they were out on the street.

'You must be joking!' cried Xandl. 'A hundred for a woman like you!' He walked along beside her for a few steps, but at the next turn-off, he swerved round the corner without a word.

'Xandl, Xandl!' cried Mizzi. He didn't turn round. She walked on down the Rotenturmstraße, then, at the Franz-Joseph Quay, she needed to sit down. It was quiet at that time of day. She could hear the rich burbling of the Danube just behind the thick laburnum shrubbery. Brazen blackbirds hopped up to share Mizzi's bench with her. They came for food, the way street musicians collect money after they've played one or two tunes. Mizzi got up to buy a biscuit from the café next door, to feed them. Like all small women, she had a soft spot for birds, and felt pathetically grateful for their trustfulness. Slowly and economically she crumbled a biscuit, in order to keep the blackbirds close to her for as long as possible. She couldn't bear to be alone that day. She wanted to hurry back to Fräulein Kreutzer, and Trummer too. She talked to the blackbirds in an undertone. She told them how wicked Xandl had been since he'd returned. ('And he was so dear when he came into the world – and after that too, when he still had his curls. It always used to make me so happy when he called me Mum. And now he never calls me Mum, it's just Mizzi the whole time, or woman. Woman!') She started crying bitterly. She felt that she had only begun to experience true humiliation after the boy's arrival. At Josephine Matzner's house, she had been maltreated by the customers at times, but never insulted. Even during the compulsory weekly check-up, at the vice squad, she had never felt dishonoured; nor later, either, in detention or in prison. It had to be her own child that came along to do her dishonour and sully her name. At that moment she was struck by the full weight of the word: sully. A word that – strange – had been in her daily vocabulary ever since she could remember, but only now did she feel its full significance. She got up and looked around, there wasn't a policeman anywhere about. She tiptoed over the lawn, went up to the parapet of the Danube Canal, and looked down into the water. A couple of years ago, red-headed Karoline had thrown herself into the Danube – a little further up, near the Augartenbrücke – and was never found. Frau Matzner used to say that the Danube was a jealous river that doesn't willingly surrender its bodies. It likes to take them all the way down to the sea. The thought of a death like that made Mizzi shudder; the longer she looked at the water rushing by, the more she shuddered; but at the same time, she started to enjoy her fear. She began to relish her fear of a watery grave. When she saw a policeman's helmet blinking up at her from the quayside, she went back to her bench.

She missed prison. She hadn't felt so lonely there, in her small cell. But out here the world was large, and a small woman felt her loneliness a thousandfold. A loneliness no smaller than the whole world itself. She had a friend in Leni, but Leni had her bloke Trummer. How can you trust a woman if she's in love with a man? The Baron would never be hers. The only thing of his she could keep was Xandl – and he was running away from her, she wasn't a mother to him. If only she could forget how lovely he had once been. Maybe he was feeling sorry for what he'd done, and was waiting for her at the merry-go-round as he did every afternoon. She crossed to the Prater, taking her time. The later she got there, the more certain that Xandl would be there already. But Xandl only arrived much later, and when he did he smelt of beer and schnapps. He was quieter than usual. There was a strange light flashing in his eyes. She hesitated for a long time before asking him for the hundred gulden. But in the end the idea that she might be able to recoup at least seventy of them decided her. 'Here it is!' said Xandl. He pulled out a bundle of ten-gulden notes. 'I spent the other twenty. A down payment on a bicycle, I'll collect it tomorrow.'

'Give me the rest then!' demanded Mizzi.

Xandl put the money back in his pocket. He went down to spur the donkey on a bit and chat with Schani. He wanted to show off his wealth too. Schani needed money. He had a silver ring with a real stone in it; but Xandl had his doubts about both the silver and the jewel. The only real valuable that Schani owned was a revolver. He sold it to Xandl – along with twenty bullets – for five gulden. They could go and fire it tomorrow in the river meadow, where the soldiers exercised, and the sound of gunfire wouldn't attract attention. Herr Trummer squeezed through the little doorway just as they were concluding the deal. He saw the notes, asked where they'd come from, called the Baron a booby and a bloody fool, ordered Xandl to give the money back to him or his mother right away. Otherwise he'd call the police: the boys would end up behind bars on account of the revolver.

'But I'm keeping the revolver, all right,' said Schinagl wheedlingly. He kept it and gave Trummer the money. Trummer told Mizzi he'd hang on to it for her, as long as the boy was in her house. He wouldn't be able to steal it from him, as he might from her. Mizzi thought the money was gone for-ever, and that made her even sadder.

She spent a couple of days looking for Taittinger. He'd stopped coming to the Prater. She couldn't find him at the hotel. She went to Schaub's confectionery on the Petersgasse, where gentlemen sometimes met. And there he was, in the company of two officers. She didn't dare approach him, not even to go and sit at another table. She stayed outside, and walked up and down the pavement. At last Taittinger came out on his own: 'Sorry, Mizzi,' he said, 'I've been busy these last couple of days. Another week. *Grüß Gott!'*

He pursued his return to the army with an assiduousness that was unprecedented for him. In a week he was to present himself to the medical committee again. To secure his transfer to the infantry, he still needed to complete a six-month course. He was as geed up as a cadet. There could be no doubt of his enthusiasm: but in his belief that the military authorities would match it with theirs, he was childishly mistaken. He imagined that the War Ministry proceeded in the manner of a regiment – with the commanding officer issuing orders, and his subordinates obeying them. In the afternoon the regimental orders would be read out, and the next day they would be put into effect. But that wasn't the way they did things in the offices of the Ministry. People didn't talk, they sent memos. Not even Lieutenant-Colonel Kalergi could prevent Taittinger's application from going on the bewildering peregrination that all documents were sent on in the old '*k. und k.*' monarchy. The 'Taittinger File' put on weight and bulk as it travelled. But it was still far from reaching the mass that might have permitted it to return to Lieutenant-Colonel Kalergi. And no matter how vigilantly he followed the crissings and crossings of the file, each time he thought he had it within his grasp again, it always managed to give him the slip.

No, no, it would be quite some time before Baron Taittinger got to appear before any medical commission.

XXIX

On one of these days he received an acutely embarrassing visit from his 'friends from among the populace'. This time Fräulein Kreutzer and Herr Trummer turned up together. Taittinger was sitting in the lobby and got quite a fright when he saw them approaching. Herr Trummer, out in the van, requested to see the Baron. At the same moment he spotted Taittinger peering over his cup of coffee. He waved his formal black hat. It looked as if he were giving signs with a flag of mourning. Straightaway he turned back towards the entrance, and waved Magdalene Kreutzer forward. He was austerely clad in black, Fräulein Kreutzer seasonably colourful. Alongside the dark and earnest man, she resembled a walking flowerbed with Death in attendance. So there they were. Within a few seconds, Taittinger had adjusted to the fact. He couldn't deny that he'd had it in mind to look them up himself one of these days.

They sat down immediately, and looked at one another for a long time, as though their eyes were negotiating which of them was to speak first. Finally they both launched into the same sentence at once, chorusing in correct German: 'There has been a tragedy!'

'What's happened?' asked Taittinger.

'A tragedy!' repeated Fräulein Kreutzer, and promptly burst into tears.

'Hush, Leni!' ordered Trummer. He took over from her, lapsed from correct German into dialect after a couple of sentences, lost confidence, repeatedly asked: 'd'you understand?' and finally ground to a halt himself.

Fräulein Kreutzer then started again from the beginning. There was a catch in her throat, and that coloured her speech, which was like the miaowing of a cat, the whetting of a knife, and occasionally the piercing shriek of a fork being scraped across a plate. Taittinger was so deafened by her din that for the next ten minutes he took in precisely nothing. Another factor was that she herself seemed not to know what she had just said, because every so often she would interrupt herself with the question: 'Now where was I?' to which Taittinger made no response, and Herr Trummer started afresh. Having decided to stick to dialect this time, he managed a continuous narrative. Even so, it was another quarter of an hour before Taittinger grasped that Xandl had done something frightful – and that responsibility for it lay with the Baron.

'The ultimate responsibility, mind!' repeated Trummer.

'With all due respect, Baron,' Fräulein Kreutzer chipped in, 'you can't just put a fortune in the boy's hand!'

'What did he do with it?' asked the Baron. Everything I do is wrong, he thought. I give him some money so he leaves me alone, and now this happens.

'He's committed a 'omicide!' said Trummer, 'but thank God it was me. And I'm alive, and I aims to be alive awhile yet!'

JOSEPH ROTH

'What do you mean, homicide?' asked Taittinger.

'He means he took a pot-shot at him!' said Leni. And then she told the story, again, of how Trummer had taken what was left of the hundred gulden from Xandl; while Xandl kept hold of the revolver. 'But on the evening of the day before yesterday, after Trummer's counted the takings from the merry-go-round as usual, and sets off for home after midnight, Xandl comes up to him, wanting not just his own money, but a whole hundred gulden. So Trummer winds up to clock him one. Then Xandl pulls out the gun and says: "Stick 'em up". But Trummer's not the man to be afraid of a little boy thief like that, and he gives Xandl a shove, and the boy falls over, and the gun goes off, and then Xandl shoots off all the other bullets like a madman, lying on his back shooting up in the air, and the police arrive, and now we're all in the soup.'

'Don't you ever read the paper then?' asked Trummer. He was offended. Yesterday the whole story was in the newspaper in considerable detail; including his questioning in the Leopoldstadt police station. And today one of those journalists even did a sketch of him, and so his picture is going to be published tomorrow. That's right. Mizzi spent the whole day at the station. There's going to be a big trial, the police commissioner said, and the charges – 'alley-gations', Trummer said – were armed robbery and attempted murder. Mizzi was questioned too, and she made a statement and explained who the father is. – And here it is in the paper, in black and white – Trummer pulled out a newspaper, and pointed to a sentence in it. Taittinger read: 'The young criminal is the illegitimate fruit of a romantic love-union between the youthful beauty Mizzi Schinagl and a titled cavalry officer who moves in the highest circles, one Baron . . .' There were three stars in place of the name.

Poor Taittinger remained seated, frozen in horror. 'If only you'd not given such a load of money to the boy!' said Fräulein Kreutzer. She was firmly resolved to give the silly Baron a piece of her mind. She set out all the dire consequences that were awaiting not only the boy, but also Mizzi and Taittinger himself when the case came to court.

The Law Clerk Pollitzer, an acquaintance of hers, spelled it out for her. 'In other countries, like America,' Pollitzer said, 'they're not so soft on juveniles. But in Austria we're just behind with everything.'

'That's so true!' growled Trummer. 'We haven't got a clue in this country. Jesus Christ Almighty!'

Taittinger pondered, but he was well aware that no amount of pondering had yet helped him to a sensible conclusion. The first thing was to lose the pair of them. So he tried a method he'd often found helpful in the army, where it provided at least temporary relief. He got up and said: 'I will see to the needful!' Feeling they'd secured their objective and defeated the Baron, Fräulein Kreutzer and Trummer made an orderly retreat from the hotel premises.

In the course of the next few days, Taittinger was forced to recognize that he was quite unable to 'see to the needful'. The Schinagl-Trummer business was already in the hands of the investigating magistrate when Taittinger looked up his friend the police surgeon. 'You know,' Dr Stiasny said, 'when things are still with us in the police, there are still possibilities. When they're with us, you know, they're at a pretty early stage, and there's a chance that they may, so to speak, miscarry. But you're too late for that now. All the time they're with the magistrate, these embryonic stories are slowly but surely growing. There's nothing to be done about it. All we can do is keep your name

226

from being mentioned in the proceedings, either directly or indirectly. I'll be happy to see to that for you: Dr Blum, the Court Officer, is a friend of mine. That way, even if they mention your name in court, I can guarantee it won't appear in the papers. But, at this stage, that's all I can do for you, Baron.'

Lieutenant-Colonel Kalergi was similarly of the opinion that things were too far gone. Taittinger couldn't quite bring himself to see why it should be harder to influence the legal system than the police. 'But you must understand,' Kalergi lectured him, 'a judge isn't like a police officer. Judges are like the angels of officialdom. But really your only reason for worrying about the whole thing is that it might hurt your application to rejoin the army. I would just go away for a while! I'll see to it that everything comes off smoothly.'

But no, Taittinger didn't go away. A curious fearfulness kept him in town. It was almost like a pang of conscience. He felt culpably and irrevocably bound up with other people's lives and businesses. He could feel that a big change had taken place in him, but once again he wasn't quite sure when it had come about. Maybe when he had run into Sedlacek on the stairs. Maybe before that, in old Schinagl's shop in Sievering. Or later, when he went to visit Mizzi in prison. Or maybe not until he had left the army. He reinterpreted the blithe insouciance of his younger days: it had been nothing but a lack of awareness. Sometimes it seemed to him as though for years he had wandered past frightful abysses with his eyes blindfolded, and the only reason he hadn't fallen was that he hadn't been able to see. He had learned to see, but much too late. Now he saw dangers on every side; great and small. Unthinking actions, harmless notions, harmlessly acted upon, casual utterances and carelessly omitted precautions – all took a fearsome toll. The world was nowhere near as straightforward as it had once been; especially since he'd taken off his uniform. His three simple categories of people: the 'charming', the 'so-so' and the 'tedious', were really neither here nor there. More than anything, people were unknowable. How easy that nice relationship with lovely Mizzi had looked once, years ago. Just one of many pleasant experiences, no more significant than a good meal, a pleasant drive, an invitation to go shooting, a bottle of champagne, a fortnight's furlough. Experiences, when one encountered them, looked bright, colourful, floating. You held on to them as to a balloon on a string, for as long as they were fun. Then, when you got bored, you let go. They floated off prettily into the air, you watched them go with gratitude and affection, and then they went quietly pop somewhere in the clouds. But a few hadn't gone pop at all. Instead, treacherous and invisible, they had hung around somewhere for years, in defiance of all the rules of Nature. And then, full of ballast, they fell back like lead weights on the head of poor Taittinger.

He no longer tried to oppose the silly sense of duty that impelled him to go to the Prater every day, and inform Mizzi, Fräulein Kreutzer and Trummer of the failures of his 'steps'. He couldn't do anything about the tormenting knowledge that he was responsible for everything: for Xandl's existence, for the hundred gulden, for the boy's hideousness. He was sinking – he could feel it – in the estimation of 'the people': (because for him those three were 'the people').

'If I knowed the bigwigs like as what you do!' said Trummer.

'It only takes a bit of bottle!' Fräulein Kreutzer reckoned.

'My poor boy!' cried Mizzi. She cried easily, swiftly and venomously. It wasn't grief, but hatred that gave her tears. The three of them formed a common front against Taittinger. Even he – no more capable of suspicion than he might be of, say, chasing a horse-drawn omnibus, or stooping to pick up some object on the pavement – even he occasionally spotted the quick, meaningful looks that shot between them.

On occasion, 'the people' had recourse to more direct methods. It spoke unambiguously through the mouth of Magdalene Kreutzer: 'If only you'd of paid for his upkeep!' and: 'A haberdashery's not much of a price to pay for a girl's virtue!' The disdain of the three of them went so far that their lapses into dialect became more and more infrequent. They were creating a distance between themselves and the Baron in correct German. He was no longer considered worthy of hearing dialect spoken.

'We'll just have to help ourselves then!' Fräulein Kreutzer said ominously one day.

She had what she thought was a marvellous idea. With the aid of Pollitzer, who for only two and a half gulden will draw up any legal document to your entire and lasting satisfaction, she decided to appeal to His Majesty in person: a plea for mercy. In the Court and Cabinet Office – says Pollitzer – they deal with everything. Write that poor Mizzi has been seduced and left with a child and no means of support. Without a father, not unnaturally, the boy grows up with disciplinary problems. What has been put in motion is the destruction of a life in its first bloom. Only the mercy of the Emperor himself can save a boy, a citizen and a future loyal soldier, from the full punishment demanded by the law. To begin with, Pollitzer thought they could wait with the petition until the case came up. But then the thought of the two and a half gulden got the upper hand, and he said: 'I'll write it – but there's no guarantee of success!' And he wrote.

A quarter of an hour before His Majesty undertook his daily drive through the streets of Vienna, dozens of plainclothes policemen posted themselves at all the corners and intersections – not to look out for suspicious characters, as you might think, but to alert their colleagues, the uniformed policemen on the beat.

The Kaiser's ritual promenade is like a familiar and well-loved holiday: heartily familiar but still always something to look forward to. It resembles the spring, which people see every year, but never fail to greet with avid joy. Shopkeepers shut their premises and go to stand by the roadside. In the big department stores that fill several storeys, the young sales girls, seamstresses and milliners, those forever curious, forever flighty sweet-toothed children of Vienna, forever desirous of change, throw open all the windows. A half-hour's holiday: the Kaiser drives by.

There already is the sound of his carriage, the two slender chestnut horses, with sensitive hooves, brusquely and gently caressing the cobbles with their tread. The footman sits on the box in minor gala uniform, and the coachman holds his whip aloft, but only as a badge of office. The Emperor's horses need no whip. The Emperor's horses always know what they must do, and whom they have in their care. It's as though they don't even need to be hitched to the carriage: they have put on harness and reins all by themselves. It is they who give the tempo and direction to the coachman, not the other way round.

On one such day, as the horses turned off the Ring on to the Mariahilfer Straße, a woman suddenly burst from the ranks of those shouting their huzzahs and 'Long live the King!', reached the carriage step in a trice, and tossed a letter in, which landed on the lap of the Aide-de-Camp. This kind of thing happened with some regularity, and His Majesty was not in the least put out by it. Generally, they were appeals for clemency, written cries for help from his subjects. He had read a good many such in his time, approved some, turned down others. But while he took such incidents as a perfectly ordinary and natural part of his office, his servants chose to see these dramatic and unpredictably delivered petitions as dangerous symptoms of a menacing anarchistic tendency in the population. The plainclothes policemen surged forward: two, three, four, five of them: far too many for a single woman. The hat was knocked off her head, her handbag out of her grip. A policeman picked the items up. The Emperor was already far away. The woman was taken to the police station in the Neubaugasse, closely questioned and her details taken, all according to the regulations. It was Mizzi Schinagl. She was warned that from now on she was under special police supervision and that she should expect a summons at any moment, and then allowed to go. None of this overly impressed Mizzi. Like all the world, she knew that she could expect two days in detention or a five gulden fine. Fräulein Kreutzer and Trummer, who had gone with her to keep her courage up, escorted her back to the Prater in triumph.

'Not a word about this to your Baron!' ordered Trummer. The Baron, it seemed, had been made into a sworn enemy, and it was open season on him. If he got wind of Mizzi's appeal too soon, he was perfectly capable of holding back the money for the waxworks.

Mizzi Schinagl felt embarrassed by the particulars that had appeared in her petition. But she told herself it was more important to rescue her son, her only child, 'all she had in the world'. That's just the way mothers are! she told herself. She decided to inform Taittinger of her action in two or three days. Give it time: wait until the panopticum had been paid for. In two or three days, they were due to complete the sale; it was to be done, following an old tradition among fairground stall-holders, in the Café Zirrnagl, the artists café on the Praterstraße.

XXX

Taittinger was due at the Café Zirrnagl at five o'clock. Mizzi Schinagl, Fräulein Kreutzer and Trummer had been there since four. Every one of them was terrified lest the Baron might have a last minute change of heart and not turn up, or, worse, that he might already have left town. We should have kept a tighter grip on him! thought Fräulein Kreutzer.

But there he was, just getting out of a hansom cab. She knew his little foible. He disliked driving right up to a place where he was expected. She had just enough time to cross the wide thoroughfare to greet him.

'I'm not late, I hope?' asked Taittinger. 'Were you waiting for me here?' He looked at his watch, he was punctual as always.

'I needed to tell you something first!' said Mizzi. She was no longer worried about the Baron's antipathy to strong personal feeling. At that moment it seemed to her that of all the people in the world, he was the only one who was dear to her. He was her lover. She loved him more than she loved her son and more than she loved her father. She saw all that quite clearly now.

'What is it, what is it?' he asked. He allowed her to take him round the corner into a side street.

'I don't want you to buy the waxworks,' she began. She said 'du' to him quite naturally, even though it was the middle of the day, and she'd only ever spoken to him like that in the darkness of their shared nights. She said she had enough money of her own, and that she didn't need any help from him. She had only been following Leni Kreutzer's advice, but that had been wrong of her. She didn't want to do any more bad in the world. Moreover, she had also delivered a petition on behalf of her Xandl . . .

'No, dear Mizzi,' he said in a tone of voice that was new to her. He freed his arm. His voice came from a long way away; each syllable was like a metal door shutting. The sentences slid home as the bolts had once done on the door of her prison cell. 'No, I pay my debts. This way you'll have a secure livelihood, and the boy too, once he gets out! – Let's go!' he said, and she followed him, half a step behind, trying to catch him up. Her heart wasn't pounding any more, though she had to hurry, and her head felt empty, though oddly heavy. It sat on her shoulders like a weight someone had placed there.

Get this over with quickly, thought Taittinger to himself as he entered the Café Zirrnagl. There they were already, all sitting down, the owner of the panopticum, and the middleman and someone else he didn't know. It was Pollitzer, the legal adviser who was going to frame the contract for them. Taittinger made no effort to follow the various points under discussion. It was all he could do to master the sense of confusion that came over him – not from within, but blowing towards him from every direction, cutting into him like a mixture of gusting wind, sleet and dust.

He had barely touched his coffee by the time Pollitzer wanted to go. Taittinger asked if they were finished yet. 'Unfortunately not, Baron!' said Pollitzer, who seemed to have the whip hand here, and was addressed by everyone as 'Herr Doktor'.

'We have to talk to old Percoli, he lives a couple of doors down from here. Would the Baron prefer to wait here?' No, something in Taittinger jibbed at that. He couldn't stay here alone, although he did feel a degree of unease faced with Pollitzer's flowing cravat, his floppy hat, his flowered waistcoat and the bundle of papers in his jacket pocket. He trailed along after the rest of them like a dutiful pet, his impatience growing the more he tried to overcome it. He climbed three flights of stairs. He followed the others through a dingy kitchen into a bright glass-roofed atelier. The old Neapolitan didn't get up for them.

Pollitzer had brought the contract with him. In it, old Tino Percoli committed himself to recreating some of the news stories of the last few months, against an advance of one hundred gulden. He was prohibited from offering the same models anywhere within the Dual Monarchy; the panopticum in Berlin might show them after an interval of two weeks. The Musée Grevin in Paris was not subject to any restrictions, nor was abroad in general. 'I'll hold on to the contract till tomorrow,' said Percoli. 'Tomorrow afternoon! I want time to read it through by myself.'

'Might I ask you at least to read those parts of it that concern the Baron,' said Pollitzer. Taittinger had to go back to the café.

It turned out that he had to pay seven hundred gulden down in cash, and promise the rest – another eight hundred – later. He was given pen and ink. He signed with a firm and cheerful hand. It seemed to him that he had managed to cast off a mighty burden, to ease his conscience, to escape from his worries and all kinds of entanglements and embarrassments. He said a positively cordial goodbye to all of them. He promised to attend the opening of the new panopticum on Sunday. It was to be given a new name. Pollitzer had come up with: 'The World Bioscope Theatre', which everyone liked. They went to have a drink. No one made any attempt to invite the Baron along. Mizzi Schinagl suddenly started crying.

'What for?' they asked.

'Oh, from being so happy,' she replied.

The opening of the new 'World Bioscope Theatre' was thronged with crowds of sensation-hungry onlookers from the Imperial capital.

Poor Taittinger wouldn't have missed it for worlds. He watched the entire programme.

The curtain rose with a quiet shriek, and Taittinger was shocked to the core to behold Mizzi seated on a red throne. It was quite impossible to tell whether she was alive or made of wax. Her waxy neck and waxy cleavage were ornamented by a triple string of heavy, silvery-yellow, blue lustrous pearls. Chunky diamonds were pinned to her earlobes. Fairy-tale illumination was dispensed by a gas light on the ceiling, set behind a blue veil. On her head, the 'Shah's favourite wife' wore a diadem in the shape of a Turkish crescent, held in place by two slender silver arrows, between which the golden bounty of her hair poured forth Mizzi – was it really her? – sat quite motion-less on her red throne.

Yes, it was Mizzi. She began to speak in her normal voice: 'His Majesty the Shah of Persia is very good to me, I once was a poor girl of the Viennese people. Now I rule over all the women in his harem, and he likes me the best of all. I think I will rule like this for many years to come. Remember me to Vienna, the Viennese people and the good old Steffl!'*

Everybody clapped. With an incontinent rattle the curtain came down. 'This vision is at an end!' announced Trummer.

The whole world seemed to press towards the curtain. Taittinger took advantage of the confusion. He left. He fled.

*St Stephen's Cathedral.

XXXI

Slowly to begin with, cautiously, and then more and more boldly, the newspapers began for the first time in many years to talk about Persia again – about the Near Eastern kingdom to which they had ties of friendship, and about His Majesty the Shah, whose last visit to Vienna was still fresh in the memory of Austrians, nay, in the memory of all the peoples in the Dual Monarchy. Russian aspirations, English diplomacy and French intrigues were faithfully reported back from correspondents in Petersburg, London and Paris.

The *Fremdenblatt* despatched a journalist to Teheran. He wrote about Persian customs, Persian women, Persian gardens, the Persian army, Persian agriculture. After a few of his pieces, the average Viennese reader felt as much at home in Teheran as he did in Döbling or Grinzing, the Leopoldstadt or the Alsergrund.

None of what the newspapers print about Persia is without special relevance, a special political relevance. The politicians, the diplomats and the journalists all know: The Shah of Persia is coming to Vienna for a second time.

THE STRING OF PEARLS

In the Foreign Ministry on the Ballhausplatz they go through the old protocols. In His Majesty's Court and Cabinet Office they investigate every tiny incident that took place on the occasion of the Shah's previous visit. They're busy leafing through the archives of the Vienna Security Police, too.

Round about this time, Lazik had the brilliant, not to say, priceless idea of offering one further news item to the 'World Bioscope Theatre' in the Prater. He still possessed all the drawings, sketches and portraits of the Persian monarch's original visit from the *Kronen-Zeitung*. Mizzi Schinagl paid him ten gulden for his idea.

There was no doubt about it: the Imperial capital and residence was preparing itself for a further visit from His Persian Majesty. All the editors knew it. So, soon, did all the footmen, all the ushers, the coachmen and the police. (The last to know about it, as ever, were the foreign diplomatic corps.)

For fifty gulden, Tino Percoli created a depiction of the 'hot news': the Shah of Persia, the Grand Vizier, his Aide-de-Camp and the Chief Eunuch. The rest of the harem was superfluous. (If need be, they could always be supplied from the already existing harem, and moved to the newly created 'Persian Room'.) In the Court and Cabinet Office, in the Ministry of the Interior and the Ministry of Trade and Transportation, in the police forces of Vienna and Trieste, in the port authority of Trieste and in the upper echelons of the Southern Railways: everyone was ready. Like tiny, uncomprehending cogwheels in the vast and incomprehensible machinery of the Empire, the small officials began spinning with pointless eagerness: searching, writing, whirring, composing and receiving memos. It was recalled that His Majesty's luggage had once been subject to an unpardonable, almost irremediable delay. But then everything was recalled. Everything was dug up: the ceremonial running order, the names, the programme of the Court ball, of the reception, the officers of the regiment from which had been drawn the guard of honour to welcome the Shah at the Franz-Joseph Station, the colonel's uniform of the Persian élite regiment that belonged to the Kaiser. Even Captain of Horse Baron Alois Franz von Taittinger was recalled, who at that time had been on secondment from his regiment and assigned to special duties. And one particularly keen official, a cat's-paw of destiny, and clueless as cat's-paws of destiny must be, conscientiously followed the traces of Taittinger's deeds and misdeeds, and faithfully passed on his findings to the police. They had a few eager cat's-paws of their own, and they sent their findings on to the War Ministry.

At that time, the Taittinger file was in the hands of Councillor Sackenfeld at the War Ministry. He was in the process of selecting the commission and naming the date for the Captain's hearing, when he received their report, marked: 'Top Secret, ref. Taittinger'. He took the file and the report to Colonel Kalergi in the left wing of the building. Both men understood immediately that now was not the moment to think about reactivating Taittinger's career.

The Baron had to be told. Lieutenant Colonel Kalergi buckled on his sabre and went.

He met Taittinger in his hotel; a much changed, embittered and as it struck Kalergi, a suddenly aged Taittinger. The small round coffee table at which he was seated in the hotel lobby was covered by an enormous rectangular poster which the

Baron was perusing with some consternation He got to his feet creakily. Though Taittinger didn't in fact have one, Kalergi could almost see Taittinger supporting himself on an invisible stick. He sat down. Taittinger dispensed with the usual formalities, the enquiry after his health and that of his wife and so forth.

'You know all about me, Kalergi,' he began right away. 'You know that stupid business with the Schinagl girl and then that *histoire*. And I've told you about my son as well. Well, two weeks ago, I settled everything. I bought the panopticum, you know, the new 'World Bioscope Theatre'. Her son, or my son, Xandl – this won't be news to you either – has been arrested for attempted murder, I think it was, and robbery.'

'Ah, that business!' said Kalergi. 'I read about that!'

'Well then!' Taittinger went on. 'Now, before going back into the army, I wanted to have put all that silly stuff behind me, of course. But just a quarter of an hour ago, Trummer, I can't tell you who that is now – but anyway he's a friend of Mizzi's – brings me this placard – and tomorrow morning it's going to be in the press and posted on walls all over the city.' Taittinger pushed the placard across to Lieutenant Colonel Kalergi, who read:

On the occasion of the return visit of His Majesty the Shah of Persia to the city of Vienna, the new 'World Bioscope Theatre' proudly presents in lifelike verisimilitude, representations of the following scenes:
1. The arrival of the great Shah with his aides at the Franz-Joseph Station (Royal train not to scale).
2. The Harem and Chief Eunuch of Teheran.
3. The Viennese concubine, a child of the people from

Sievering, conducted to the Shah by important public figures, and subsequently enthroned as ruler of the Harem in Persia.

4.   The remaining retinue of the Shah of Persia.

Lieutenant Colonel Kalergi carefully folded up the big poster, very slowly, without looking up. He was afraid of the despair he would see in Taittinger's eyes. But he had come to tell him the truth. He wanted to make a start. He patted down the folded poster, and wondered how to begin.

'I'm impatient,' said Taittinger. 'Can you understand that? All my life I've behaved like a fool. I can see that now, but it's too late. Listen to this – I looked at myself in the mirror today, and I saw I'm an old man. Looking at the poster just now, I realized I've always been an idiot. Maybe I should have got married to Helene. Now the army's the only place for me. – What's the latest on my petition?'

'That's what I've come to see you about,' said the Lieutenant Colonel.

'Well?'

'Well, my dear chap! That old business, your *histoire* as you call it! I just had a word with Sackenfeld about it. You're going to have to wait, that dolt from Teheran has come at the wrong time. The police are digging around in their old files, and you're in the news again. All I can advise is: be patient!'

'So I won't be able to join – ?'

'No,' said Kalergi. 'Your wretched story is back. Best keep a low profile.'

Taittinger merely said: 'I see,' and 'Thank you!' Then he was silent for a time. The evening was getting on, the lights in the lobby were being lit. 'I've had it, haven't I?' said Taittinger.

He was silent again, and then, shrilly, in a voice that seemed not to have come out of him at all: 'So my appeal hasn't got a chance?'

'Not for the moment!' replied Kalergi. 'Let's sit tight till the Persian business has gone away again.' And, to lead his friend back into ordinary life, Kalergi added: 'Why don't we go and have a bite to eat at the Anchor!' and he looked at his watch.

'Fine, I'll just go and clean up!' said Taittinger. 'Won't be a moment. I'm just going upstairs.' He got up.

Five minutes later, Kalergi heard a shot. Its echo rolled around on staircases and down corridors.

The Baron was found beside his desk, dead. Evidently he had been trying to write something. The revolver was still in his right hand. His skull was shattered. His eyes bulged out. Lieutenant Colonel Kalergi had difficulty closing them.

Taittinger was buried with customary military honours. A platoon fired a salvo over the grave. Among the mourners were: the manager of the Prinz Eugen Hotel, Mizzi Schinagl, Magdalene Kreutzer and Ignaz Trummer, Lieutenant Colonel Kalergi and Ministerial Councillor Sackenfeld.

Afterwards, the Ministerial Councillor asked: 'Why do you think he killed himself? You were there, so to speak.'

'God knows!' replied Kalergi. 'I think he lost his way in life. It happens. A man can lose his way!'

That was the only obituary for the ex-Captain of Horse, Baron Alois Franz von Taittinger.

XXXII

This time, band leader Nechwal of the Hoch-and Deutschmeisters was given just three days to rehearse the Persian national anthem with his musicians. The order had come down to him so suddenly. There was nothing for it but to rehearse out of hours.

The day the Persian monarch arrived was a mild blue spring day; one of those spring days which the simple souls of Vienna claim can only be found in their city. The usual three companies that made up the guard of honour stood – one on the platform, the other two drawn up outside the station – in front of the usual mixed crowd of onlookers, wild enthusiasts and conscientious joiners, and looked, in their blue uniforms, like an integral – martial – part of this highly particular Viennese spring. It was a spring day much like that other, long before, when the Shah had come to Vienna for the first time; the resemblance was like that of a recently born brother to his elder sibling.

This time, it wasn't a tumult in the blood that had brought

the Shah West, nor was it curiosity nor again a perplexing thirst for variety. For some months now he'd lived in complete bliss with a newly purchased fourteen-year-old Indian girl by the name of Kalmana Kalinderi, a gentle and delightful creature, a brown doe, a pet from the faraway banks of the Ganges. She was the only woman he brought with him this time, and, to look after her, he brought his Chief Eunuch. A new Grand Vizier was there (his predecessor had been packed off with a middling pension after the Shah had suddenly turned against him). But the Aide-de-Camp was still the same; it was still the playboy Kirilida Pajidzani, who over the years had become a favourite with the Shah, and, still quite young, had been promoted to the rank of General, with the honorary title of Commander of the King's Household Cavalry.

Alas, poor Taittinger had been in the ground for ten days now, and the worms were already gnawing at his coffin. In his place, another cavalry officer, an Uhlan this time, had been seconded to Vienna on special assignment, a Pole by the name of Stanislas Zaborski, who took his duties more seriously, if only to prove to his superiors that the reputation of the Poles for unreliability was unjustified. Nor did First Lieutenant Zaborski wait, as the charming Taittinger had once waited, at the bar of the station restaurant, but on the platform next to the goods train. The Imperial luggage arrived in good order this time. Zaborski introduced himself – also in good order – to the Aide-de-Camp of the Grand Vizier, General Kirilida Pajidzani. Pajidzani, whose temples and thin side burns showed just a matt flash of silver in them, remembered the amusing Captain Taittinger, and asked whether he was still in Vienna. 'Excellency,' replied First Lieutenant Zaborski, 'the Captain died ten days ago, quite suddenly.'

Pajidzani had a glib heart and a tough nature, but he had a strong fear of death too, especially of sudden death. He said: 'But the Captain was still young?' thinking all the while that he himself was still young.

'It was a sudden death, Excellency!' repeated Zaborski.

'A heart-attack?' persisted Pajidzani.

'No, Excellency!'

'Suicide then?'

Zaborski made no reply. Pajidzani heaved a sigh of relief.

For some years now, Pajidzani and the Chief Eunuch had been on almost fraternal terms. They had intrigued together to undermine the previous Grand Vizier. They had succeeded, and now they were, perforce, lifelong allies. Pajidzani had not been named as the successor to the Grand Vizier, but he had been promoted to General anyway. The Chief Eunuch had grown fond of the harmless Kirilida Pajidzani. There was a man after his own heart. Harmless, easily led, unthinking, often naïve and grateful for any scrap of advice; on occasion a willing tool. A superb friend!

Two days after their arrival found them strolling, both in Western suits, through the sparkling spring streets. They looked at the colourful shops, and made frivolous purchases, walking sticks, opera glasses, boots, waistcoats, panama hats, umbrellas and braces, pistols, ammunition, hunting knives, wallets and briefcases. As they walked down the Kärntner Straße, the Chief Eunuch suddenly stopped and stood transfixed in front of the windows of the Court Jeweller Gwendl. On a broad, dark-blue velvet cushion, gleaming opalescently like a hail cloud, white as the snow on an Alpine summit and yet pinkish-blue like a sky threatening a storm, were three rows of heavy pearls, which were as familiar to him as if they'd been his sisters. He had an incomparable eye for gems. Rubies, emeralds, sapphires, pearls – once handled, or even once seen, he never forgot. These pearls – he knew their provenance. These were the pearls he had once taken on his Master's orders to a certain house. 'You told me yesterday,' said the Chief Eunuch to the General without taking his eyes off the pearls, 'about your friend the officer in the dragoons, who took his own life!'

'Yes,' said Pajidzani.

'Well, now, there's a thing!' said the Chief Eunuch. 'Come with me! I need you to interpret! I want to talk to the man in the shop.'

They went into the shop, and asked to see the owner. The General gave their name and rank. Court Jeweller Gwendl came slowly down a steep flight of stairs.

'We are from the retinue of His Majesty the Shah,' said the Chief Eunuch. And the General interpreted for him. 'Where do the pearls in your window come from?'

Gwendl replied truthfully that, having first received them from Efrussi's Bank, he had then sold them to Amsterdam. Now they were back with him on commission. 'How much do they cost?' asked the Chief Eunuch, and Pajidzani translated.

'Two hundred thousand gulden!' said Gwendl.

'I will buy them back,' said the Chief Eunuch. He pulled out a heavy blue leather purse, slowly untied the thick strings, and poured its contents out on to the table – lots of little golden saucers. There were fifty thousand gulden. He demanded that the pearls be taken out of the window immediately, and be put aside for him till tomorrow. He didn't need the receipt that Gwendl had begun to write out for him. He looked at the piece of paper for a moment, ripped it up, and let the white scraps float down and cover the reddish-gold ducats. 'I'll be back at the same time tomorrow!' said the Chief Eunuch, and Pajidzani translated.

'Why did you do that?' asked the General.

'I love those pearls!' replied the Chief Eunuch.

Pajidzani stopped at the corner of Kärntner Straße and the Stephansplatz. There was a large wooden billboard in front of him. A motif of little Persian flags bordered an announcement in eye-catching red letters on a black background:

His Majesty, the Shah of Persia,
Lord of all faithful Worshippers of the Prophet
In true and lifelike representation.
The Harem of Teheran.
The Secrets of the Orient.
All on show in the 'World Bioscope Theatre' on the Prater-
    Hauptallee!

'What are we waiting for!' said Pajidzani.

XXXIII

In accordance with long-established custom, the Shah called for his Chief Eunuch in the morning.

The monarch was sipping his usual Karluma tea. His pipe, as long as a walking stick, leaned against the low table: it seemed to be smoking by itself.

'You saw the world outside yesterday, didn't you!' the Shah began. 'Well, what do you say? Is it much changed since the last time we were here?'

'All things change, Sire,' replied the Chief Eunuch. 'And all things remain the same. That's my opinion!'

'Did you see old acquaintances from our previous visit?'

'Only one, Sire, a woman!'

'What woman was that?'

'Sire, she was your lover for one night. I had the inestimable honour of taking her a present from you.'

'Does she think of me still? Did she talk about me?'

'I don't know, Sire! No, she didn't talk about you.'

'What present did you take her?'

'The most beautiful pearls I could find in our chests. They were a worthy gift. But . . .'

'But?'

'She didn't keep them. Yesterday I saw the pearls in the window of a shop. I bought them back.'

'And how is the woman?'

'Sire, she is not worthy of being asked after.'

'What about then? Was she worth more then?'

'It was different then, my Lord. Your Majesty was younger, but even then I saw who she really was. A poor girl. By the standards of the West, an object for sale.'

'But I remember liking her then!'

'Sire, it wasn't the same woman; it was a similar one!'

'Are you telling me I'm blind?'

'We are all of us blind,' said the Chief Eunuch.

The Shah felt uncomfortable. He pushed the dishes with honey, butter and fruit to one side. He thought, or rather, he gave the appearance of thinking, but his head remained as empty as a hollow pumpkin.

'Well, I see, I see!' he said. And then: 'But she made me happy!'

'Indeed, indeed!' affirmed the Chief Eunuch.

'Just tell me,' the Shah began again, 'be candid: do you think I make mistakes, mistakes in other . . . more important matters as well?'

'Sire, candidly, yes! You err because you are human!'

'Then where is there any certainty?' asked the Shah.

'Beyond!' said the Chief Eunuch. 'Beyond, after we are dead.'

'Are you afraid of death?'

'I've been waiting for it for a long time now. I'm surprised I'm still alive.'

'Begone,' said the Shah, and a moment later he called: 'Bring me the pearls!'

The Eunuch bowed and slipped out, a plump shadow.

XXXIV

A week later, the Shah left the Imperial capital again. Band-leader Nechwal conducted the regimental band of the Hoch-and Deutschmeisters on the platform. The guard of honour presented arms. First Lieutenant Zaborski took cordial leave of General Kirilida Pajidzani. Little Yalmana Kahinderi slipped discreetly into the next carriage, escorted by an old, plump but still alert-seeming gentleman. His Majesty the Emperor took leave of his foreign guest with practised cordiality. The other side of the window in the stationmaster's office, the artist from the *Kronen-Zeitung* made a sketch of the parting, a possible theme for Maestro Tino Percoli or some successor of his.

As far as the 'World Bioscope Theatre' was concerned, it was allowed to open its doors again for business the day after the departure of the Persian monarch. Mizzi Schinagl sometimes sat at the till in her pearls. Sometimes she thought of the trial that was awaiting her Xandl. Sometimes she visited him in the remand prison to bring him some cheese or salami to keep his strength up and, on occasion, behind the benevolently turned back of the guard, cigarettes too. She never came away from any of these occasions with any sense that Xandl was her son, and she his mother.

Very rarely did she think of her beloved Taittinger, but when she did it was all the more forcefully. It made her sad. But seeing as it wasn't in her nature to be sad for very long, she forced herself to think cheerful thoughts instead, of the two thousand gulden that she had safe and sound in the post office bank, and of the brisk trade that the 'World Bioscope Theatre' was doing. She was healthy and cheerful, on occasion even boisterous. She was the kind of woman who, on account of their appetizing fullness, are sometimes described as voluptuous. Now and again she looked out for a husband for herself.

Old Tino Percoli, who still supplied waxworks for the 'World Bioscope Theatre' and who knew the story of Mizzi Schinagl, would sometimes say: 'I might be capable of making figures that have heart, conscience, passion, emotion and decency. But there's no call for that at all in the world. People are only interested in monsters and freaks, so I give them their monsters. Monsters are what they want!'